Island of the Mad

Island

of the

Mad

A NOVEL

LAURIE SHECK

COUNTERPOINT

BERKELEY

Library of Congress Cataloging-in-Publication Data

Names: Sheck, Laurie, author.
Title: Island of the mad : a novel / Laurie Sheck.
Description: New York : Counterpoint Press, [2016]
Identifiers: LCCN 2016020231 | ISBN 9781619028357 (hardcover)
Subjects: LCSH: San Servolo Island (Italy)—Fiction. | Quests
  (Expeditions)—Fiction. | Hospital patients—Fiction. |
  Sanatoriums—Fiction. | BISAC: FICTION / Literary.
Classification: LCC PS3569.H3917 I77 2016 | DDC 813/.54—dc23
LC record available at https://lccn.loc.gov/2016020231
ISBN 978-1-61902-835-7

Cover design by Kelly Winton
Interior design by Domini Dragoone

COUNTERPOINT
2560 Ninth Street, Suite 318
Berkeley, CA 94710
www.counterpointpress.com

Printed in the United States of America
Distributed by Publishers Group West

10 9 8 7 6 5 4 3 2 1

Everything passes away—suffering, pain, blood, hunger, pestilence. The sword will pass away too, but the stars will remain when the shadows of our presence and our deeds have vanished from the Earth. There is no man who does not know that. Why, then, will we not turn our eyes toward the stars? Why?

—Mikhail Bulgakov, *The White Guard*

We learned that our universe is not static, that space is expanding, that the expansion is speeding up and that there might be other universes all by carefully examining faint points of starlight coming to us from distant galaxies. But because the expansion is speeding up, in the very far future, those galaxies will rush away so far and so fast that we won't be able to see them...So astronomers in the far future looking out into deep space will see nothing but an endless stretch of static, inky, black stillness. And they will conclude that the universe is static and unchanging and populated by a single central oasis of matter that they inhabit...Sometimes nature guards her secrets with the unbreakable grip of physical law. Sometimes the true nature of reality beckons from just beyond the horizon.

—Brian Greene, *Is Our Universe the Only Universe?*

"You're not Dostoevsky," said the citizeness, who was getting muddled by Koroviev.
"Well, who knows, who knows," he replied.
"Dostoevsky is dead," said the citizeness, but somehow not very confidently.
"I protest!" Behemoth exclaimed hotly. "Dostoevsky is immortal!"

—Mikhail Bulgakov, *The Master and Margarita*

Table of Contents

PART I

REFUGIUM
IN PERICULIS

I, Ambrose A., having no family or worldly attachments, though at times ghosts have visited me, and far-off waters still swell inside my mind—the Adriatic, the canals of Venice—; I who carry voices of the dead, or are they of the living?; who have traveled far or have I traveled not at all?; I who have read the secret pages of others—the sleepless woman, the epileptic—; who have felt the world come to me in fragments but never whole; who have known myself as one of those fragments, "a mis-shapen piece" (though isn't all that comes into the mind mis-shapen, partial, hurt?); I who dream even now of the one who can't sleep, and the one seared by wild joy in the moment before seizure; I who have loved facts as others have loved bodies—I don't know if what I leave is part of the material world, if it's burning or not, ashes, dust, lit only in the mind or not.

I have loved the facts of things. The lists, accumulations.

The way, for instance, I can type the words "magic characters" into Google and what comes up has nothing to do with anything I might have thought, but a page from a "hyperlatex manual" in which "magic characters" are explained as "meta characters used as single-character marks for various kinds of layout directives in a text, as where a paragraph break should occur." There are also those that "protect a text from being interpreted." But how is this so?

And what is "hyperlatex"? The site says it is "a software package that allows you to prepare documents in HTML and, at the same time, to produce a nearly printed document from your input."

I, of course, know nearly nothing of these things.

Or I can open a book and find: "Among Venice's many relics is the body of St. Lucy, protectress of the blind."

Or: "In the 14c, Venetian paper from the workshop of _____ was embossed with such emblems as eyeglasses and gloves."

And for a few moments I am less preoccupied, less restless. I have felt the world touch me with its strange, unpredictable hand. And for a few moments have not doubted or recoiled from that hand.

Should I say my name is Ambrose or Anselm? Even this, which should be so simple, is unclear.

In the foundling home they named me Anselm. A name plucked for convenience from the alphabet's beginning. Or could I have been named for the Duke of Friuli who became St. Anselm in 805? As a child I considered various options, looked up what I could.

I learned that St. Anselm withdrew from the world at the height of his political power. Founded a monastery at Fanano, then another at Nonantula. Built hospitals for the poor. I liked him for this, was pleased to share his name.

But after a while the caregivers began calling me Ambrose. So what was my true name? They said I was quiet like him, liked to read only to myself, like him. Augustine had written, "When Ambrose read, his eyes scanned the page and his heart sought out meaning, but his voice was silent and his tongue kept still. He never read aloud..." By then I was often in the infirmary for weeks or months at a time, waiting for my bones to heal. And even when well enough to walk, I mostly sat in a corner, reading and thinking, my back more hunched and twisted by the year.

And so my quietness seeped into my name; they had re-named me.

Over time I learned more about Ambrose. How as an infant in his cradle (around 337 AD) a swarm of bees settled on his face, leaving a drop of honey on his cheek which caused him to feel deeply the sweetness of words. And how decades later, when told he was to be named Bishop, he gathered his loved books and stole out of the city by night, concealing himself as best he could, but lost his way and wandered for many days until he came upon the house of his friend Leontius who reluctantly turned him in. Still, even as Bishop he remained an ascetic—gave away his land and money to the poor. For them he melted the church's gold collection plate: "The church possesses gold not to hoard but to scatter...It is not from your own goods that you give to the beggar; it is a portion of his own that you restore to him. The earth belongs to all."

In the face of attacking soldiers, he said, "My only arms are my tears."

"The poor are my stewards and treasures."

"Wars and the Sea, not thoughts, destroy lives."

(Yet I wondered even then, was this true? Hadn't thoughts destroyed many lives? Don't they still?)

Nights I turned his name over in my mind, liked that it was mine. Thought of the drop of honey and the poor. Touched my own hand to my cheek. Wondered if it could be true—that the earth belongs to all. If this was so, what forms might this take outside the walled grounds where I lived?

I pictured him hiding, not wanting to be found. Dressed in rags and homeless.

"The earth belongs to all....It is not from your own goods you give to the beggar..."

All this I spoke only quietly and to myself.

If you could see me, what would you see? A hunchbacked man in a frayed, camel-colored coat, his large balding head seeming to protrude from his chest. And if I tried to look into your eyes (but it is rare that I would try) you would see a face straining sidewise, as if struggling to lift itself out of some dark, viscous liquid. A face half-drowned and yet still breathing, twisting upward as if seeking some small, indiscernible speck in the distance. Something, maybe, it could love. I have glimpsed from the corners of my eyes sudden fright in the eyes of those who've watched me.

I don't blame them for their fear. Maybe we are all made of a secret, tender chaos not visible at the surface of skin, and I remind them of that chaos. Though I think what I am to them is more mysterious, unquantifiable, variable, complex.

I don't pretend to know what I am to them.

Inside my hump a bird has grown completely silent; its dark lidless eyes don't understand why it's not free.

Each week I pass a parade of worn shoes, dropped paperclips, sales slips crumpled into rough, irregular balls. The knobbed bottoms of tree trunks. Mismatched socks. Hems billowing or tightly folded. The fragile, sinewy rivers of torn stockings. I track the cracked sidewalk's intricate, unmeaning damage.

So much that is despised, discarded, overlooked.

I was eight when the doctors first told me the name of my illness as I lay in the infirmary waiting for my bones to heal. *Osteogenesis Imperfecta,* they said—and those words opened over me, a Luna moth's papery blind wings trembling, almost breathing, though there was a harshness in them also.

One brown helpless eye on each green wing.

Gradually the doctors gave me to understand (but what does it truly mean to *understand*?) that my bones would break over and over. That this wouldn't change. The improper formation of cartilage and bone simply part of what I was. And without sufficient collagen, the whites of my eyes would turn blue, blood-filled capillaries leaking from beneath the surface: two small seas but waveless—all turbulence hidden.

Then gradually the hump began as well.

"So much averse I found and wondrous harsh." Which of my books had said this?

Is all seeing inseparable from the interruptions of seeing, all thought from the distortions and contradictions of thought?

Though I write these things, I speak of them to no one.

But why write these words at all? Why leave these pages filled with streets of water, sleepless eyes?

Why speak of the places I have seen, the islands I have traveled? The sleepless woman? The epileptic?

How explain that a voice I barely knew led me to the Lagoon of Venice? And that I feel even now a tenderness for that voice. That I would bring it if I could news of these frail islands once known as *Refugium in Periculis,* Refuge in Peril.

But I suppose I must go back to the beginning, or at least as close as I can get to what might pass for a beginning.

For a time (often poorly, I admit, but still I managed) I worked as a book scanner in a digitizing company's cramped offices.

There were two of us in that basement room, myself and a quiet brown-haired woman.

I knew it was only a matter of time before robots would replace us. But the technology was still developing, the few robotic scanners too expensive to be widely used.

I began each day by placing a book in the scanner's metal cradle, then flattening its first page against the glass. After setting the camera and pressing the scan button, I watched its light flare sideways, up and over. Page upon page of histories, geographies, fictions, biographies in white heat before my eyes. 20 or so books per day.

Sometimes I still think of all the strangers who have come across my scanned, mistaken handprint on the page—that irregular gray island not unlike the islands of the Venetian Lagoon.

From a few feet away my office-mate scanned as well, her motions near-shadows of my own.

The signs over our work stations read: OUR DIGITIZED WORK MUST BE CAPABLE OF BEING DELIVERED IN A VARIETY OF MEDIAS, SOME OF WHICH HAVE NOT YET BEEN INVENTED.

I often wondered what this meant. Sometimes I'd just sit there imagining things that weren't yet invented: Print encoded into skin? Books inserted into infants' brains at birth? Whole tomes like DNA within a single cell? Things that wouldn't happen in my lifetime if at all.

The company's marketing brochure spoke of "freeing the printed word from the books that bind it...moving knowledge from books to bytes by digitizing the vast, worldwide depository amassed over centuries of human history—this is how the printed word is freed."

But I didn't think of us as "freeing" anything. It seemed almost the opposite was true—that we were banishing words into air, sending them into some desolate restlessness, dematerialized, ghostly, wandering far from any shelter.

Evenings, walking out into the dimming light or the dark if it was winter, I felt the scanned words traveling beside me, something homeless and disoriented in them, though I told myself this was foolish. Or I'd see in my mind's eye a bit of marginalia the computer program had systematically erased. I wondered then, and still do, if she felt as I did, the printed words and the erased beside her.

Every morning I heard the hum of her machine, smelled her morning coffee.

The lights from our machines slid back and forth without memory, and yet they appeared to enact a kind of memory.

Much too often they seemed more solid to me than myself, and I just a shadow. Wasn't my memory more helpless and troubled than theirs, less manifest, effective?

The books smelled of dust and darkened rooms, dampness and neglect—or maybe it was a kind of privacy I smelled—the way they managed to go on year after year unopened and untouched as if existing for themselves alone. Unread and yet still filled with words.

Wasn't this what partly made them beautiful? I thought of them as beautiful.

The spines were cracked and torn, hanging or unglued. Inside were watermarks. Food stains. Tabbed-down corners. Ink blots. Marginalia.

On one a winged lion held a tablet. On others there were fishes, dogs, celestial bodies, all kinds of creatures—as if to read were to step into an un-summarized, still-forming world.

A few were held together only by brown twine or household string; there were no cover-boards at all.

Every now and then from the corner of my eye I noticed her pausing to read a single page—was there sadness in her face, or perplexity, or pleasure? But I barely ever looked into her face.

The dictionary says that to be silent is "to cease giving out natural sound," and yet I *heard* a sense of who she was even as we didn't speak. And how reticence is also speech—layered, various, highly detailed. That *this*, too, is *natural*. In any case, I'd lived for years within silence, and still do— felt the scars in it and voices, damaged pathways moving back and forth inside the air. My name tied from early on to silence. And sometimes even now when I think about my breaking bones, I remember how silence is said to either *break* or to be *kept*, as if one can't exist beside the other. But what breaks is also kept, I know this. We never said good morning or good night and yet I sensed in her a kindness, a way of thinking strong and fragile as the islets where I'd later walk.

This, too, I also learned:

The Sanskrit root for "man" means "think, concentrate, be silent."

Nights, back in my room, I listened to noises drifting up from the alley (my one window faced the rear exit of a restaurant kitchen)—garbled talk and laughter, whirring sounds, garbage cans dragged along concrete, clanking metals. Every now and then, an odd whimper appeared that seemed neither animal nor human, I could never figure out what it was. Often I spent a few hours at my computer. I'd type in a word, then see where it might lead.

One night I chose: "brittle." (As a boy I'd looked this word up often.)

"Brittle" led to: "brittle star":

"An echinoderm that crawls across the sea floor using its five, slender whip-like arms for locomotion,"

which led to: "abyssal fauna":

"One of three divisions of marine fauna...Many are blind, while others see by means of the phosphorescent glow emitted from their bodies and the bodies of others. Their organs of touch are often highly developed. No plants can grow in the abyssal depths..."

Then "abyssal" opened onto: "unfathomable," and "abyssal zone": "the portion of the ocean deeper than 6,600 feet."

"The abyssal realm is very calm. It lies far from any storms, and is marked by neither diurnal nor seasonal changes. There is only darkness, calm water, sediment-soft bottoms. Oxygen is scarce."

That night I crawled along the sea-bottom, my phosphorescent bones signaling and probing for any sentient creature nearby, but there was nothing. After a while my green glow grew terrible with wordless shame. All I knew was that 6,600 feet of black water were flowing over my hump and clumsy head, my twisted body.

Then one day this came:

Dear A,

It is hard to know where to begin. Please forgive me ⧸ I sleep little now, in time I will sleep less, then probably within a year not at all. Mine is a strange malady, poorly understood, which is said to have its origins in Venice. There is a doctor there whose specialty is epilepsy, though he studies this as well. I expect nothing of him.

In my sleeplessness many things have begun to happen. Does it matter how or why?

I see pages being written, then burned. The canals of Venice and St. Petersburg. A man in a stone room feverishly scribbling. Other hands writing as well, sometimes warming themselves, sometimes touching, though rarely, the hand of another.

Do you know of Mikhail Bulgakov, author of the novel The Master and Margarita? Lately his book has been coming into my mind, I don't know why. It is said he burned his unfinished manuscript, then wrote it all over again. This was under Stalin. From 1928 until his death in 1940, he hid it in a drawer, worked on it in secret. In the book there is a character called the Master who also writes a book and burns it.

With Bulgakov many questions arise. For instance, the novel's first paragraph as transcribed by his wife, can be found nowhere in his surviving notebooks. So did he dictate it to her before he died, or did she alter it after his death? Such things can never be known. What can be known is the compassion of the text. And the Master's love of books and for his companion, Margarita. The many strivings, transformations...

Sometimes my mind wanders ⧸

I believe there is a certain notebook in Venice, now lost, not by Bulgakov, but by someone else. I don't know why it comes to me or why I care, though

I sense in it many feelings not far from my own. A hurt presence like the Master's. A person struggling with his body as I struggle with mine. Sometimes I see the hand that writes but never the inked pages. So I know nothing of its contents—only that there's suffering in it, and gentleness, and deep care for another.

Turgenev worried that one of his ghost stories was too fantastical, but Dostoevsky countered that in fact it was not fantastical enough. That the ordinary is stranger than anything if only we could see it.

I think about this often.

In my mind's eye I see you walking in Venice, though I know it is hard for you to walk. I see you climbing up stone steps and finding in a drawer—or somewhere—the pages of that notebook, but how can I even say this to you?

Una notte bianco—a night in white—this is what Venetians call a sleepless night. So much whiteness in me now, so much distance.

You will understand now why I can no longer come to the office.

Think of how fragile they are, the islands of the Venetian Lagoon. So thin and unprotected.

I believe you understand such fragility. I have sensed your kindness.

If you go there I will write to you, I promise—

I'd lived a solitary and bookish life to be sure, one with a particular malady that lent itself to long periods of immobilism and wondering, contemplation. Still, what could have prepared me for this letter? All that silence between us, and then this. It's true, I noticed for some weeks she seemed paler, thinner, her left hand often trembled. (The small bird inside my hump gently watched this.) But I thought I was most likely mistaken as I never looked straight-on, and in any case mistrusted my assessments of most everything outside me. Those frequent interludes as a child in the infirmary and then later in my own bed healing, had made my mind restless, sometimes feverish, "too active"—a crack in the wall became a spider or the checkpoint to a foreign land; a bed-crease a sinuous, blind creature. Words in my book broke apart, their letters flying to link-up with letters from other, broken words: *ste* pulled free from *listen* and hooked up with a solitary *p* much farther down the page (itself loosed from what other crumbled word?) where they melded into *step*. *K* broke off from *back,* and "*n*" from "*no*" and both flew sidewise to find *own,* which then was *known.*

Yet even as I mistrusted my own eyes, I noticed books she kept at her work-station to read on her lunch hour and coffee breaks: Pavel Florensky's *The Imaginary in Geometry,* guidebooks to Venice and Moscow, Filippo Pedrocco's *Titian,* a biography of Dostoevsky, a thin volume titled *Architectonics: Line and Meaning.* I wondered what she was thinking—what she might say if we could speak. Wondered what went on inside her mind.

So when that morning her typed note appeared at my work-station, neatly folded and tucked into a plain white envelope with an inked red "A" at its center, what was I to think? To this day I don't know how it got there.

That night, I ran my hands over the white, believable surface, crisp and lightly flexible. Read it again and again. A plain sheet of multi-purpose copy paper filled with small black marks that seeped into my brain and lodged there. What was I to make of what she wrote? Did it require an answer? Who was she and now where? We who'd never even spoken.

That night's dream comes back to me clearly even now:

I was standing at my work station scanning a passage of Nansen's *Farthest North* where after months of being alone he sees "above the southern edge of ice a red lantern inexplicably moving." Then I wasn't in the office anymore, but in Venice where bolts of red cloth hung outside the dyers' shops to dry. I felt someone beside me. After a while I understood it was the painter, Titian. "I died in a plague year," he said, "Yet my name doesn't appear on the Health Office's list of the 164 citizens who died of plague on that same day, August 27, 1576. How can I explain this? And many of my works no longer exist. Of my frescoes for the Fondaco dei Tedeschi only one crumbling fragment remains. Salt and time ate the rest. I can see it is hard for you to walk. But the red cloth is beautiful, isn't it? Now that I am dead I miss the keen outlines of things, the touch of wet cloth, a stone wall's irregular edges."

That was all.

Why had I let myself walk the streets of Venice, even if only in a dream? The thought of going seemed absurd. Yet the more I thought about it, the more I began to wonder if maybe I should go. After all, aside from Ambrose who was born and died many centuries before me, she was the one I felt closest to on earth, though it was a closeness I couldn't explain. Still, something about who she was—or what I *sensed* or *believed* of who she was—the hurt tenderness in her, a stubbornness and kindness, a withdrawal much like my own—had come to live within the fault-lines of my bones. Even though we didn't speak.

On the envelope there'd been no signature or initials, no return address. Could her name be on some memo I'd discarded?—a joint email, maybe, with new rules for handling damaged books, or an update on the latest technology? But all I could find was the email she'd had at work that was no longer in use: mmwys@Proscan.com How could she have learned my name when I didn't know hers?

I imagined her wide-eyed, unable to sleep, maybe feverish and pacing, watching Bulgakov's manuscript burn, a hand writing in a notebook.

Was it possible my going could in any way help her?

Over the years I'd made little money. Had little use for money. But had saved some nevertheless. I'd kept my brown coat for 20 years, my few shirts for almost as long.

For the next week her work station stayed vacant. I was sure in a few days they would replace her.

How to speak of where I went and what I did? Though verbs and their tenses line up like obedient soldiers, I think now they're wounded at the core. Conflicted, hobbled, partly lost. Something shuddering outside them they can't catch, a rougher, truer breathing not bound by the clear coordinates of time and space I once believed in (even as minutes glow on my computer screen, and mapping-sites calculate routes from starting-points to destinations).

All time and space more vulnerable, more porous, than I thought.

Unstable, thin, erratic—this is the Lagoon of Venice. In 1894 Horatio Brown noted the stone pines, *Pinus pinea,* that once covered the islands, a protection for the soil, but by the time I arrived few remained. Brown marveled at the strife and inconclusiveness inherent in the islands' shifting forms and porous boundaries, mud-banks alternately covered and laid bare. 160 square miles in the shape of a fallen crescent moon.

The ground beneath my feet drifting fragments of shadow and light as I walked.

At first much of what I learned came more from books than what I saw—how tamarisk and sea lavender thrived years ago, and Venice's earliest name was *Refugium in Periculus.* But haven't so many of the facts I've come to love first come to me like fictions overall?—things believed in, felt, trusted to be real, but not experienced first-hand.

Even so, I saw much from the moment I arrived. I thought, for some reason, that Venice is an isolate city, but quickly realized I was wrong. There are 118 islets scattered within the Venetian Lagoon, and though I never went to all, I've felt on my skin the soil and stones of several.

Some believe these narrow islands—none more than a half mile wide—were severed from the mainland when the ocean-force on one side, and the Brenta, Sile, and Piave rivers on the other, shuddered them apart. The Adriatic swept landward while the rivers swept toward the sea. Or could it be that the islands are "a bar built by the rivers across their own mouths"? As if they began in self-inflicted muteness—restraint across the lips, imprisonment, enclosure.

(How could I not think of the one across the ocean and myself?)

Tintoretto could never envision them apart from their watery destruction.

I had gone where she asked me to go. Had brought my computer, a few books.

But why was it called Refuge in Peril? It seemed so imperiled itself, water always threatening to overwhelm the fragile boundaries. So how could it possibly provide protection, and to whom? Yet it had been a refuge for those who fled the mainland when the Goths and Huns invaded in 452, leaving everything charred, in ruins. The first island to be settled was named *Isola del Rialto* and the next *Isola della Citta Deserta (Island of the Deserted City)*. What great power would want to conquer such a place? Desolation would be its sole protection. One settler wrote: "the unnerving isolation of the waters, this strange barrenness that keeps us safe."

Before that, there had been only a few clusters of rudimentary huts, and for work the harvesting of sea salt, and fishing. Cassiodorius, the earliest official visitor, noted, "Thus you live in your seabirds' home all under equal laws, none too rich or too poor; house is like unto house. Envy, that curse of all the world, hath no place here."

Juvenal pointed out that the rough cape, *bardo cucullus*, was worn by rich and poor alike. And Herodotus, that every year when the virgins were gathered together to be chosen for marriage, neither the "deformed" nor "less fortunate" were excluded.

"What is the sea?" Alcuin asked his pupil, Charlemagne's son. And his pupil replied, "It is refuge in danger." "Yes," Alcuin answered, "but the sea is also danger. It is both."

How many nights did I fall asleep hearing Cassiodorius in my mind? And how he said, "Yours is so frail a bulwark. You live like sea-birds. You have not tried to straighten your streets or overpower the wildness of the sea..."

On my first day I found myself a room on a narrow winding street by the bus station where syringes and cracked vials lay scattered on cobblestones and sills, thinking *How could I have come here, what could I possibly have been thinking, what have I done?* The room held a single bed, a wooden nightstand, a lamp with a green shade. In my mind I'd go over the books I saw by her work station, thinking maybe I should read them. That maybe in some way they'd help to bring her closer, make my mission less strange. Who was Pavel Florensky in any case? And why would she read him? And *The Master and Margarita*—that book she wrote of in her note—I supposed I should read that also.

Meanwhile, I tried to make sense of where I was. I soon learned the city is divided into six *sestieri,* each with its own consecutive street numbers reaching into thousands. There were dozens of alleyways with the same name but in different districts. So I would see a white street sign (ninzoletti, "little bed sheets" as they're called) marking a certain street, only to wander into another sestieri and find the same street name on a different street. A few had more than one name; on those there was an "o" between each choice.

Rio Tera degli Assassini, Calle delle Procuratie, Salizada San Pantelon, I walked as best I could, my cane often in my hand though I disliked using it and it was difficult to raise my head enough to truly see what was in front of me.

Stone faces. Two baskets of eggs in a doorway. Shining pyramids of oranges and eggplants. Warm loaves in bakery windows.

When I think back to those first days, they seem a frayed, confusing tapestry given to me by a hand an ocean away. What was it doing, that hand, as I walked?—pushing back sweaty hair from a forehead, or turning pages, or fastening scotch tape to the rim of broken glasses—restless, feverish, not sleeping?

All around me, a language I could barely understand.

Those first weeks were a strange mixture of Venice and Russia. By day I was in Venice, learning, exploring, thinking about canals, the lost notebook, the doctor, but at night when I read I was also in Moscow with Bulgakov—I had found a copy of *The Master and Margarita*.

Sometimes I imagined I was her as I read, back home across the ocean, waiting, maybe, for some word from me. But how could she expect me to find her when she gave me no name or address?

Some things exist in silence only.

Increasingly the words I had for time and space and whatever is claimed to separate the two, seemed ever more inadequate, confusing.

I was still just beginning to learn the many streets, their crookedness not unlike mine, and their many bewildering inconsistencies, the histories behind them. Why was one stretch of a *calle* Santa Margarita, and another stretch Santa Margherita? Why did Santi Giovanni e Paolo suddenly turn into San Zanipolo? There were streets named after long-lost trades: Calle dei Saoneri (street of the soap-makers); Calle dei Fuseri (street of the spindle-makers), etc. Five centuries ago on Riva di Biasio, a man by that name, a sausage-maker and murderer, suffered a terrible death by beheading. Campiello de Cason was the site of a prison, and Agnello Participazio, one of the Republic's first doges, had lived there long before. I had loved that doge's name for as long as I could remember, having stumbled upon it in my boyhood reading; its sound of peacefulness, inclusion.

Meanwhile in Bulgakov's book, the devil had arrived in Moscow. He sat on a park bench by Patriarch's Pond where he conversed with two men of letters. He seemed not devilish at all, but more like a distinguished, somewhat elderly scholar from abroad. A gentleman, well-educated, thoughtful. His name was Woland.

In my sleep, I heard the soft lapping of the canals.

Then one day—I'd never really believed I'd actually hear from her again—another letter came: But how could she have found me?

Dear A,

Sometimes I wonder, what is kindness? Where does the word come from, from what is it derived? Isn't there a strong sense of attachment in it, kinship with another, and yet there is also this distance, this xxx

Such separateness I cannot cross   and yet you crossed an ocean out of kindness

Now that sleep is strange to me, I spend many hours sorting papers. Things I clipped or wrote yet barely remember.

Today, for instance: a black and white photograph of a bronze head of Bellini, believed to be genuine, though much injured.

Maybe your eyes are now seeing what he saw. Even when quite old, each day he rode back and forth in his gondola from the Lido. Always he wore the same thing—a black cap and long black robe, a slender chain around his neck holding a bronze medal that the senate had bestowed on him in honor of his painting, The Transfiguration. It's said he ate only ripe figs, coarse bread and nuts, and shared these with his servant, a hunchbacked man who took care of the boat all day while he painted. The old man was deaf, and though his back was deeply hunched, for hours he scoured the gondola, straightened its awning, saw to its white cords and tassels, polished the two brass lions on its sides. Yet every evening when Bellini returned it was he who took on the role of servant. He insisted the hunchbacked man recline on a pillow, and Bellini, standing erect in the stern, ferried him across the water, humming quietly to them both Te Deum Laudamus.

Why do we need to believe these things, picture them, repeat them? And yet the air would be so empty without them—

I still see the lost notebook.

I wonder what you have found in Venice. I still think of your kindness—

But ~~I am so~~ tired now xxx I xx

Her note, in a plain manila envelope, was on the small oval table in the cramped entranceway of the building where I stayed.

I still had her other note in my pocket; each day I took it out, read it, then put it away.

Though I was baffled she'd found me, I soon realized another part of me wasn't surprised. For a moment I worried she was toying with me, playing some odd game. But in the end this just isn't what I felt. Even so, I didn't know how to look at what was happening. As if the troubled sweetness of words I had long associated with Ambrose had fallen away and left me in some stranger, coarser place—though it was a place I somehow sensed all along.

Liste are main streets, and *crosere,* crossroads. But most of the streets were called *calle,* and as I walked I noted that this was a feminine word: *la calle, le calli*—and so felt at times that I was walking through the labyrinth of the thoughts of the one who had sent me—mysterious, without summary. The way I couldn't say she was one thing or another, one truth or falsehood or another. (I sensed in her a truth, but then thought about the ways truth itself is mysterious, unsteady.)

Of course much of Venice is in its essence largely hidden. Over one hundred thousand supporting wooden poles stand submerged beneath the Basillica della Salute. And though St. Mark's appears secure and formidable, it's held in place by a raft built on stilts.

I wondered, would I hear from her again?

I was still reading *The Master and Margarita,* but hadn't yet been able to find anything by Florensky.

How was I going to search for the notebook? How could I even begin?

What Venice did she hold inside her mind? The real one where I walked in which one of the few remaining kindergartens had recently been turned into the island's 231st hotel, or another made of words as much as buildings? In 1850, Gautier wrote of the "four species of blackness" he observed as he moved through a canal at night for the first time: first the water's oily darkness; then the tempestuous darkness of sky (he arrived in a storm); the black opacity of narrow walls on one side of the canal made briefly erratic by his boat's reddish light; and finally, on the other side, looming and disappearing at once, the darkness of grilled doors.

I wandered the February streets. Decided I'd look for the doctor, see what I might find on my computer.

All I knew of the doctor was what she'd mentioned in her note—that he was an epilepsy specialist in Venice who also studied her condition. And though she claimed he couldn't help her, how could I not try to find him? But as I searched the internet, no one in Venice fit that description. I came to believe she was slightly mistaken—the man she had in mind was Dr. Elio Lugaresi, Professor of Neurology, but in Bologna, not Venice. I downloaded his CV:

> Birth date: July 1, 1926. Marriage: August 24, 1959.
> Children: Alessandra, Nicola.
>
> Editorial Board: Journal of Sleep Research
>   Italian Journal of Neurology
>   Sleep
>
> Membership in Medical and Scientific Societies: Italian Society of Neurology, Associazione Italiana di Medicina del Sonno, Ambassador for Epilepsy for the International League Against Epilepsy, President of the Italian EEG Society, 1969-1972, President of the Italian College of Neurologists, 1996-2000

Etc.

He had published 500 scientific papers in international journals. Was co-editor of: *Abnormalities of Sleep in Man* (Gaggi, 1968) and *Evolution and Prognosis of Epilepsies* (Gaggi, 1972).

One of his specialties was Dostoevsky syndrome, a form of epilepsy with ecstatic seizures.

On the last page of the CV, I came to this:

> Responsible for the discovery of a hereditary autosomnal dominant disease characterized by loss of sleep.

I was sure this must be the man she meant.

Then:

> Current work includes conducting ongoing studies of *Agrypnia Excitata:* a term that aptly defines a peculiar clinical condition characterized by loss of slow-wave sleep.

Agrypnia Excitata sounded feverish, archaic, almost desperate. By then it was late at night when the sounds and shapes of words most frightened and unnerved me.

I reminded myself she wanted me to find the lost notebook, not the doctor, though I still wondered if the doctor might help her.

I resolved that the next morning I would try to think about the notebook as she asked. Then I turned off my computer, listened to the slowing rain, its gray erasures.

The task was absurd, I knew this. How could I possibly look for a notebook I knew nothing about?—not one page of it, not one hint of its condition or contents—except that it was written by someone in Venice who seemed to be suffering in some way. True, she had hinted at a canal in St. Petersburg, but how could that help? And besides, who knew what kind of fever she was in all those weeks of not sleeping?

Yet I also knew that, viewed from certain angles, I, too, seemed improbable, even absurd: the endless cycles of breakages and silent cracks; the blue sea around each pupil, no eye-whites at all. So how could I judge something on improbability alone?

By this time, I noticed that the devil in Bulgakov's book also has strange eyes, each a different color, the right one black, the other green. What would he think of mine? I noticed, too, that, being a traveler and historian, Bulgakov's devil understood there is no such thing as safety, and that all plans are in a certain sense ludicrous, futile, though some, of course, can still be beautiful.

I suppose I believed, in the end, that my task, though ludicrous, was also in its own way beautiful. My searching would enact a kind of faithfulness, a promise made and kept, some sort of striving. I wasn't sure, but on balance it seemed best to press on. At the worst I would know more of Venice, and maybe of my own mind, my ways of thinking; also maybe more of hers. (I touched the envelope beside me). And when I considered all the minutes, hours, days, I'd "wasted" in my life, as almost anyone does, just hanging around being bored, or complaining, worrying, would doing this be any worse? (Again, I wondered what opinion the devil in Bulgakov's book might have on the subject. He seemed rather thoughtful, informed.)

After more hunting on the internet I learned that the doctor who lived and worked in Bologna sometimes came to the Venetian Lagoon, to the small island of San Servolo, where there is a conference center and an annual seminar on epilepsy. Still, how would that help me find the notebook? I didn't know. But "knowing" seemed so little of anything, and myself more and more a stranger to the wisdoms and attitudes of reason.

And then my right ankle broke. Or more precisely, the right talus—that small bone between the calcaneus and the tibia and fibula of the lower leg. Such terms had accompanied me since childhood, and though I tried to find in them some hint of Ambrose's sweetness, in truth they tasted more of bitterness or the acrid, industrial smell of burnt computers.

I didn't want to live again within that acrid taint. But what choice did I have?

The first time I broke my talus I was 10. After it was bandaged I looked up "talus" and found it had "an odd humped shape, somewhat like a turtle." That night I lay awake for many hours marveling at how, concealed within the outer humped shape I was beginning to develop, and with which I met the world—and by which the world largely saw and judged me—there was another hidden hump, and not just within myself but others. That it was *normal* to possess a small hunched site within the body. I stared at the ceiling with a sensation that felt new to me and strange, but which years later I came to think of as a kind of almost-comfort born of that new knowledge.

But now I looked at my four walls, the rigid lines of my confinement. My ankle was unbruised but swollen. I knew to wrap it in a splint from toes to upper calf. And though I knew that staying immobile is often harmful to the injured body, I also knew my fractures, bred in secret quiet, were different from those in normal bone. Experience had taught me I'd have to stay in my room at least a week, maybe two, before I even tried to go outside.

I already missed the street names I was learning: Calle della Mandola, Calle del Scarliatto, Calle de Riformati. And the *fondamente,* the bridges, the canals. The ground beneath my feet an odd echo of her voice, her longing, though I reminded myself I knew almost nothing of her at all.

My ankle throbbed. The walls grew dim, then dark. All Venice seemed a world away.

How would I spend my time within that room? My search for the doctor would have to wait, and the lost notebook. Whatever wandering I did would have to take place inside my mind.

Or maybe she would send another letter.

Dear A,

I suspect by now you will have read The Master and Margarita (though maybe you read it years ago before I even mentioned it). Why do I go over and over it in my mind? All these sleepless hours, and I trace the plot again and again, though "plot" I suppose is the wrong word—rather, I move inside the world Bulgakov made, its scents and textures, events, characters, chapters, shifting back and forth through time—many centuries can pass between two chapters.

I find it very beautiful how he begins a new chapter with the words that ended the chapter before it which took place in a completely different era and location. As if he is sewing a thread between the two, a kind of tenderness of mind—subtle, receptive linkages, connections.

It comforts me, this threading. (I wonder if it comforts you.) As if everything were somehow not separate after all.

Even in my sleeplessness I hold the book's brief outline in my mind. It begins in the 20th century with the devil as a visitor to Moscow, sitting on a bench, conversing with two men of letters. By the end of this first chapter, the devil has claimed to be a specialist in black magic, a consultant, a historian, the only expert in the world who can authenticate a certain manuscript, and has pulled from his pocket an enormous gold cigarette case while predicting one of the men's deaths in gory detail. So of course the men are thinking he's insane or an imposter of some kind, maybe even a spy. In any case, his voice softening as if offering a fairytale, the devil begins to tell Pontius Pilate's story, "Early in the morning of the fourteenth day of the spring month of Nisan, wearing a white cloak with a blood-red lining..." And as I said, the next chapter begins with the same words—but who is speaking? Is it still the devil or someone else? Who is the narrator of this book? Is there one, or several?

In this second chapter we are no longer in Moscow but Jerusalem, which Bulgakov calls Yershalaim. Pontius Pilate is meeting with Yeshua Ha-Nostri, who will be put to death beside two others, crucified for his subversive acts (though those acts are forms of love).

Over the course of the book the chapters move back and forth between what happens in Yershalaim—Pilate's torment over his cruel treatment of Ha-Nostri, who he's sentenced to death yet feels a pained attachment to, and the adventures of the devil in 20th-century Moscow who comes to know the man who calls himself the Master, and his companion Margarita. The Master has written a book about Pontius Pilate and suffers for that book. Burns it, walks out into the cold. Gives up Margarita and his name (though in the end Margarita finds him, helps him to heal, but only partly).

Throughout, there are many strange, fantastical acts. A large cat rides a streetcar, Margarita rubs a magic lotion into her skin. The sky over Moscow blackens with storm clouds and soot from raging fires. In Yershalaim there are also many storms, and when they come Pilate sickens with migraines, even the scent of roses makes him ill.

Underlying all of this are many questions which Bulgakov weaves in and out like the sentences linking his chapters. Among them: what is peace, what is tenderness and care, what is good and evil and can one wholly separate the two? (The devil himself does many kind deeds in this book.)

Of course there is much I have left out. But you see, in my sleeplessness these people come to me and these places. How Margarita comes to feel suffering and joy and deep care for another. How the Master's burned book somehow endures.

I still picture you in Venice. Like Bulgakov's threaded sentences, this comforts me.

This not-sleeping still feels strange to me. I suppose I will never get used to it—will just see more and more before my eyes (even now I smell the scent of Pilate's roses) then slowly, maybe, nothing. I don't know.

There is so much to come to in this sleeplessness, this silence—so many places I can go, must go—

I am tempted to sign my name, yet for some reason I can't bring myself to do it. Why did the Master give up his name, why do I?

I think of you somewhere among the many canals of Venice, their many beautiful names—

To this day I don't remember how that letter came.

But I remember that from the moment I read it, it was as if for a second she was beside me, even as I knew she was an ocean away—even as I didn't really know her. Not one word had ever passed between us. But in her sleeplessness, she used the word "comfort." She wrote of questions threading through storm clouds and fires. Of subtle, receptive linkages, connections, and subversive acts that are a form of love. Of a life she would never get used to, yet it was hers.

I once read that our DNA is a series of folds precisely structured for the efficient storage and accessing of information. But that night in my room, her thoughts were like Bulgakov's tender threading, but through a text I couldn't see.

Confined as I was to my bed, I kept thinking of how she'd written *tenderness of mind*—in some sense wasn't that what I felt for her? As I thought this, I pictured Margarita, alone after The Master's disappearance, walking through Patriarch's Park where she finds herself in conversation with a stranger who, unbeknownst to her, is the devil's representative. Though she's been desperate, bereft (I touched the letter in my pocket, thought again of the one across the ocean) shortly afterwards she discovers she can fly.

There's such joy in her flying.

She sails over Moscow's rooftops, over oil shops and traffic lights, over "rivers of hats" and lit windows, street signs painted with black arrows— she doesn't have to follow their directions.

I wanted to picture the one across the ocean flying like Margarita. But the thought of her sleeplessness and weakness wouldn't let me.

If only I wasn't stuck in my room...if only I didn't break so easily...if my foot weren't damaged and bandaged...I could seek out the notebook and the doctor from Bologna, though she'd been adamant he couldn't be of help.

After a few days, I tried to stand for a few minutes, and glimpsed by mistake my humped back in the mirror. With a rawness that surprised me, I felt a sudden hatred for what I saw.

The longer I stayed inside my room, the more confounding the notions of absence and presence became. In many ways the absence of the one across the ocean seemed a kind of presence. Challenging, accompanying, haunting. Prior wrote of a "Presence which no space can bind." And I felt nearer to her than when she stood just a few yards away in the office. Still, I understood I didn't know her. Didn't feel the air between us as a kind of skin—something I could know or touch—but as an element that held the absence of another and made palpable that absence; only the slightest hint of pulse moved through it.

Yet if one meaning of presence is an *influence felt,* then how could she be absent? It seemed to me there was a different word I needed, a word I didn't know. My mind was knotting.

And still I kept the few letters in my pocket. Read them, put them away. Waited for my bones to heal.

Each day of my confinement I learned more about the city I lay in but now missed:

"Venice was viewed in the Romantic and Victorian eras as the embodiment of erasure and decay."

"During World War I, the city suffered greatly. 'Bombers from Pola buzz over us nearly every night, dropping bombs for half an hour. Everything that shines is covered. Our gilded angels are dressed in sack-cloth. Our spires are dirty gray.'"

"Every hotel but the Danielis has been turned into a hospital." This was in 1915.

"For 400 years Venice was the greatest trading power in Europe. Thus, it is just to compare the Republic to a joint-stock company for the exploitation of the East—the board of directors was the Senate, the citizens of Venice the shareholders, and as the majority of senators were men of business, their requirements and beliefs brought forth the regulations which governed all of Venice."

"Although Titian was born in the Alpine district of Cadore with its rough terrain of gorges and defiles, he left at the age of ten to learn his trade in Venice."

Again Titian appeared to me in a dream.

"For decades I was one of the most celebrated artists in all of Europe. My work was commissioned by Popes, Emperors, Kings. I soon learned to play one against the other, ingratiated myself, was comfortable with power. Often I worked on a grand scale, gave King Philip just what he wanted. But my late paintings are different—a certain mournfulness in them, a rougher finish. But no one sees this as mostly they've been lost, so how can anyone realize who I was?

And for all my maneuverings, nothing could save me from the plague (though some say I died of other causes).

I died just like the others. What swept through my city swept through me.

Thousands upon thousands were struck down, including my dear son, Orazio.

The silence you feel in yourself, surely it isn't so different from the isolate silences that have plagued so many others over time.

These bolts of red cloth are still beautiful, aren't they? So much brightness rising and drying in the wind—"

Outside my windowless room, I imagined the lagoon rising red with the legacy of plague.

Surely Bulgakov's devil, Woland, that most polite and gentlemanly historian, would have witnessed the plague through his dark eye and seen a suffering beyond anything I could fathom.

Even though he now wore a well-made suit and spoke calmly while holding his walking stick, what redness still lived behind his eyes?

Titian's cloth was red and streaming, the sky behind it tinged with faint pink blotches.

And the canals were filling with red water. Even a few cobblestones were staining, and the lower steps of the foot-bridges.

I felt my own walls growing red, then darker, redder.

The entire second chapter of Bulgakov's book is also drenched in red—first as the "blood-red lining" of Pontius Pilate's cloak, then the scent of roses that plagues and torments him.

He stands in his garden, helpless before "the hellish trace of roses," that causes him such pain he's afraid to turn his neck. Blood pounds in his temples, leaves streaks across his eyes. At the height of the migraine, Caesar's head floats before him, a red sore on his forehead festering and spoiling. More and more he lives in a red torment, and the longer he feels this the more he's filled with an overwhelming love that baffles and distresses him for the prisoner, Ha-Nostri, who he's condemned to death—the one who wears a light blue chiton and a white bandage on his head—while the sight of Caesar conjures only revulsion.

What Pilate knows but can't quite let himself know is that Ha-Nostri has shown a deep tenderness toward him, an uncanny understanding.

Once, when Ha-Nostri is brought before him, he refers clearly to the procurator's pain. (But how can he possibly know this about me, the procurator wonders, then enquires if perhaps he is a doctor.) Ha-Nostri continues, "You are too isolated. Your life is impoverished," then points out that his only earthly attachment is to his dog. "But how can you know I am thinking of calling my dog?", and the prisoner replies, "That's very simple...you wave your hand in the air as if you are petting something, and your lips..."

As he leaves, Ha-Nostri says to Pilate, "Every kind of power is a form of violence."

As I read, I wondered what the redness might mean to Pilate. As it pounds inside his head and seeps relentlessly from roses, and even swims in the sore on Caesar's forehead, couldn't it have something to do with the power Ha-Nostri mentioned? A power Pilate knows he furiously desires and fought for, but something inside him senses that even at its mildest it's still a form of violence and injustice...

When Pilate is once again alone, all he can think is "I am standing in my garden among roses and marble statues, yet nothing seems real but the kindness and wisdom of a prisoner I ordered beaten and condemned to death."

He looks out from his balcony with "dead eyes," wondering bitterly at this defiled closeness.

In my dream Titian loved the red cloth. But Pilate imagined hoarding white bandages, blue chiton, anything untouched by redness.

There is much redness, too, for Margarita.

After the Master's disappearance, she flies above Moscow's dreary streets until she finds herself in a strange room where she's washed with rose oil at the hour before midnight.

The devil's entourage is preparing her for his annual ball, to begin within the hour.

But unlike Pilate's, Margarita's red doesn't hurt her. Her skin is lighter, freer, the air sweet with the openings of roses.

Rose petal slippers are sewn onto her feet.

And although he is the devil, Woland says to her in a voice mild with compassion, "You are so enchantingly kind. Perhaps there is some sadness or anguish from which you suffer as from a terrible poison?"

She thinks of the Master's disappearance but says nothing.

Earlier she'd glimpsed Woland's globe in a corner. "I don't like listening to the news on the radio," he said, "this is much more convenient...Do you see that piece of land washed on one side by the ocean? Look how it's bursting into flame. A war has broken out there. If you step closer you will see it in detail."

When Margarita stepped closer she saw a whole country in flames—every leaf of each tree, every bird and worm in the forest, each brick of each small village; its inhabitants, their faces, their possessions. Blackening smoke. Piles of steaming rubble.

I wondered what the one across the ocean felt as she read this. (What would she feel if I could speak to her of Titian and his love of red cloth?)

Meanwhile my walls were growing even redder. I wanted only to go outside, but the redness wrapped me even tighter.

If I could know almost nothing of the one across the ocean (though the fact that she used the word *kindness* seemed some sort of indication), was there some way I might come closer to her through Margarita?

After all, she had mentioned her in her letters. Wasn't it reasonable to imagine her turning the worn pages like me, feeling the fate of Margarita as she looked into a globe or sat on a park bench or studied her few photos, lonely for the Master.

And that feeling of *kindness* which concerned her—how could she help but notice it in Margarita?

So it interested me to think about Margarita's kindness toward the dead woman, Frieda, who she meets at the devil's ball after midnight.

After the devil appoints her Queen of the Ball, Margarita stands for what seems like many hours (time is always illusive in Bulgakov's book) greeting the specters of the dead, invited guests. Hundreds of poisoners, traitors, perpetrators of all sorts of terrible acts. One hobbles in a cumbersome wood boot. Another covers her neck with a green bandage. But, of all of them, it is only the young woman, Frieda, who she can't forget.

As the dead twirl away and dance, Frieda stays nearby and looks into her eyes, desperate with imploring anguish. What is her punishment, Margarita begins to wonder, what was her specific crime? The devil's assistant explains that each night for the past thirty years a maid has laid a white handkerchief with a dark-blue border on the night table beside her, and each time she sees it, it drives her to despair.

This is the handkerchief she used to smother her newborn baby. "She was a waitress in a café...her boss lured her into the storeroom...nine months later she gave birth to a baby boy, carried him into the woods, stuffed the handkerchief in his mouth, then buried him...At her trial she said she panicked, fearing she had no food, nothing, no way to provide for him."

When the ball is over, Woland asks Margarita what single wish she'd like granted. She can choose only one. Of course she thinks of asking for the Master's return, that he be healed and beside her once again.

But when she speaks she speaks instead of Frieda.

"I want them to stop giving Frieda the handkerchief she used to smother her baby."

Though at first he's dumbfounded and thoroughly disapproves of her request, Woland grants her wish. Margarita insists her concern for Frieda has nothing to do with her own kindness.

"I am a thoughtless person...I asked you on Frieda's behalf only because I was careless enough to give her real hope..."

Yet even now, I find Margarita's description of herself unconvincing. After all, it was Frieda she noticed above all others, Frieda's eyes she couldn't forget.

The one across the ocean, pacing, not sleeping, did she think of this too? Did she watch the blue-bordered cloth finally vanish forever, though the crime remained, and memory, and the dampness of the forest floor—

Day after day I breathed red ocean, red air.

Titian had rubbed red pigment into eyelids, collarbones, garments, foreheads, lips, sometimes even into the whites of eyes. Had used, in the end,
his bare fingers.

The love of red cloth never left him.

As I lay in my red room, the air seemed both flower and flame—a tenderness but also what harms that tenderness. It was a silence that held me,
mute and burning, in its arms.

The mirrory disks of gondolas on water. In the church of San Geremia, Saint Lucy's mummified face covered by a silver mask.

For the first time in weeks I had ventured outside again. My shin muscles taut, my footsteps, tenuous, unsteady.

I looked up what boat to take to San Servolo: Public Boat Line 20 with departures from San Zaccaria (at Riva degli Sciavoni, in front of the Londra Palace Hotel) at ten-minute intervals throughout the day, and had decided on the 8:15 AM; arrival time 8:25. Maybe at the Conference Center I would stumble upon something more about the doctor. I didn't really know what else to do. Or maybe by chance he'd even be there and I could meet him. It was unclear what this had to do with my search for the lost notebook, but at least it seemed a place to begin.

I wasn't used to being out on the streets. Not red walls but pale sky all around me. Gray clouds of pollution rolling in from Maghera. Yellow, roughened stone.

I looked down into calm water. The boat's seats were mostly empty, the ride to the island short, uneventful.

By then I had found a copy of the book by Florensky I first noticed on the desk of the one across the ocean. Though it was hard to understand, it seemed to do with his idea that our linear thinking is wrong and that all time and space exist at once. I didn't know what to make of this, or what it implied about the distances inside me and between myself and others.

But soon I was raising my eyes from the water. The Conference Center stood a few yards beyond the dock—a stately, restored complex of cream-colored buildings. (Later, wandering inside, I counted 11 meeting rooms, an auditorium, a small theater.) One wing housed nearly 200 bedrooms; a white terrace overlooked the lagoon. There were several outdoor areas for gatherings—the "English Court," the "Cloister," "Baden Powell Square"—I wondered where those names had come from.

For a few minutes I walked down empty halls, past rooms filled with rows of red plastic chairs, white screens for presentations, podiums, long wooden desks.

The booklet I held announced "the transformation of the island, once a place of isolation, into a space for dialogue between culture and experience..."

(And yet couldn't isolation provide "culture" and "experience" as well? I chastened myself not to wonder at such things—to just stay focused on my task. Though I still wondered, why assume isolation needs to be "transformed"?)

Air conditioning. Internet. ATM machine. Bar. Laundry. Even a small general store.

Press office. Floral decoration. Shuttle boat service. Publicity. Poster designing. Simultaneous translation.

I passed a line of shut doors with bronze name plaques beside them:

Chiara Ballarin, Events Supervisor
Massimo Busetto, Reception Supervisor
Carlo Castiglioni, Facilities Supervisor
Manuela Cracco, Congress Department

What could that last one even mean? But I didn't dare knock. If someone answered, would I ask for the doctor, explain that I knew he sometimes stayed there, but how could I explain?

Outside again, I could see across the water to San Marco. The whole city slowly sinking. My legs ached, bones twig-like, too narrow. My plan seemed suddenly ludicrous, sheer folly. But just as I was going to step back onto the boat, I suddenly turned and walked toward the building, went inside and randomly opened the door, #9, of the first conference room I came to. I sat down in a red chair—waited for a long time doing nothing, stared at the red drapes, the window.

What would she think of what I was doing?

I walked over to the desk beneath the screen for presentations, and pulled open its long, narrow drawer, already slightly ajar.

Right away I could see that it was full of papers. Leftovers, I assumed, from some past conference. Why hadn't the custodians thrown them away?

I picked one up, touched its crinkled surface:

INTERNATIONAL SCHOOL OF NEUROLOGICAL SCIENCES IN VENICE

PRESIDENT: GIULIANO AVANZINI   DIRECTOR: FRANCESCO PALADIN

Then:

ADVANCED INTERNATIONAL COURSE   JULY 28–AUGUST 8

There were lists of sponsors, explanations of application requirements, and the course's main objectives. Then finally at the bottom of the page the list of faculty, but I didn't find the doctor's name.

I reached into the drawer again and took out the official listing of conference topics:

Auras and Clinical Features in Temporal Lobe Epilepsy: A New Approach on the Basis of Voxel-based Morphometry

Unilateral Thalamic Lesions on Lateralized Spike Wave Discharges

Mozart K.448 and Epileptic Form Discharges: Effect of Ratio of Lower to Higher Harmonics

What was I to make of that? Then I noticed, in the right-hand margin: *the results suggest listening to mozart k448 for two pianos may reduce epileptiform discharges. it is possible to reduce # of discharges by optimizing fundamental tones & minimizing higher frequency harmonics*

There seemed something beautiful in this, though I didn't really understand. Quickly I read on:

A Novel Perspective in Treatment: Is it Possible to Repair an Injured or Malfunctioning Human Brain?

A Preliminary Investigation Into Chromosome 17q.

Delusions, Illusions, and Hallucinations: 1. Elementary Phenomena 2. Complex Phenomena

The list went on and on, probably over several pages. What was I to do with what I found? No matter how much I thought, I didn't see how anything I came across could help her.

What I did next is simple to relate, though none of it *felt* simple at the time—the physical manifestation of an act being, I've come to think, so little of the act itself.

I made sure the door was tightly shut, then scooped up the entire mess of papers and shoved them into a plastic bag I took from the wastebasket beside the red curtains. Then slowly, quietly, holding them as if they were my own, I walked out into the hallway and past the row of nameplates, wondering would someone see me, then headed farther down the hallway until I exited the building, reached the dock, and took the public boat across the water.

In my room I would unpack them.

But as soon as I stepped off the boat at San Zaccaria the thought of returning to my room and its red walls unnerved me.

Cafes, grocery stores, tourist shops—my foot was swollen but I kept walking. After a while, I came to the old fish market at Campo Margherita where a centuries' old stone tablet detailed the daily terms for sales of fish. Had Titian often passed this, I wondered, as I looked idly at the list of fish:

Red Mullet, Grey Mullet, Sardine, Anchovy	Cent 7
Sea Bass, Gilthead, Umbrine, Sea Bream	Cent 12
Eel	Cent 25
Oyster	Cent 5
Mussel	Cent 3

Then ever so faintly but distinctly, a voice emerged from somewhere near me: *Who could condemn me more than I condemn myself?*

I looked around in each direction but saw no one. I can't stand here any longer, I said to myself, it's time to get back to the room even if I don't want to. I clutched the bag of papers tightly. After weeks of not walking, I had tired myself badly.

That night I was wandering inside one of Pontius Pilate's migraines. Even as I dreamed this I noted the absurdity of the act, told myself one can't walk *within* a neurological event. Yet that's what I was doing. A festering redness throbbed inside soft walls I took to be the tissues of his brain. Then I saw sudden streaks of blackish light—were his nerves misfiring, or had I come upon a lesion? At the crest of a reddish cliff Pilate's dog raised its pained eyes to the full moon. I realized it was blind. A brief, terrible howl broke from its mouth. The air was flooding with the scent of roses. Even the moonlight grew sick with it, even the few stars.

The red of Pilate's migraine still burned in me as I poured my morning coffee, my legs aching from the day before. For a moment I touched the thin stack of letters from the one across the ocean, but knew I should turn to the bag of stolen papers and walked over to the table where I'd left them.

Then I heard that female voice again, the same as from the fish market the day before:

I am on the island of Lazzaretto Nuovo. I want to go to Lazzaretto Vecchio where the plague victims are suffering and dying, but so far this has not been possible. How can I convince the white boats to take me?—I must keep trying until one of them finally agrees. Do you know what cries sound like through damp earth? How dead cries shudder and scrape through damp earth? My hands still stained with it. My handkerchief still stained though I have washed it many times. I want to tend to the sick on Lazzaretto Vecchio, the ones who will never get well—I'll dip a cloth into cold water, wipe their burning foreheads. If in their delirium one of them mistakes me for a loved one and murmurs words I'm not meant to hear, I promise not to betray them. When will the white boat come across the water? How long must I stand on this shore looking out in all directions? The wind is still tonight. The water empty.

I realized it was Frieda.

It was impossible that she could be beside me, and yet she was beside me.

Ovid had written: "All the things which I denied could happen are now happening."

I thought again of Florensky, his strange theories. How he believed time and space merge each into the other, that geometry as we know it is misleading, and that past, present, and future aren't separate.

Then once again the voice was speaking:

Maybe you sense the weight of my footsteps like the restless pacing of the one across the ocean. You want to help her, you want some relief from your own mind, but what if there is no end to harshness? Look at Lazzaretto Vecchio— so many horrible deaths, the ill thrown half-alive into dirt pits. Do you know what that plague island is used for now? It's a sanctuary for abandoned dogs. But a new sports complex is being planned, so what will happen to them when their refuge is taken away? Already the few trees are being cleared, the remnants of old walls hauled off. Profit. Concealment. It's all par for the course. Contests and cheering will replace the silence of charred bones. Why expect anything different? I know you would rather think about Margarita flying in the air in her red freedom, wind streaming through her hair. It's true she arranged for the nurse not to bring me the white handkerchief anymore, but how much does it really matter in the end? I still see it in my mind. I should leave you to your bag of papers. I must stay vigilant on this shore, must watch for the white boat that's coming.

Maybe I had been reading too much Florensky.

His essays were titled "Fictions in Geometry," "Reverse Perspective," "Beyond Vision."

Of course I found his writing mostly baffling. But I'd been trying to understand his points about the limits and misuses of perspective; how he believed we are wrong to view the "absence of perspectival unity" as a "failure or <u>sickness</u>" (he often underlined his words) or any flaw of seeing. Rather, our common notion of perspective is only one of many truths.

"First and foremost, space turns out to be <u>extremely diverse</u>." (Again, his love of underlining.)

"How very different the actual, lived system of our space-sensations is from the geometrical...the world is life, not frozen stasis..."

"We should have doubts that our world exists in Euclidean space which is just one particular, though privileged, instance of many heterogeneous, diverse spaces, all possessing the most unexpected characteristics."

And finally:

"What lies past the single horizon, single scale?"

But as I read, unexpected grief flooded over me. If space and time could collapse and blend into each other, why did so many smaller boundaries still remain? My hands isolate in air. The one across the ocean pacing far away and all alone, burning in her silent, private fevers. And Frieda's voice alive in my red room though she stood alone on some far island. Florensky seemed not to have written of these pained boundaries among the diverse, shifting planes he depicted.

The stark distances I'd accepted as the inevitable given texture of my life suddenly felt like a series of small cuts and taunting questions.

And still I thought of Frieda. How she was waiting for the boat to take her to the island. And how, though I couldn't see her, she didn't seem unreal. Her voice a raw skin. My own skin suddenly too raw, uncovered.

I know you want to get back to your bag of papers, not think of me at all. But what can I do, I still have things to tell you. I was so young when I committed my despicable act, so young when I died for it, so what can I even know of the actual world, how can I even speak of it, having lived in it so briefly? What could I possibly have to say to you at all? What right do I even have to speak? I watch your red walls, and ask myself these questions. Still, I can't bring myself to leave you. Maybe you think I am buried in Moscow, or outside the small village near the forest where I killed my baby, but how does a voice come to be buried? Does it? How do thoughts? I feel my questions press against your walls, my words growing slowly darker, redder. There are soft turnings in me also, and a sorrow I can barely name and have no right, I know, to feel, yet it lives like my white handkerchief inside me.

The island is cold tonight. It's said a new cargo boat arrives tomorrow morning. The crew will be quarantined for 40 days to make sure none are carriers of plague. All the cargo—wooden crates of spices, dried fruits, metals, hundreds of crates of colored cloths—will be taken to the storage sheds. But I think those sailors will not need me. They'll check off the days with thick brown chalk against the walls, bake bread in the stone ovens, wait out their days walking, building, thinking. Time and memory won't blacken or speed up inside them unlike those on that other, farther island from which no one returns.

The seabirds are circling tonight—their wordless flying.

Now that Frieda's voice was coming to me, the silence of the one across the ocean whose letters I still hoped might come but didn't, felt even louder, sharper, more confusing.

That night a hump moved beneath the water's blackened surface. When finally it emerged on shore, I saw that it was Pilate's dog. A stained white handkerchief was sticking to its back, and though it tried to shake it off it couldn't. I walked over to help, but when I reached out my hand, I saw the handkerchief was covering a triangle of raw skin, so how could I pull it off without hurting the dog further? The dog grew thinner and thinner, trembling like a palsied hand. Even if Pilate was a cruel, tormented man, or just a trapped, ordinary man flung into circumstances wildly beyond him, why couldn't he come help his dog, why couldn't he at least try to take care of it and feed it? I knew I should take it to my room, give it food, clean water, but also knew this was impossible, though for reasons I didn't understand.

Then for a few days I heard no voice at all, though at times there was the sound of quiet weeping.

Today I am remembering that on the island where you live there is the Ospedale degli Incurabili—or should I say it was there in the plague year of 1575—I believe it has since been abandoned. So what is it now?—A ruin? A music school? An empty lot? But in 1575 it was inhabited by the ill who weren't sent to lazzarettos. And it was there that one day a man with a horrible pestilential mange called out in anguish for one of the young fathers. These were the years, of course, when everyone was afraid to touch or draw close to another. The young father was terrified but scratched the patient's back as was required, then violently convulsed with nausea. But even then he didn't draw his hand away. This man is suffering, he said to himself (he wrote this down later), I must not shun him, what would I be if I shunned him? Then suddenly, almost without thinking, he lifted his pus-covered finger from the man's oozing back and placed it in his mouth and sucked it.

And what of my own mouth? What of yours?

And this white handkerchief inside me...

I wonder what you think of what he did. Are you awake now, watching your red walls, hoping that my voice will leave you?

Maybe you don't even hear me at all—

What does it mean to truly feel the living flesh of another, the presence of another? I ask myself this often.

I still need to find a boat to take me to Lazzaretto Vecchio. I'm not sure why I have told you what I have—

Though I tried to consider Florensky's theories, and maybe even accept them, I couldn't get used to the way her voice kept coming even as she brought me the idea of a man willingly touching his lips to another man's blistering, contaminated skin.

In my whole life I had barely ever touched another. I wasn't sure I could even remember the last time. Maybe it was when my hand grazed the hand of a salesperson giving me change.

From my childhood reading, I knew that "contamination" has its root in the Latin "contigere"—"to touch." How that gentlest, most unguarded act can lead to defilement and horror. But the more I thought about the young father, I saw what I should have all along: that what he did was beautiful, his defiled mouth more gentle and tender than I could ever understand. I moved my right hand along my lips, the thin, ignorant borderland of skin.

Sometimes I spend hours thinking about skin, how I carried it into the world as if I weren't moving through fire and the shadow of fire. That was before my hands became contaminated by my brutal, cowardly act—my skin a place of harm and sorrow. And now, when I think of the plague first entering Venice, I wonder how the newly infected could have even begun to understand what was happening to their skin, their very bodies. The earth and sky no longer benign. The sun suddenly shredding itself, darkening over every visible thing. As if even life itself were shredding. Even thought.

If thought is infection, how could I ever have felt any hint of peacefulness on my skin, and yet I did.

There are so many suffering and dying on the Lazzaretto island. I keep telling you this as if my words could burn or scar you. But why would I want to hurt you? Why would I want to do that to you? Sometimes I suspect I secretly want you to soothe me, though it's wrong to seek this from you, I know, or to feel I could in any way deserve it. Why do I keep coming to you? Why have I found you at all?

What is trust in the face of damage and contagion? What is love?

I understand that I am nothing. That my suffering is nothing.

This morning a new ship arrived from Malacca. I stood beneath a stand of trees and watched the crew unloading cargo, the Captain chalking inventory onto the barrack's farthest wall: porcelain, nutmeg, silk, camphor. Afterwards the men played cards, told stories. Now every hour or two a guard walks by, checks off their names against a master list: Antonio Trivisani, Vicolo da Ponte, Zeno Planta, Marco e Antonio di Batista. The date on the page is Sept 13, 1576.

They will stay here 40 days. I wonder who waits for them, not knowing where they are, why they are missing.

I believe you also think about such things.

A soft rain's beginning, gray seabirds lifting.

I thought again of Ovid's words: "All things which I denied could happen are now happening."

Yet wasn't I supposed to think what I was hearing was my mind's projection? (Was there a pill for it? Should I be taking one each morning?)

Neuroscience and progress would say this was so. But I wasn't sure that I believed in progress. Didn't humankind seem to move from one muddle to another, from one kind of ignorance and misunderstanding to another? Each age a different kind of cage—and those cages truly visible only from a gap of time and distance.

But though I felt the *fact* of her voice, I didn't know how to accept it. Even so, more and more the pores of my skin grew alert and taut with waiting.

And with her words the lengthening shadow of the plague moved toward me.

Then I was walking along a busy Venetian street which turned into a barren plain. A few yards away, someone half-naked lay face down in the dirt. I couldn't tell if it was a woman or a man. As I drew closer, I saw black sores oozing, split open like the ones the young father had tended even as he grew sick with nausea. *(...I must not shun him, what would I be if I shunned him?...)* But I was on a barren plain and not knowing what else to do, I ripped off a corner of my shirt, moistened it with bottled water, and swabbed the sores as best I could. I didn't know if this would help or maybe harm, and felt my ignorance, how little I knew of the real pain that moves through the real body of another. Suddenly I understood I was touching the back of the one across the ocean, though I couldn't see her face and couldn't tell if she sensed the cooling water.

Why do I even believe that you can hear me? These small waves are louder than your breath, my own mind louder, harsher. If my hand touched your hunched back, would I feel a yielding softness or a cage of brittle bone?

Now that I have found you, I hear my voice entering the air again like a strange, unseeing bird. Wings jackknifed, wary. It is so odd to hear it after all these years. So many years without speaking, so much dark...

This morning on my island, Lazzaretto Nuovo, the plague doctor has arrived to do his weekly rounds. I haven't seen him before (I don't know how long I've been on this island—sometimes I'm convinced it's been months or even years, but then wouldn't I have already seen him?). He's wearing a broad black hat, and a black coat that's covered with suet or wax to fend off infection; it extends from his neckline to his shoes. Both hands are covered with white gloves—I can see this from beneath my stand of trees—and he's carrying a white stick for measuring distance and fending off infection. He refuses to stand close to anyone, no matter how healthy. He knows that skin is precarious, untrustworthy, deceiving—it can change from pink to black in a few seconds. It's more dangerous than a mind, and quicker. More willing to erupt and vanish. But I haven't told you about his mask which looks like the gas masks of your century, but with a beak-like protrusion, the beak long and curved, its cavity filled with rosemary or camphor for detoxifying the air. In your century you know this is useless, though of course you have your own delusions. But it's too frightening to feel helpless for more than a few days, or often even a few hours, and the plague shows no sign of abating. On the mask are two round eye-pieces of red glass. It's believed infection enters most easily through the eyes...that anyone can fall sick from just looking at an infected person. And now the doctor turns his eyes from the shore and walks toward the barracks... he's stepping among the rows of narrow beds, lifting the sheets with his white stick, poking and probing, looking for abscesses and pustules. What does he see through his red lenses?—Our skin and the whole island drenched in redness. Everything flaring, festering, decomposing. Every few minutes he pauses to write in his ledger, then indicates with his hand who can stay another week, who will be sent to Lazzaretto Vecchio to die. And now the boat arrives to take him back, and just as quietly as he came to us he leaves us.

I reminded myself that everything she spoke of had once happened.

That the suffering was real, the bodies poked at by the doctor, real.

During my first days in Venice I noticed the plague doctors' masks in the shops around San Marco, had realized they were souvenirs of carnival, but the rest of their meaning escaped me.

Now, as I thought of Frieda's words, my walls burned red as those glass lenses.

I want you to hear me, but maybe I am wrong to want this...Maybe a voice is mostly endangerment and risk and best kept to itself...If speech is a kind of infection...and the desire to be heard, infection...but I don't know...I watch your closed eyelids' delicate membranes, their faint pulsations as you sleep. But your voice is unknown to me. I have never heard your voice.

I wish that you would show if you could hear me.

Titian had brought me his love of red cloth, so why couldn't I turn my head toward Frieda? Why wouldn't I try to comfort her, as Titian had tried to comfort me?

Though she kept coming to me, and I kept waiting, I wouldn't show that I could hear her.

Each time, I refused her any gesture. Acted like I didn't hear her or even know she existed.

(Though more and more I woke to her white handkerchief, its worn edges and blue border.)

.

Why won't they let me go to Lazzaretto Vecchio?—I want desperately to go there. Maybe you think it's cowardly and selfish of me to want this—that I am trying to soothe my suffering with the suffering of others. I say I want to tend them, but is this true?—Maybe I'm only trying to tend myself. (My mind still fills with black dirt and wet leaves, the white handkerchief on the forest floor.) But I can't imagine going anywhere else on earth. The plague doctor wears red lenses over his eyes, tries to cover and protect the deepest recesses of his eyes, but it's as if my eyes are covered with glass lenses also—only mine are tinted a deep black, or sometimes a blinding, glaring white. But never any other color. And I can never take them off. So what is the world of the thriving to me, the ones who see in colors? What is your Venice to me? There is no place for me among them. And even though Margarita stopped the handkerchief from being brought, I still feel it. I can never forget my terrible act. But if I could finally put my hands to good use, my eyes to good use...I need to go to Lazzaretto Vecchio. To the ones who are suffering and will never return. To those whose eyes are hurt animals violently exposed, with no lenses to protect them. Is it wrong of me to want this? They are falling away from everything they know, even their own names. If I could go to them...if I could tend them...my white cloth dipped into cool water...I would touch their burning skin, every cell in their bodies raw and unprotected—

Why do you keep your lips so tightly closed? Why do you avert your face and never answer? Why do I still believe that you might hear me?

Even if you don't show that you can hear me, I believe if I gave you the white handkerchief to hold in safe-keeping for me, and you agreed, you wouldn't speak of it or palm it off onto another. But maybe what I <u>believe</u> has little to do with anything. Maybe who you are is a truth beyond my comprehension, different from what my brain can hold. Maybe what we call knowing is more like angles but not a single point or center. Maybe there are only angles, and those angles keep changing. What if nothing is simply reducible?—but as I say this, my skin grows cold—I take the white handkerchief out of my pocket. It never changes color. Nothing about it ever changes—

As the illness keeps spreading, everyone in Venice is afraid. Windows are shuttered, even the thoroughfares are deserted. Letters are soaked in vinegar before being read if they are delivered at all. Often many months pass without reply. Children are made to carry birds which are thought to bring some small measure of protection—but how?

Sickness comes in waves, grows quieter in winter.

Always the suffering is the same.

Each day more merchants flee the city. On October 7th, 1575, a barrier is erected in the middle of the Rialto Bridge. Those in the worst three siestri may no longer pass into the other three.

The quiet of the streets is broken only by the howling of dogs and screeching of cats being slaughtered, then tossed into the canals.

The red silks that you saw hanging from the dyers' shops to dry—they're gone now. Weeds are sprouting up among the cobblestones.

In one year your Titian will be dead.

What does he think of the empty streets, the blank facades of the dyers' shops, the way the rich have taken the red silks and fled north?

When the senators meet they wear perfumed gloves, a sackful of rue around the neck, grains of arsenic secured above the heart.

Though the law requires that they stay to administer the crisis, soon most of them have fled. Only the poor remain in the city.

I stand on my shore and feel the black lenses hardening over my eyes. A black wind grazes my face.

Will the white boats look black now if they come? How will I even recognize them? Why can I still see your red walls when all else drowns in blackness?

Xenopsylla cheopsis.

Pulex irritans.

These are the names of the fleas that carry plague.

White clouds of insects rise like fragile cities from the bed sheets.

Such softness kills.

Did you know that fleas can jump for hours, even days, without resting? That although they feed on rats and humans they inevitably die of starvation?

Black infested rats invade the dwellings of the poor, multiplying quickly in vast numbers. Imagine dirty wells over-spilling, families huddled in close quarters. Everyone too afraid to go out.

The authorities issue a new edict: All suspect clothing must be burned. But the poor hide what they can. What else is there to use against the cold? Sometimes they bury their coats in the cold earth—

I tell you this as I watch your closed eyes, your face turned to the blank wall.

Think of the shut houses of the poor, black pustules suddenly appearing. The chaos that replaces thought—

Though I told myself I was hearing Frieda's voice, was I hearing it or seeing it, or both? It seemed to exist in some realm between the two. How could sound have skin?—and yet it did. Frieda, who was a voice and not, a color, a visitor, a wall, a presence and absence and not, a wound and poultice and not, came as a kind of sound-form I had no words for saying. My sense confused me. Her plague-facts building—endless blackening.

That night Frieda's face was beside me, her eyes covered with black lenses. In the dark I could make out almost nothing, yet I was sure it was her. I wondered if her lenses made me more distant, smaller, obscure; my refusal less vibrant. And if maybe this calmed her. What new fact about Venice would she tell me? I heard her clear her throat, and waited. But instead of speaking, she picked up a rock (where were we?) and started digging. When the hole was two feet deep and just as wide, she reached in to retrieve the pile of contaminated clothes she'd hidden—hundreds of miniature white handkerchiefs, stained and meticulously folded.

For many hours she unfolded and refolded them. The sun was black, and the few clouds.

Then she raised her hands to her temples, and started tugging to remove the black lenses. But nothing she could do could get them off.

.

Even behind the plague doctors' red lenses nothing is safe.

Though they try to understand what is happening, soon they see they're as helpless as anyone.

For months the physician Paolo Belletini meticulously documents every case he oversees: patients with boils so virulent that when those beneath the neck push upward they cause death by strangulation. Grotesque glandular swellings and brightly-striped rashes. Sometimes redness covers the entire body, or a single hemorrhaging blackens every inch of skin. At first he believes such extremity is the surest sign of imminent death. But after thousands of cases he notes that time and again it is the relatively small undramatic bumps called morbilli that are the most consistent indicators of nearly instant death.

So the very thing that isn't so terrible to look at, that doesn't repulse the watching eye—this is the most treacherous, most fearful.

The way some thoughts move quietly, almost blandly, yet cut more deeply than the cruelest word.

Why should anything be what we expect?

I lived so briefly in the visible world, touched it so briefly. There is little I can understand—

From this island of small trees, I can't touch the broadsheets being posted through the city though I know they're there. Notices of the election of plague guards. New regulations governing burials, bell-ringing, funerals. Penalties against the sale of contaminated goods. Advice on the washing of the face, the hands, the mouth. Instructions on how to perfume letters and books. The proper way to make a fire. The sale of second-hand clothing is forbidden.

Inside the government buildings arguments persist. Where has this suffering come from? Could it have been born of dead fish in the sea? A bad crop of wheat?

The city orders its doctors to gather in the Gran Consiglio. How can the air be corrupt when the stars are of great beauty? Could a single leather jacket passed from one person to another be responsible for the 25 most recent deaths? Might salt water be a disinfectant or is it a destructive carrier? Is there some way it might be both? Why does affliction dance most wildly among the poor?

No birds have abandoned their egg-filled nests. No serpent has emerged from the earth.

The merchant Panizzone Sacco, the gate-guard Besta, and the proofreader Borgarucci all retreat to their separate quarters to chart each day's death-count and chronicle the unfolding events.

Why is there so much sickness in Venice when the nearby islands of Murano and Guidecca are unaffected?

As I tell you this, as you sit in your red room, how can we understand such harshness as befell the city? And my voice that comes from afar and tries to find you—if you can hear it I still wonder what it means to you—or does it mean anything at all?

For years I lived only with black dirt and the white handkerchief that wouldn't leave me, my hands pressed to the forest floor, my skin rough with rotting leaves. My voice far from me. Even the trees were dust. And the ferns along the forest floor.

Why do I still come to you? Why do I still wonder if you'll see me?

How can I understand the separateness of your face, the quietness you live in, your closed, unmoving lips?

And now, throughout the city, even silk is being confiscated, set on fire and thrown into the water.

But why should anything I say know how to reach you? What could that shore with its ashes that hiss for a few minutes and then there's nothing ever give you?

Why did I ever think that I could know you?

But if I could understand how kindness moves from one body to another, from one mind into another...

As I listened, I tried to understand what it must feel like to spend centuries in silence and dirt, then suddenly hear your own voice emerge from your throat, your eyes suddenly aware of a stranger's face and body.

It was as if she had no gravity to hold her, nothing but her body which in itself had become a site of wrongness and injustice.

So by bringing me her plague-facts, was she trying to construct some vague simulation of gravity, a kind of tether, a connection between herself and things outside her, though she sensed this was a feeble imitation?

Wasn't she in need of something to hold her to the earth and the reality of another?

And still I didn't turn my head, though my refusal pressed like her black dirt inside me.

.

If there is a shard of brutality at the core of every word, a ruthlessness embedded in the plain fact of every word, wouldn't even *kindness,* that softest and most gentle, be infected like the rest?

I remembered the word *kind-cruel*—I'd read it but had never heard it spoken—how it seemed to point to a pervasive complication that felt true.

As even now, though I thought of her need to construct her makeshift gravity, I didn't picture myself trying to help (though often I thought of her dead child).

I didn't imagine removing the black lenses.

If I could come all the way to Venice for the one across the ocean, why couldn't I turn to Frieda, let her know her words had reached another, that in fact she wasn't alone? Sometimes in my sleep I even walked beside her, felt the rhythms of her breath, the wind blowing her hair—she wasn't wearing the black lenses. But then the white handkerchief would stretch to a black scrim between us, our footprints dissolving, and Frieda, though so close I could have touched her (though of course I never did), seemed unable to sense I was there, her eyes suddenly cloudy, as if blinded.

I haven't spoken for several days, I know, and must get back to the facts of the plague-city. I don't know why I feel them on my skin, restless, pressing in.

In September, 1575, after a delay of many months, the Venetian government finally officially acknowledges the epidemic, though still refuses to label it a plague: "We have understood that within two days twelve persons from the parish of San Zeno have perished..."

By October, the first quarantine houses are being built.

Winter, as usual, brings a brief reprieve.

But in the first week of June, the deaths suddenly quadruple. 270 patients are housed on Lazzaretto Vecchio, and another 580 on Lazzaretto Nuovo. 25,000 have already fled the city.

Of those who remain, 171 die in the first week of July.

By late summer, Lazzaretto Nuovo is "found to be so full of people that there is no space for anyone else." The lazzaretti are expanded to the islands of Mazorbo and San Erasmo. The Robbe Amorbate, "Sickened Things," are transported to various monasteries throughout the lagoon.

Shipbuilders from the Arsenale are instructed to produce more housing for the lazzaretti as quickly as possible. On my island alone, this increases the capacity "to a total of 2,000 souls."

A new law forbids all physicians from fleeing the city, though few actually obey.

Chalked on a stone wall: "Everything I've held close has vanished into whisper and ruin."

Who will bring food into the city?

Keys, doorknobs, windows, gates, everything touchable is suspect.

"Dress in pleasing silks or in cloth with light, sunlit colors," one authority advises. "Look at beautiful paintings without fear."

But the poor possess no "pleasing silks," they only plead that their few goods be spared.

In Milan the Cardinal fasts for three days, walks barefoot three times around the city, dresses "for sadness," a hood over his head, a metal cord hanging from his neck. He drags his cloak behind him on the ground.

Even on Lazzaretto Vecchio the terror increases. Rotting food and refuse are no longer swept from the rooms. The dying are thrown into the death-pits with the dead.

Does your Titian still dream of his beautiful silks, mix his red pigments? Is his garden still tended as before when it thrived as the grandest, most magnificent, in Venice?

In the face of all that is happening, how do eyes not blind themselves, how do they tolerate their ongoing ability to see?

I wish I could ask you...I wish that I could talk with you...though why should I wonder what you think when I've seen much more ugliness and darkness than you have...Yet I still wonder.

No new boats have arrived on my island.

Even as I speak to you, I try to remove these black lenses, but though I lift my hands and start to tug, I understand they will never come off. Is it better not to see all the plague-colors? The reds of the morbilli, the purple stripes of festering skin? Yellow eyes and pus-covered cloth?...Still, I think I'd rather see...But why am I able to see your red walls when everything else remains drained of color? How can your walls slip free from all this blackness?—Why don't these black lenses tint them?

I lived so briefly in the visible world, touched it so briefly. There is little I can understand......

Pontius Pilate was standing before me wearing the plague doctor's beaked mask and long black coat. Red lenses covered his eyes. "Can't you see the roses won't stop growing?" he said. "I have tried to seal myself against the world, I have wrapped myself in resin and blackness. Yet my mind still sickens with the scent of roses. Why do they fill up the sky like this, and my terrace, and every road into the city? Even my dog's coat is covered with roses, so how can I let him come near?" Then I was in a forest bordering a shore. I thought I heard the one across the ocean pacing back and forth, maybe waiting for some word from me or lost in her thoughts, but when I turned my head, Frieda was standing on the shore, her eyes covered with black lenses. She held a white cloth and pail of water. It was clear she couldn't see. Suddenly I had no idea who I was or why I was living. Waves broke on the shore. Gray seabirds circled.

Though my sight is growing dimmer, the times I glimpsed you haven't faded. I still see your pained walk, and how you read with open books around you, the computer screen glowing. I see what I saw then—scattered angles into open pages:

"worked as a seamstress and waitress in"

"St.Gallen"

"On a hot spring evening, just as the sun"

"is very fragile and easily destroyed."

   "hemicrania, meaning"   *"<u>half skull.</u> This was transformed"*

"<u>migraine</u>"

"My voice, although harsh"   *"nothing terrible in it"*

You read for many hours. Once you brought a document up on your screen but I couldn't read it.

Those thin slivers of words were the only ones I saw. I never glimpsed your books again. And now that I've said those words aloud—now that I've told you—I can feel they've left me. I stand here alone with my black lenses not knowing what words remain or how to speak them.

I waited for many days, but heard only quiet weeping.

Although for many days her words weren't coming...and although I didn't try to show her I could hear her...and although I knew any thinking I kept to myself did no good...each night before I slept I imagined lifting the black lenses from her eyes and washing her face with cooling water.

It's been many days since I last spoke, but I'm still walking this shore, still wondering why no boats are coming.

And I still have much to tell you about Venice.

As the city continues to suffer, there are many troubling signs and occurrences:

Titian's paintings are on fire in the Sala del Maggior Consigilo in the Doge's Palace. Other paintings by Bellini, Veronese, Carpaccio, Pisanello and Vivarini are also up in flames. No one knows why this is happening—Is it the work of arsonists? A sign from God? The trailing tail of a great comet?

Near the stalls for the Ascension Day Fair a fire breaks out in a small shop. The boy standing guard is burned alive.

Many begin to reconsider the famine of 1569, the War of Cyprus, the previous Great Fire of 1574—maybe they were portents, each one a sign of some unspoken wrongness.

Could the plague have been waiting dormant all along, a soft infected heart?

How will Venice ever heal itself? What flaw lies festering within the city? Despite the years of silks and proliferating riches (or could it be because of them?) what is it that's so terribly wrong?

Other signs are also noted:

On May 26, 1575, a "monstrous birth" is recorded in the Ghetto: "one body but with two heads, four arms, four legs, and in the middle one hole through which the filth is purged."

"It seems as though it is one body united against another."

The "monster" is put on display for eight days (it dies on the ninth) to be viewed by the general public for the price of admission.

Is this body our Republic, many ask—grotesque, divided, ailing?

When I was a child I sometimes walked through Patriarch's Park, bought ices and apricot juice from the stand that said BEER AND COLD DRINKS, didn't think about such things. Still believed in safety. Believed in my own goodness...

What did I know of thought's unstoppable lesions, of how time complicates itself and wrongness builds its hidden structures?

Given your fragile bones maybe you thought about such wrongness from the start. How comfort holds within itself the seeds of its own crumbling.

Do you hear Titian's voice or is he lost to you? Do you miss him as you look at your red walls? His kindness of red silk. His burning paintings—

These black lenses are pressing even harder onto my eyes. Always I feel their rigidity.

Even your red walls are darkening.

.

All night your silence laps against this shore.

As if silence is a form of listening, though I know it's not.

But why does the thought of you still calm me even as you give no sign that you might hear me, even as your red room grows darker?

The thought that she was growing unable to see me pressed down on me like the weight of her black lenses.

Where was the Venice I once read of where in honor of King Henry III of France, a banquet was set out on a sky of blue-gold cloth, and all the plates and cutlery, the goblets and napkins, were made of spun sugar?

As Frieda's plague-facts kept building, everything around me, even the most solid, seemed vulnerable, hurt, fragile.

The one across the ocean had written, *Think of how fragile they are, the islands of the Venetian Lagoon. So thin and unprotected.*

But where was she now...what was she doing? Was she still pacing? Was she even able to move?

Had her sight turned black like Frieda's?

Then one night when Frieda's voice still didn't come, I wondered if maybe she hoped I would be like the merchant Panizzone Sacco, the gate-guard Besta, and the proofreader Borgarucci—a chronicler who locked himself away to document the ongoing history: her forest floor, her handkerchief, her isolation. Maybe she wanted me to be her witness. But then I thought of what she told me: that she trusted me, if she did, because of my silence and aloneness…I could hold the white handkerchief, but never speak of it or pass it to another…

Even though I am no longer able to see you, I still want to bring you the facts of the plague-city.

Despite the ongoing suffering, the Venetian government still refuses to label the pestilence "plague"—a word that would halt trade ships and incite economic disaster.

Instead, they recruit two outside "experts" from Padua who demand exorbitant rewards for their services: "housing, gondolas, and all other conveniences of life for ourselves and our families."

After some days of examination, they offer their acceptable advice: "Not any house should be sealed. The transport boats to the lazzaretti are unnecessary and must immediately be disbanded." The government hopes this will calm the terrified city.

The Senate is eager to concur: "It is best for the public benefit to accept our experts' most honorable findings. The Sanitation Board has made the plague an invention to serve the purpose of its own self-aggrandizement."

But suffering doesn't bow to words. It doesn't heed evasions.

Soon there are over 100 deaths per day.

One night I watched you look up 'fact' on your computer. "In a neutral sense: a course, a deed, an act of conduct."

Why does the mind fight such neutrality, such conduct? I believe you think about such things as I do, but what proof do I have, why do I sense you'd understand? (Your face in shadow now, your walls...)

The two experts return to Padua where, for their "good works" in Venice, they are each honored with a raise of 250 florins, then after 10 years, one is granted a prime post in Bologna and subsequently appointed First Physician to the court of the Grand Duke of Tuscany.

We say "the body politic" but what happens when that body falls ill? Soon it's not one body but several. There is the body of those who are able to flee, and the body of those who are too poor and must remain.

So why does your Titian stay put in the city? He who could so easily cast his lot with the privileged...

The magistrates have fled, the councils have emptied.

The Medical Collegio is now granting numerous dispensations to the wealthy: this one's "melancholic tendencies require a change of air," while another must leave Venice because "in order to survive" he "needs to live in good and happy places."

Signs appear in store windows: CLOSED TO AVOID THE PLAGUE

IF I DON'T WANT TO SELL WHAT ARE YOU GOING TO DO ABOUT IT

THE MAESTRO IS AFRAID

Once your Venice took great pride in its "unanimitas"—its identity as "the single, unified will, the body and soul of the Republic."

The writer Pietro Barozzi asserted, "Our city is one body old and new, noble and ignoble, poor and rich...If any part of this body were to seek disproportionate aggrandizement it would deform itself and become like a body with a nose five feet long, or one whose hand wishes only to be an ear or eye."

But now baskets are lowered from windows in the hopes that someone will leave food. But who is there to leave it?

I try to look through this black air into your room and although I search for a long time I still can't see you. Did you ever hear me at all? I know I should stop asking this but I still wonder and can never quite decide.

Are you still in your room or have you left for somewhere else? Maybe you are far from here...

Where is my white boat? Why is this black shore so quiet?

For most of my life I thought my quietness would never be heard by another or matter to another. Though the caregivers had renamed me, their noticing seemed clinical, almost a kind of scientific observation.

But the more Frieda spoke of it and of how she sought but couldn't find me, the heavier and less private my quietness became.

Sometimes I still heard—as if from somewhere farther than her words— her quiet weeping.

———————

And from farther than her words, there were other things she'd brought that were real. I knew they were real, but how close could I truly bring them?—

I thought of the ones dying on the lazzaretto islands. How they suffered with an extremity that in health they could never have imagined and was beyond anything they could have borne.

And yet for a short time they bore it.

What could I know of their minds? What could I know of her shore, her black lenses, the way she hoped that silence is a form of listening?

"Our inconsolable city," the Patriarch Giovanni Trevisan writes in a letter as winter brings with it increasing sickness.

The Senate issues a notice seeking out "remedies from all quarters...whether they be physicians, surgeons, barbers, or any other man or woman who has knowledge, practice, or a secret for treating this mal contagioso."

In response, the physician Giaccomo Coppa offers his "special expertise" in exchange for the exclusive licensing and sale of his "incomparable remedies."

And for access to his "marvelous experimental secret," the Senate accedes to the demands of the French Priest, Mansueto, that he be compensated with a lump sum of 500 ducati with an additional 25 ducati for life.

To the Paduan nobleman Ruggerio dei Conti who proudly asserts that although he is "neither physician nor doctor," he has come upon a cure, they agree to "give exclusive rights to any profits resulting from his marvelous remedy."

But one Emilio Manolesso (profession and qualifications unrecorded) requests only that in exchange for his solution "a certain book be given back to me."

In July, 1576, the Consigiliore Dieci pays several hundred ducati to the physician Francesco Rodoano for his "secret remedy," as well as 400 ducati to an "anonymous person" who promises to "liberate the city within a few days without need of barbers or physicians."

Even on Lazzaretto Vecchio, the senior presiding physician demands "at least 3000 ducati, plus 30 ducati tax-free for life and through the lives of my children" in exchange for the "cure" his father-in-law bequeathed to his daughter's dowry.

These terms are also accepted by the Senate.

What happens to facts when they move through money and through fear? In what ways are they no longer true?

If I could talk to you, if I could ask you...

I wonder if I will ever see you again, your red walls, your coffee cup, your books...

A light rain is falling on my shore. I pace back and forth not knowing if I'll ever leave here.

Though I can't see you, I still want to bring you the plague chroniclers' luminous names: Vincenzo Tranquilli, Muzio Lumina, Girolamo Mercuriale—

Each one a comet streaking through black space—

I speak into this air where I once saw you—

For a long time I thought I might grow used to these black lenses, the grass a stiff black-gray beneath my feet, the sand gray also—But suddenly I'm not sure how to go on anymore. Even as I speak to you I feel I'm drifting farther and farther away into black space and don't know how to get back. And your room far from me, and your voice I never heard.

I couldn't find a way to hold in my mind her small, unprotected body drifting farther and farther away through black space *(I lived so briefly in the visible world, touched it so briefly. There is little I can understand...).* I'd been renamed for silence and separateness, I'd barely ever touched another's body—a store clerk's hand, a doctor's—so how could I know how to comfort, or ever convince her to come back...Like her, I knew almost nothing...

For some time I'd noticed she liked to say *your Venice* and sometimes even *your Titian*, as if I belonged to them and they to me, as if she wanted to reassure me that even though I felt alone, unlike her I was still bonded to the world—and that I shouldn't forget this.

Even as she drifted farther, she still offered me this kindness.

For several days I heard only quiet weeping.

If she had truly drifted away, how could I have heard that? I told myself that even though she wasn't speaking, the sound of her crying meant she hadn't left me.

But it also meant she felt deeply alone.

Even now, as I'm drifting farther through black space, I don't understand how I am on my island where I wait for my white boat and feel I can still talk to you, though my throat burns raw with antiparticles and a harsh, metallic odor.

Even on Lazzaretto Nuovo many are now dying.

A fleet of 3,000 boats surrounds the shore. Inside them, 10,000 patients brought from your Venice.

All night the soundless weight of anchors in dark water.

Grass continues to spread between the cobblestones of the city's streets. No one walks there anymore. All the way from the Rialto to San Marco, not one single soul.

And on Lazzaretto Vecchio, the number of confined has reached 8,000.

Each night at the sounding of the Ave Maria, there's singing from the barracks.

How long has it been since I first stood beneath these trees to watch the quarantined going about their days—the healthy working to improve the buildings, preparing meals and trading stories, the ordinary world still firmly lodged inside their bodies. But for the ones who've fallen ill so many bonds are crumbling...

Some leap from their beds, stumble madly through the makeshift gardens, fling themselves into the water.

It's true a small number still get well and are able to leave. I've seen whole boats of them setting out across the water. Calm light on lifted faces.

They return to a city where new approaches are being tried: textiles will be boiled instead of burned. But what difference can that make?

Great plumes of smoke rise constantly from Lazzaretto Vecchio: the incineration of the dead.

Now that the water is no longer unbroken and the boats heavy with suffering have drawn near, why do I still dream of leaving? Why wait for my white boat? Why head to that other, farther island?

Meanwhile the new ordinances continue:

Suspected or convalescent cases are permitted to emerge from their dwellings for two periods of ten minutes each day but must paint their faces white and carry a white stick 1.60 meters long.

Blind beggars who sing on street corners must henceforth stay indoors.

(But who is even left to beg from? Mostly it's the poor who remain, tightly locked inside their houses—)

Those who beg in front of churches or go from house to house will be punished by imprisonment or whipping.

Coal carriers, rag dealers, and repairers of old shoes are no longer allowed to take their business to the city's streets.

The families of the dead may not accompany the body to the grave.

"We must learn to find beautiful laws," one plague-chronicler writes. "We must understand more fully the nature of order."

But what laws can save the city? And in what ways might they be beautiful?

And what beauty is there to be found in the new ordinances that turn against the poor who are blamed for spreading the sickness through the city?

"Fear leads to extreme sadness of the soul," Leonardo Foravanti writes in his plague-tract, white X's on the doors increasing, the plague-silence spreading.

But there is also kindness.

Cardinal Borromeo encourages his priests to move among the poor and visit the plague huts: "Do not desert the afflicted."

He makes this list:

"We thank and grant plenary indulgence for all their good actions to:
Physicians who take the pulse of the plague-stricken.
Nurses who aid those physicians and touch the feared bodies.
Barbers who bleed or treat the infected.
Wet nurses who nourish the infected infants.
Those who lead or carry the sick to hospitals or huts.
Those who visit and console the suspected.
Those who bring messages, medicine, and food to the afflicted and suspected."

In Milan, the friar Paolo Bellintani calls for the distribution of daily rations to the poor.

500 additional wooden huts are built to shelter the new suspected cases.

"What is the price of terror?" the Venetian notary Benedetti asks. "How might we think of a soul condemned to isolation, sent off to suffer alone?"

Pilate's dog was walking over miles of barren earth. A red thorn was lodged in its right, front paw, and with each step the gash grew deeper. Had Pilate sent it away because he could no longer stand the scent of roses on its coat? Or had it wandered off on its own and been unable to find its way back? Or maybe a stranger had lured it away from the only one it loved. It was clear the dog was starving, its ribcage jutting waves. Then Frieda was beside it. In one hand she held a white cloth and in the other a bowl of water. But as she kneeled to hold its bleeding paw I saw that she was bleeding also—the blood pooling on her collarbone and neck, though the site of the wound wasn't visible. Her face was white with grief, her eyes blinded. Even so, she washed the dog for many minutes, then held it, gave it food. All the while her wound continued bleeding.

Isola.........isolation........i.......

―――――――――――

It's been so long since I've witnessed any color. Are your walls still red? Does Titian's hand still sometimes come to you in kindness?

I wish I could show you what I've found.

It's a curious document from the year 1576 (the year of your Titian's death, remember?).

At first it seems just an ordinary plague ledger:

"August 21: 40 year old man dies within a day. Towards evening a carbuncle breaks out on the right side of his mouth, followed by a high fever. By morning a bubo has formed on his right groin. His heart stops that afternoon."

"August 22: 23 year old pregnant woman dies. On Monday morning falls ill with fever. Wed night the fetus has aborted. Black morbilli all over her body. This afternoon ceases breathing."

The entries proceed in this way for many months. Hundreds of cases of the nameless dead. And always at the bottom of the page, the signature of the attending physician, Gaspare de Comité.

But the last page is different.

Here the doctor records his own symptoms:

"Wednesday: fever / Thursday through Saturday: there seems to be a reprieve / Sunday: a milky urine, red morbilli / Wednesday: black morbilli covering entire body."

Beneath this, he confirms and signs his own time and date of death: "Magister Gaspare de Comité. Died at approximately 5 o'clock in the afternoon. October 23."

That night I felt a hand moving over my face. It was the hand of Dr. Gaspare de Comité. First it erased my right eye, then the right corner of my mouth, my right cheek, the jaw bone beneath my right ear. It moved on to my left eyelid but left the eye intact, then erasing the few strands of hair on my forehead, edged down the left side of my neck.

The hand smelled of camphor, burning coal. In each place it touched me I heard the sound of coldness. How could cold be audible?—yet it was.

Then I realized Titian was standing beside me, though I couldn't hear his voice or see red cloth. Could he see that the doctor had erased parts of my face?

When I turned to ask him, my mouth was a shadow, impotent, half-vanished.

After some time I realized Frieda was there also. *How could he have signed his own death date like that?* she asked into the air, of no one, her eyes staring off into the distance.

For a split second I thought I sensed the one across the ocean pacing back and forth like Frieda, her eyes clouded over. I wanted to tell her about the bag of papers I had found, how I'd learned the doctor's name and had been to San Servolo.

But of course when I woke I was alone.

For the next few days I lived within Frieda's silence and the silence of the one across the ocean. I touched the worn letters.

In my sleeplessness many things have begun to happen. Does it matter how or why?...I've seen much more ugliness and darkness than you have...I would touch their burning skin, every cell in their bodies raw and unprotected—

My black shore frightens me, as if there is no softness left in the world anymore, only suffering and harshness and coarse sand.

Everywhere the innocent are wrapped in desolation. Nearly 50,000 Venetians have now died.

Even within one illness there are so many types of swellings: eminenta, apostome, carbone, bubone, antrace, dragonzello.

But what words are there for what goes on inside the mind?

I know I have no right to speak to you, or to believe that if you heard me my words would be anything you'd want.

How could I have ever hoped to shed this wet dirt, this odor of decaying branches?

Why did I lift my eyes to find you?

What if Venice can never be healed, the white boats forever rocking?

What if a black cloth has settled over this marsh covered by centuries of hauled stone, and nothing can lift it?

What if the paintings in the Sala del Maggior Consiglio won't stop burning, or this white handkerchief inside me?

And Titian's hand immolated in that light, your memories of him, his words, his garden?

What if there is no end to sorrow?

I ask too many questions, I know. As if these streets weren't deserted, the doors not locked and marked with X's.

In the days when I could see you, I watched one night as you looked up "heal" on your computer: "To become whole or sound, to recover"; "To save, clean, mend, purify, repair."

Water can be healed. And suffering. And earth. And bodies.

I hadn't known that "heal" can mean to "hide, conceal, keep secret"; "to cover over as with earth." So seeds are <u>healed</u> inside the ground. And roots in winter.

But your Venice doesn't heal.

Once it was known as "a site of purifying Air emanating from salty canals...this special Air that brings life to the near-dead, joy to the living, health to the sick, strength to the healthy." It was said that "Nowhere in all of Europe do people live more healthily than in Venice."

What if healing is by its very nature transitory, fragile, a passing stage within a greater wounding?

Wherever you are, I believe you must wonder about this also—

Though she said she'd endured much more ugliness and harshness than I had, and I hadn't disagreed, now, even as I listened to her speak, I imagined her skin merging with the lagoon's too-thin, eroding shores, or fading further into the blackness she drifted through, its acrid smell of burning metal.

Though I can't see you anymore and don't know how to find you or even know if you're in Venice, and though my skin is turning thinner, papery, my bones less protected, my eyes more like the eyes the plague doctors imagined, I still want to talk to you. I want to believe that you can hear me.

Before I grew lost within this blackness, before I put on my black lenses, I saw the blue sclera of your eyes. I'd read about such eyes and the fractured, twisted bones of your illness, the word "incurable" applied to your condition. I'd read about a surgery involving the insertion of a metal rod into the bone's internal cavity. How even when the bones heal they often heal crookedly and wrongly.

This aspect of you so visible, and yet you treat it like a secret, so I think it deeply hurts and shames you. But it's why I noticed you that first day at the fish market. Though your head hung heavily, I could still glimpse the bluish whites of your eyes. And the hump, irregular, lumpy, beneath your camel-colored coat, the awkwardness and worse you have no choice but to carry. I had read about body casts, something wrong with the DNA, children forced to lie in bed for months at a time, the silence too loud, bones fracturing in the middle ear, a quick snap, just like that, each part of them breaking. Even music can cause harm. Even a kind gesture, a wrong turn of the wrist opening a bottle.

I thought of how you will never stop breaking, your DNA won't let you. I wondered what it's like to live in minutes spiked and broken, each one too unwieldy, too unpredictable for your body. To have to think of the breakages, how you never stop breaking.

And in that split second I first saw you at the fish market, in my mind you were a child lying in a body cast white as the white handkerchief I carry. A sudden, inexplicable hurt went through me, and then my voice was back and I was speaking.

I had lived for so long in silence and black dirt. But when suddenly I could speak again I meant to speak of you, yet spoke only of myself—that I condemned myself. I was looking at you, thinking only of you, yet when I opened my mouth I said, "Who could condemn me more than I condemn myself?" And even if I hadn't spoken of you, there would have been so many things more interesting and more important to speak of than myself—conductivity, electricity, man's relationship to animals, the Arctic, silkworms. Why didn't I speak of them?

I told myself then I would speak to you of Venice, of the suffering here, that I would bring you anything but my own narrowness.

You were alone...I would bring my facts to you...I didn't know what else I could offer, what else to do.

I thought to myself: it is 1575, 50,000 souls have died in Venice. The Senators have fled. But Cardinal Borromeo walks among the poor with his head uncovered and says to anyone who will listen: "Do not desert the afflicted." And the notary Benedetti says, "The price of terror is isolation." He says, "Carry the sick to the hospitals and huts"..."Nourish the infected"..."Touch their feared bodies."

Though I had been thinking about her drifting away, and how her shore frightened her, nothing could have prepared me for what she just said. I didn't know how to take it all in.

All I knew was that I felt more naked than I ever thought possible, more exposed, frightened, ugly.

I needed to shut my eyes. I needed to run, but couldn't.

Then I was sleeping, or maybe thought I was asleep, but wasn't. I'm not sure what it was. The words kept coming and coming...

I think of the breakages........you never stop breaking.............

.........a wrong turn of the wrist.............even a kind gesture.............
.............inexplicable..........twisted.............your DNA won't let you.............
.................................no choice but to carry.................................
.....crookedly.....wrongly...............to carry the breaking.....the hump...............
to carry.............................to carry.............................alone and wrongly.............
.........minutes spiked and broken.............lumpy...unwieldy.........................
...you have no choice but to carry...........

And even after that—how many hours or days had passed, were passing?—
more words kept coming—

touch their feared bodies...............carry to the hospitals...............................
.....................................nourish............................touch...

       I think of the breakages......you never stop breaking..................

...........touch their feared.................................carry to..............................
even a kind gesture.......................crookedly...wrongly..................................
......touch fear..............................fear touch...................touch isolation...........
no choice but to carry..alone...lumpy........................
........................feared bodies................feared bodies....................................
.......carry to...................and fear...................and carry.................................
do not carry.................do not nourish...................do not touch....................
...carry feared touch..
...........fear their feared bodies.................................feared touch................

touch their and carry their......................their ugly hump..............................
their crookedness.................their twisted..........alone..............isolation...........
their hump...their ugly hump.................................

I was drifting away into black space...I was on earth with my ugly hump,
but I wasn't...on earth with my twisted bones, but I wasn't...or...no...I
closed my eyes and all I could see was black space and inside it a body, my
body, no more than a speck but still broken...The body was drifting away
through black space to where no one could touch it or know it existed,
its smudged mouth almost nothing as it drifted farther and farther away
into black space, black soundlessness spreading...

For several days I heard nothing. No words from her. No quiet weeping.

Was I in the world as I had been before?—That same world she'd reassured me I belonged to: *Your Venice. Your Titian.* Had I ever belonged, did I want to?

I didn't know if I would ever hear her again, or how I'd feel if I did. If I'd listen or maybe turn away.

Why would I want what she wanted to give me?

I have painted my face white and am carrying a white stick. I am on your island. Why is it so hard to find you? Though I'm away from my shore I know I must go back very soon to the white boats that still don't come or the black space I drift through among particles and infrared radiation, moving farther and farther away, though always I come back. But for now I am here and I wander past the Military Bakeries, and then along the Riva degli Schiavoni, not thinking, not planning—then I look up and see in front of me the old Orphanage that Pero Tafur noted on his visit from Spain in 1436: "There are few weeks or even days when the fishermen do not untangle dead babies from their nets...and so the rulers have taken counsel and founded this hospital with a hundred wet nurses so that those who seek to abandon their children do not kill them but leave them to be raised."

At these words, my skin grows cold, the white stick turns to ice in my hand. The air is a forest of damp leaves.

Then I am back on my small island.

An endless quiet over the whole earth.

Though I still wait for my white boat, making sure to look out across the water (I couldn't bear it if it came and went without my knowing), every now and then I still turn toward the barracks. As now, five "suspected cases" are being led from one building to another where the "confirmed" are being kept. I can't see their faces, only their shaved heads, their gray clothes loose shadows. When the plague doctor comes, will he send them across the water—though with so much sickness in Venice and no sign of it stopping, where is there left to even send them?

Do they exchange a few words as they walk? Or do they walk in a silence closed as the barracks door behind them—

Finally there comes The Day of the White Page. Imagine. After two years and over 50,000 dead, on January 1st, 1577, not one death is recorded in the Health Board's register.

After so many thousands of pages of symptoms, victims, times and circumstances of death, suddenly there is only blankness—

The city officially proclaims its liberation.

Hearts are filled with "incredible joy"..."emptied of past horrors."

Celebrations and processionals crowd the streets. The doge walks in humility, bareheaded, without his crown.

But within days the plague chronicler Rocco Benedetti is already noting in his journal: "Restored from the damage of suffering, people are busily funneling into the law courts litigating and fighting. We laugh easily as we stroll down streets still lined with the houses of the dead as though our great tragedy, the near-perishing of our city, never happened..."

How strange it must be to touch again the skin of another, the lips of another.

But what is Time to me? What is the White Page to me?

As she spoke, I found I could listen. When she walked alone and came upon the old Orphanage, or stood isolate outside The Day of the White Page that she could speak of but it would never touch her skin or mean that she could touch another, or as she watched the gray shadows of the confirmed walk from their old barracks, I could feel the same black space I'd drifted away through days before lingering on her body also, its odor of gunpowder, burned metal.

Frieda walked with her face painted white on the Calle de L'Ofizia de la Seda where the dyers' shops once stood. She had painted her black lenses also, but the whiteness that covered them was filmy, thinner, more sheer. Now that the plague was finally over, why hadn't she wiped the white stain from her face? Why hadn't she discarded her white stick?

All around her, laughter and singing from the canals and bridges: *Venezia rassomiglia ad una sposa...sposi ed amanti, buona fortuna...Venezia nostra, sei il piu bel nido...*

But in her whiteness she seemed almost to hear nothing.

What might it mean to her to feel another's hand cleansing the paint from her face, loosening the white stick from her grip?

Yet stripped of their covering, wouldn't the black lenses still remain?

My hand was drawing a damp cloth across her face, trying to cleanse and soothe what she couldn't cleanse herself.

But I held no cloth. My hand wasn't moving. And in that moment's stillness I felt inside my body the blind, isolate whiteness of her body.

Now that the rich have come back to reclaim their abandoned houses and factories, and all the streets that for two years were left empty and untended, the poor are being driven from the city.

"Everywhere the poor go around interrupting"—this from an official report on the current well-being of the city.

Hospitals for beggars are relocated to outside the city's limits.

Within the year, the Governors of the Mendicanti have banished over 800 paupers. The 300 or so who remain—the elderly, children, the sick—are sent for incarceration to a remote island hospital.

Why does getting rid of the poor feel like freedom to the ones in power?

And why must harshness reassert itself so quickly, with such ease? Has so little been learned from all the years of suffering?

I think of how you can't hear me or don't want to—does that also help you to feel free? Though my eyes are black with guilt and I know I shouldn't ask you.

I'm still standing on my shore, watching for my boat and waiting. Maybe it makes no sense to want to leave for that farther, harsher island, now that the plague has finally ended.

And still I want to go there. I don't believe the suffering is over.

You who have wondered about kindness, I would ask you why you think there must be so many forms of blindness, so many walls.

Do you believe I am wrong to stand on my dark shore still waiting for my boat to anchor? Though I ask you, I expect no answer—

I imagine, if you could hear or see me, you'd think me foolish to be standing on my shore and waiting, the black lenses fastened over my eyes. Why wait now that the plague is over? But everywhere the danger is still thickening. If Time as we know it is a construct of the mind, then is it wrong to think the dying are still waiting, that somewhere on an island they're still suffering, wondering if a tenderness might find them? Or maybe they're not wondering at all, despair having wiped even that from their bodies as they wither toward their unmarked graves—

Why should the white boats not last forever?

Why has this shore become so quiet? What is the meaning of "to mourn"?

That "our" in mourn—why hadn't I noticed it before?

Yet, like before, I still offered her no gesture.

Pilate stood on his stone terrace watching an eclipse of the sun as he burned in his red migraine, the slow isolate destruction of his mind. Through the darkening streets, tall lamps were being carried. Hadn't this same phenomenon followed Augustus's death?—"A total eclipse, then the sky on fire, blood-red comets, glowing embers in free-fall." Pilate shuddered as he thought this. Each time he tried to calm his migraine a red hand nailed to a cross appeared before him; he understood that it would stay forever. An attendant brought him his red robe but it was made of cobwebs. He put it on. Even the clouds were heavy with the scent of roses, even the sick sun.

―――――――――――――

The abandoned barracks are black now, and the gravediggers' makeshift implements, the brick ovens and stone cisterns, the grass covering the nameless graves.

Does Titian's hand still come to you? Do you feel the kindness of red cloth? Do you think about the one across the ocean and carry her letters in your pocket? Are you in Venice?

Maybe you still wonder about kindness, and why harshness reasserts itself so quickly. Why the poor are being banished from the city.

Do you walk these cobbled streets where I can't see you?

How does thinking hurt the core of seeing? Or is it seeing that hurts the core of thought?

My eyes wander over the small island of San Giorgio in Alga, and then to another, smaller island, San Giacomo in Palude, but everything is dark there also.

Then I am on the streets of your Venice, though I know I am also on my island, still waiting for the boat to come, and the air still smells of burning metal.

It is Carnival—"Carne Vale"—the "giving up of flesh."

These are the weeks before Lent. Masked faces swarming everywhere for miles.

There are Lion Heads. Suns. Veils draped from hooded caps. And the mask known as "la Muta" held in place by a disk between the teeth.

In the gambling hall of the Rialto, the players watch from behind white larvas, their cloaks fashioned from old sails.

There's also the mask known as "la Ganga" behind which men disguise themselves as women.

Even rich and poor can no longer be sorted as they stand beneath the wooden dove releasing flowers into the crowd, though at night they return to different lives, different houses.

Eight harnessed bulls drag a golden boat across the square followed by spangled acrobats and dancers.

The word "I" dissolving, the white X's washed to nothing—

For many weeks the pageants and spectacles continue.

Pigs are chased in circles, then slaughtered in the front-most Piazetta of the Ducal Palace. The Devil bursts from a fiery ball rolled into the square. Miniature castles are smashed with wooden clubs.

Turks balance on tightropes strung all the way from the boats in the lagoon to San Marco.

Peasants appear in glittering jewels as if from nowhere.

Even the doge watches from his window as the vast pageantry unfolds, his head no longer bare in a gesture of humility but adorned with a gold crown.

I grip the disk of the Servetta Muta between my teeth and stand in an alley not knowing how to belong.

The masked suns are twirling, dimming.

The black lenses ever blacker over my eyes.

The wooden dove still releasing all her flowers.

I believe now that you never heard me.

It had been weeks since I last picked up Bulgakov's book, but I remembered how, long after Pilate condemns the prisoner Ha-Nostri to death and finally finishes with his earthly life, he sits alone in a stone chair on a desolate summit and stays there for two thousand years.

Mostly he sleeps, but when the moon grows full a terrible agitation overtakes him. He rubs his hands spasmodically, his eyes jerk from side to side. Always he longs for the same thing—a path of moonlight where he and Ha-Nostri can walk side by side, at peace, finally speaking.

Though Frieda was on her island, waiting, and sometimes drifting through black space, she also sat alone in a stone chair on a parched summit overlooking a dry plain.

Maybe this is partly what Florensky meant by the limits of geometry— that there are ways we aren't ever in just one place. Or that our idea of place is too limited, too narrow.

I looked across the desolate miles to where she sat, the Servetta Muta covering her face, her white handkerchief folded in her lap. A few strands of hair lifted lightly from behind her mask as a cold wind moved in from the surrounding peaks that stood without echo and would never be destroyed.

If I could see color again...if I could know the meaning of to kneel. The meaning of kindness. The meaning of tenderness, to tend. The meaning of to give.

Again I saw Frieda alone in her stone chair on the far summit. She looked at the full moon with blinded eyes. No wind touched her skin or brought to her the slightest sound. Just once she briefly raised her hands to her face, adjusting a mask that wasn't there.

There's a boat on the shore, I can see it.

But when I try to walk toward it, my feet sore and burning from the heat, why do I suddenly seem not to be moving at all, even as I'm trying to go forward?

Thousands of black masks toss among the small, declining waves.

If I could know color again, if I could see, even for one second, white sails cutting through blue sky....

Even my white handkerchief is black now. And your quietness, all the ways that I can't find you.

How could I have ever hoped that you might hear me or turn in my direction?

If I could see into the deepest structure of chaos, would I glimpse an order beyond our human comprehension? Or would I find no order at all, but that what's real is even wilder, more baffling, than anything I could have thought?

Maybe my white boat will stay forever distant.

How can a black moon grow blacker? This black moon growing blacker, this black wind—

PART II

SAN SERVOLO

Frieda was gone.

I missed her voice, or whatever the various strands of light and dark I thought of as her voice were made of.

Her white boat, her handkerchief, her waiting.

Her love of the word *tend*.

How she tried so hard to see through her black lenses.

Even as she drifted through black space (the smell of burning metal on her skin) she wanted me to know that unlike her I still belonged to the world and it to me, and that I shouldn't forget this.

If Venice could outlast its own fragility, or at least manage, beyond all reason, to continue to exist within it, was there some way she might come back to me, that I might hear her once again?

But it was too late to undo my refusal—all the gestures I withheld, my silence.

My room an alien skin, my hands at my sides brittle, unthinking.

I tried to get used to not waiting for her voice. To understand it wasn't coming, and that silence was itself again, not the intervals between her speaking.

But my sense of time and space felt blind, too narrow. I turned to my Florensky.

"When an opaque body intercepts light in space, the <u>isolation</u> of that body occurs from one side..."

Was that what was happening to me? My body isolate, opaque, and yet I'd come to care for Frieda. And the one across the ocean—I still wished that I could hear from her and know her.

"In a sense all light is active, all matter passive."

I looked down at my hands, those two persistent lumps, passive, without recourse, brute matter plainly trapped.

Then I came to:

"This passive medium of matter, in its finest and most tender manifestation, is a <u>creature</u>."

I held the word *creature* in my mind, thought of the tender vulnerability within it. It seemed Florensky was expressing an almost-protectiveness toward matter, its unguarded limitations. Though most of what he wrote confused me, the words *tender* and *creature* moved in me, a wind that stung but also partly warmed and calmed me.

I knew I should put down my Florensky, and return to the bag of papers I had taken from the island. That it was long past time, even as my hands felt heavy with the weight of Frieda's absence.

But as I held the bag from San Servolo, my thoughts swerved again to Frieda—how I'd wanted to turn to her yet something in me didn't. And my love of facts, was that even true? Hadn't she laid them out before me—the plague islands, the history of Venice—and still I acted like I didn't hear her. My hands untrustworthy, besieged, deceitful. The room's surfaces subverted and undermined themselves the moment I even looked at them or touched them. Thoughts tied themselves into tight nooses.

Titian had brought me his kindness of red cloth, but what had I brought Frieda?

Then Titian was standing near the ruins of a castle among pines in a place I didn't recognize. "I am in Cadore," he said, "the village of my birth. Though I wrote many letters, little of what I said was personal, so much of who I am is lost. But what can anyone truly know of another? Take my painting 'Man of Sorrows' for instance. Vassari attributes it to me, then turns around and at the same time claims it was painted by Giorgione without acknowledging the contradiction. And as to my early life, some say I apprenticed myself to Gentille Bellini, but others say no, it was to his brother, Giovane, and still others say it was in truth to Giorgione, or even to Palma Vecchio, father of the beautiful Violante who I am said to have loved. My biographers write of the 'darkness that prevails' when they try to piece together my early life before the new century brought me fame. You may wonder why I am no longer holding the red cloth—but so much remains unknowable, mysterious, obscured. Think of the fragile land you stand on. The hundreds of thousands of pillars hidden beneath the water and St. Marks."

I tried to accept that there are many things I would never understand. That this is what a life is made of. Hadn't Florensky tried to say this? And now Titian?

Again I reminded myself it was time to turn to the bag of papers. After all, I had "given my word." Had promised to follow any hints, however unlikely or absurd, that might lead to the lost notebook or even an idea of what it was or why the one across the ocean sent me.

I needed to believe she was still alive, maybe pacing or waiting for some word from me, but when I tried to picture her all I could see was a white mist.

Titian spoke of Venice's fragility. But isn't all thought and intention also fragile, a form of contingency, and to "give one's word" as vulnerable and imperfect as skin? Why shouldn't the one across the ocean be lost to me, and I wouldn't even know it?

I waited a few minutes, then reached into the bag of papers. My hand touched something hard. I had found a thin bound volume.

The Island of the Mad, they call this. San Servolo. Each morning I walk the few steps to the shore and look out at Venice's buildings in the distance. But to step onto that soil would be like stepping from one skin into another, one mind into another.

And now we've been told we have to leave here, that after centuries of use this hospital will be closed forever.

The seizures come more frequently each week. For years I wanted nothing more than to stop them, but something's pulling me in ways I can't explain. The air splintering, slowly burning. Light/Dark. Each time one comes I fall through and fall through. A quick glittering, then blackness. Thin rips in the smallest particles of air. The world no longer real, or maybe it's the opposite—everything suddenly more sharply what it is, bluntly present, yet filled with a strange peace. As if space is scarified yet at the same time wholly composed. My mind watching from some farness, alert but coldly blind. Cells flickering, untethered.

The world wounds and soothes itself in ways I can't explain.

What are words in the face of this? What is thought?

If there is a dark joy I don't know how to think of it. But sometimes it comes to me like this light spreading over the lagoon.

I'll burn these pages before anyone can read them. Maybe weeks from now, maybe years.

What do I even know of this island where I live?

Only some dates, a few names.

In the 7th century the Benedictines fled the Franks and found refuge on this rocky soil. They built a monastery, a bell tower, planted medicinal gardens. Over time, they added cisterns, stables, workshops, many walls. They stayed for 500 years.

When they left it became a dwelling place for lepers.

After that, three centuries of hospitals began—first for wounded soldiers, then for the contaminated and frail, and now this one for "the mad and epileptic."

This morning while helping to sort the hospital's records for storage, I discovered the first admitted patient was one Lorenzi Stefani, "a fine Nobleman from Venice, confined in 1725." "Most illustrious," the official ledger says—but then goes on to call him "mad." I've been unable to find out anything else about him. Still, I wonder what it felt like to set foot on this island before any other patient had arrived. His footsteps through the halls echoing, too present. His eyes staring out from the cell window at the rows of empty cells. Who sent him here and why? Did he walk the few feet to the shore as I do now and look out across the water at the island he'd been sent from? Was he ever allowed home or did he die here?

I never expected to find the lost notebook, not really, not even for a minute. My eyes were blurring, I grew dizzy. When finally I steadied myself, I tried to accept what I was holding. All my years of reading had taught me a mixture of skepticism and enchantment, the nature of facts and the limits of my eyes before them—how they are more enduring, less corruptible, than the human mind. Now this new fact was before me, but it was something I could barely accept or understand.

For a moment I almost felt the one across the ocean, tense with mysterious waiting, but quickly the white mist replaced her.

All my life I lived within one form of brokenness or another, one aspect of disruption or another—my fragile bones, the blue fissures in the whites of my eyes—so how could I not notice that the pages I just read existed within a fracturing somewhat different from my own but also close to me, familiar. Each seizure a quick slash of lightning.

Then once again my eyes grew blurry.

Again I opened the notebook, started reading:

This morning among the hospital's uncatalogued documents, I found the "admission of the second mad, Giacomo Marini Baldassarre," which took place on September 3, 1732. By then the asylum was run by the Fatebenefratelli, the religious order of St. John of God, summoned by The Most Serene Republic of Venice to "provide care and solace for the wounded and afflicted."

He died in confinement on the 10th of May, 1749. He had lived here for 17 years.

"What is man? What is this sense of sorrow that continues always to exist?" I found this on a sheet of torn, blue paper.

And on another folded scrap: "compassion alone cannot discern the distance."

———————

"Think of the fragile land you stand on."—I remembered Titian said this.

But the more I tried to get my bearings, the more fragile the floor beneath me seemed, and the stone streets, all the words inside my mind, as if even a soft wind could break them.

Tonight looking out across the water I thought back to the first time I had a seizure. I hadn't known the world could be so broken. Always before, when I looked at the sky I saw sky, when I looked at a rock I saw rock. There was weight, mass, equal signs, right answers—the word "is" stronger and steadier than any human brain—all of that made sense, or seemed to. But afterwards everything was different—information no longer a series of locked or open boxes, the earth more a site of threat and de-coherence than of building. Particles of air sizzled in the too-bright light. The ground suddenly vulnerable, almost desperate, as if even my small weight could hurt it. I missed how before it had seemed almost despotic, oppressive, more durable and impermeable than thought.

There's a tingling in my right arm now. The red fire's starting in my eyes.

Now that the red fire is starting, how am I going to read to the one across the courtyard? I promised I would go to her and read each night I could.

And when I think of her, why do I need to compare her to something else—a nameless island in some far-off sea etc.—as if it's too unsettling to acknowledge her simply for what she is: singular, mostly unknowable.

I wonder if I can still go to her even though the fire's spreading. Maybe I can manage it for just a short time.

Pilate's migraine spilled in red waves from his terrace onto the dry plain below. He wanted to pick up the notebook on the stone table beside him, but knew if he did it would crumble to red dust. The sky flared red, and the hills in the far distance. His temples pulsed like a heart that disdains the body it belongs to, wanting only to break free, but air unmediated by lungs is alien, unwilling.

The notebook still open in my hands, I remembered the epileptic's promise to read to another and wondered who she was.

When she first asked me to read to her I was perplexed. I'd glimpsed her a few times in the courtyard, always with a book in her hands, either walking or sitting on a tree-shaded bench. A small woman with shoulder-length brown hair. She'd probably seen me working on and off in the hospital library, but didn't say this, just came up to me one day and said her eyes were failing, that she needed a reader and believed I might help her. "It's Dostoevsky, I've been reading his books but my eyes are weak and now the print is blurring." She was holding a worn copy of The Idiot.

I had suffered a seizure the night before—everything still slightly unreal, the ground wave-like, oddly alert. My head pounded, my neck muscles ached. The air jumped with a slight, nervous glitter, as if straining to recompose itself after hours of tireless breaking.

I don't remember if I answered or what I said. Here, take these, read them and then think about it, she said, as she handed me a few sheets of folded paper. Just burn them when you're done.

My right arm is still tingling. The red fire is spreading in my eyes.

As I read, I felt I'd opened a door of veins and skin, something softly beating I had no right to listen to or touch.

And then, in that soft beating, the white, glaring light of my childhood infirmary came back to me, the doctors' faces unreal in that harsh whiteness, tainted in a way I couldn't name, their words tainted also, much too real, as they explained the reasons my bones had broken and that this pattern wouldn't change.

Ugly consonants hung in the florescent air. My book in my hand, my eyes averted.

When they were finally done, I turned toward the small window and the grass, but something in me flinched and turned away. My eyes suddenly wary, unprotected.

Did the notebook writer feel this also in those hours after he seized and fell?—how even the word "is" grows lost and maimed at its pure core, unsteady.

I should burn these notes as she asked me to, I know. But instead, I keep taking them out, reading them again and again, and now what's worse, I've started pasting them into my notebook. I tell myself this keeps them safe, that no one will ever look for them or find them, but in truth my feelings are more suspect and less clear, more selfish. The red fire's still spreading through my eyes, even this air is stained with redness—

~~~

How can I explain why I need you to read to me?

If the doctors had their way I wouldn't even be writing this at all. They say it is forbidden for me to keep any private diary, any notes or journal at all, that I need only to rest. That if I were ever to write something down I must immediately hand it over. They will study it, place it in my records. They want to know why I am as I am, and the others before me.

They would think my secrecy a form of evil, or at least a blatant recalcitrance, a problem to be solved.

But to me it is the strongest flower.

If I can't live among words, what am I? And this book of Dostoevsky's I carry with me and take out even at night when the doctors insist I try to sleep....If they knew they would confiscate it also.

Can Time frighten itself? Each night I hold the book and wonder.

(They say I need to calm my mind, treat it as one treats a fevered child...)

But I know perfectly well why I am here. I know what is happening to me.

I still haven't really explained what I need from you and why. I will try again later—

This is what is happening to me:

There are malformed infectious proteins known as prions spreading through my body, opening and folding like strange fans.

This movement is called "conformational influence." Each day inside my brain, prions hollow out the thalmus.

"Sleep," Robert Burton wrote in The Anatomy of Melancholy, "moistens and fattens the body, concocts, and helpes digestion, expels cares, pacifies the mind, refreshest the weary limbs after long work."

But I no longer sleep. Or sleep only briefly, tense as these wrong wings inside me.

It's said there is no cure. Since prions aren't technically alive they can't be killed by radiation. This is hard for me to understand...

My pupils will shrink to the size of pinpoints. Already I shiver often. My sight blurs, my forehead's moist.

For centuries there was no name for this. My ancestors waited in shame to see which one would sicken next. Was it a form of insanity? A punishment for evil deeds? They pulled into themselves, walked with lowered eyes, barely stepped onto the streets of the Veneto. Spoke of it to almost no one. Not even to each other.

Pico della Mirandola called man "plasteis et factor"—"maker and molder of himself." But I see now this is wrong. There is so little we control, so much mystery and harm inside us.

In the coming months I will sleep even less. Maybe I will grow unable to use my arms or legs, my pulse quickening, my hands agitated, shaking. Some lose all speech and fall into a coma, others hallucinate, but a few remain lucid until the end. I don't know how it will be with me.

Sleep is a soft covering, I see this now. A place of safety. It's one of the first things the brain learns even before birth, inside the womb. How does one live without such safety? I guess I will find out. Sometimes I leave my books behind, walk down to the water, try to think about this, but my mind mostly goes blank—

Long ago those who died of this were buried in nine-foot-deep graves. It was thought this might protect the living. The bereaved were warned never to touch their dead—As if staying apart could keep them safe, as if suffering must inevitably come from the outside...

Now that my eyes are failing I would be grateful if you'd read to me. I have been rereading many books by Dostoevsky.

Finding the notebook had been unsettling enough—but now this. How could I possibly accept what I just read?—this illness that echoed so closely the condition of the one across the ocean. It was as if every fracture in my body had come back at once. I longed for the real bridges of Venice, the clear sounds of the canals, anything palpable and likely. But the longer I thought, the shallower my breath became. My body ached. My sight grew dim again, and wary.

When finally I steadied myself, the first thing that came to mind was that Dostoevsky once traveled to Venice. (I learned this years before while scanning.) Given all that had been pressing in on me—prions, fire, seizures, blurring eyes—why focus on this one small fact? And yet I did. It had been years since I'd thought of *The Idiot* or *The Brothers Karamazov*, each with its epileptic character, or of how Dostoevsky suffered from the same affliction.

What year had it been when he stopped for a few days in Venice before heading to Trieste, then on to Prague? Nearly destitute, wanting only to go home. "This total isolation is difficult to bear," he wrote. *The Idiot* was finished by then, his newborn daughter several months dead. In his diary he noted the time and duration of each seizure. In those months they came often.

"What most people regard as fantastic I hold to be the inmost essence of truth," he wrote. "In any newspaper one picks up one comes across reports of wholly authentic facts which nevertheless seem completely extraordinary, yet they are the truth for they are facts."

(As I read that, I pressed the scanner's stop button, copied it down.)

Then I thought once again of how Frieda said I loved facts, and that each time she said it something in me flinched and wondered.

But the world's facts kept pressing in.

For several days my eyes kept blurring. My walls crumbling, dissolving, reassembling—

Titian was walking over miles of red cloth. "It's as beautiful as ever," he said, though thousands of small holes glared up from it like ragged eyes. Then Frieda was beside him, holding a red handkerchief, the moon red and full above her, her face turned toward a shore I couldn't see. I felt the epileptic's notebook in my hands, but couldn't see it. The term "conformational influence" ran through my mind but no matter how hard I tried I couldn't remember what it meant. How could I think if I couldn't understand the words? Then I realized the notebook was also pocked with holes, small roughnesses I couldn't mend. The longer I looked, the more numerous the holes became. I wondered if Titian would finally despair at the millions of blind eyes he stood among, but his face was calm, his hands open.

Often I wonder, how will I take my place among those who came before me?

The first suspected case was a physician who died in the Campo Santi Apostoli near the Jewish Ghetto in 1765. For a year his breathing grew increasingly labored until finally he took to his bed.

In his delirium he gathered Caterina Quirini's spilled pearls from the ballroom floor before the King of Denmark could grab them for himself, insisted on exchanging his red leggings (the color of revolution) for the safer black signifying piety, knocked on his own window thinking it a golden door.

For brief moments he almost came back to himself, pondered the beauty of mathematics, science, reason. Scrutinized and wondered. Jotted down what he could. After all, his teacher was Morgani who had been taught by Valsalva, who himself had been taught by the anatomist Malpighi, who had been taught, in turn, by Borelli, pupil of the monk Castelli, who had been taught by Galileo.

He remembered standing in the Acquapendente in Padua, the most famous anatomy theater in all of Europe, watching the miraculous wand of Morgani's scalpel. He was so young then, ideas didn't frighten him.

But in his bed hundreds of pearls rolled across the ballroom floor. Caterina Quirini spun faster and faster, her hem churning to white foam.

Finally everything grew still. The anatomists stood faceless, without hands. The ballroom was empty.

Pearls didn't exist. Anatomy theaters didn't exist.

Why do I tell you this? I want only for you to open Dostoevsky's book and read to me of Prince Myshkin stepping off the train in Petersburg after many years away in the sanitarium in Switzerland—everything he once knew pressing into him again, his face curious in the dirty light—

These errant proteins inside me are named for a genus of small petrels, *pachyptila desolata*, also known as the avian prion, found in the south seas. "A fluttering thing of pale gray-blue and white...a flightless bird...a ghost..."

It's marked with a black "m" across the back extending from one wing-tip to another.

Sometimes I feel those flightless wings with their black "m" inside me.

But mostly I feel no wings at all. I think only of what's fact: that among the many hundreds of genes on Chromosome 20, some for the regulation of insulin, others for the control of childhood eczema etc.—one is misfiring inside me.

Dostoevsky had one black eye and one brown eye, did you know this? The black one—his right—was said to have resulted from an epileptic fall or maybe from the treatment that ensued (some say it was a needle in the eye) which left the pupil enormously enlarged, the iris almost entirely obscured.

Often I think of that dark eye. He wrote in his notebook, "My nerves are unstrung in the extreme...Yesterday I pawned my overcoat...I sit at my desk night and day but still need to work faster. The fit has left me very tired. I have ruined my own joy like a hawk attacking a small bird."

The less I sleep the more I need the books I can no longer read. I believe you can help me.

Forgive me, I xxx   it's not that I expect things to make sense

"Strange facts are before us in abundance," the elusive, unnamed narrator of Dostoevsky's great novel, The Idiot, says, "but far from making things clearer, they obscure every explanation."

How can I explain why I need this so badly?

"The soul of another is a dark place," Prince Myshkin thinks to himself as he walks in his own darkness, "and what chaos is found there."

Today I found a copy of The Idiot in the hospital library, and although I've just barely started skimming, I can see it's the story of a young man, Prince Myshkin, who after years away from St. Petersburg for treatment for epilepsy struggles to adjust to the world he has returned to. But much trouble befalls him. He is a good man but unworldly. When moved by the tormented, beautiful Nastasya, he wants only to help and comfort her. But the more he tries to understand the ways and motives of Nastasya and others around him, the more his fragile steadiness begins to crumble. Often he feels different and apart. By the end of the book he has seen many terrible things and can't find his way back from that knowledge.

Why did she choose this book for us to read? Does she know that like Myshkin I also seize and fall?

How could I even begin to absorb what I was reading?—her need, the history of her illness, how she asked for help though she didn't even know him. His willingness to go to her, how he listened and didn't turn away.

And how could this not be shadowed by what happened between Frieda and myself?

The notewriter said Dostoevsky believed he ruined his own joy. But what wrong did he believe he committed, what violence inflicted on himself? Did he believe his fits were his own fault?

Once again, I remembered my childhood infirmary. My left leg had broken (a break that came mysteriously and quietly, as if a furtive creature lived in me who hated me but wouldn't say why, and every now and then would hurt me). Thin fractures started spreading through my spine. I learned very young that clamor often does less harm than what takes place in secret quiet. And now, in the infirmary, I had to stay still for many weeks.

I was reading a book called *Phillips's New World of Words.*

At "J" I came to "joy":

"Joys of the Planets are certain Dignities that befall such planets."

"Every planet, according to Ptolemy, is in his joy when another is dignified and when each planet can exist according to its nature."

But what, exactly, was a Dignity? And how could it "befall" a planet? What had this to do with joy? Right away I knew I couldn't understand. But though I couldn't say just how, those words felt to me like balance and justice, maybe even peace. As if somewhere the universe is deeply kind and can communicate that kindness. For a moment I pictured my body not breaking, and the others around me unhurt within their given natures.

Already we've made our way through the first few chapters of The Idiot. And last night before I left she spoke briefly about Dostoevsky's life—his childhood in Moscow and Daravoe, the prison years, his travels through Europe, though the whole time she kept her eyes averted. Often when we read she asks me to double back and go over the same passages again, or even parts we finished days before—so it's as if I'm thrown back into a darkness I've struggled hard to leave, or a patch of mottled sunlight I never expected to set eyes on again. I try not to think about time, the ways it can feel torn and broken.

But this morning I had a seizure that's left me too tired to go to her tonight. Hours of black waves washing over me. A feeling of great thirst.

Last night when you didn't come I tried looking through the book myself, but the letters blurred and spread across the page. I've been thinking about how Dostoevsky wanted to write a novel about a truly good man, but I'm not sure in the end he did this. Doesn't Myshkin become more and more like the others, his pure goodness and compassion confused, his thoughts contaminated and contorted, until a darkness overtakes him.

In the beginning he sees and feels so clearly but gradually arrives at a seeing that is torn and desperate.

I wonder what you think of this. Is it impossible to live unruined in the world?—

I have noticed throughout the book the word "ruin" appears often.

I don't know if it is day or night now. I don't know why you're not coming.

Frieda was sitting in her stone chair on the parched summit. Behind her, miles of jagged peaks jutted up from the rough, untended soil. The Servetta Muta lay like her white handkerchief in her lap, and from the tilt of her head she seemed to be staring at the moon, though I couldn't see her face. Black miles between us, miles of cold, degraded air. Then I thought I heard her speaking, though knew also she was far from me and silent, *He goes to her whenever he can, reads page after page even as his world swerves and breaks and a red fire spreads inside his eyes. Even as he fears the words will hurt her. I imagine much tenderness in his face. His hands turning pages.*

I told myself her voice was a small vessel that would crack if I touched it. But when I looked at my hands I saw only two fingerless stumps, blunt matter cut off at the wrists, the blotched, purple skin sewn shut with coarse black stitches.

"Here are the islands of the painful," Pompeo Molmenti wrote in *Venice: Its Individual Growth from the Earliest Beginnings to the Fall of the Republic,* his monumental 5-volume work from 1905. Over 2,000 pages, but less than a paragraph on San Servolo.

In all those thousands of pages he passed over the small islands so quickly, with not even a pause to explain why he chose the word "painful."

But now as I pictured the epileptic and the one he read to, each alone but still thinking of the other, I thought of how Dostoevsky understood more than anyone that dailyness is a form of extremity, and instability and pain live within the most ordinary hour.

He wrote in a letter, "Writers don't invent or fantasize but document what is."

Why did I ever think of sleep as stillness?

Sleep spindles are synchronous brain waves that come in bursts in stage 2 sleep. I know this now, though when my brain could still make use of them I didn't know the term or that they even existed. They show as eye-shaped clusters on the EEG. It's said they enable the integration of new information into our existing knowledge, but what happens when those eyes begin to vanish?...

Today I had a waking dream. I was in a stranger's room, bare except for a small writing table with a carafe of water; a divan draped in worn brown fabric; also a round table covered with a small red cotton cloth. I realized this was Dostoevsky's study. There were many papers on the floor but of course I didn't touch them. For hours I waited, hoping he might come. Then I felt his dilated eye watching from outside the window. But the more I felt it, the more it dawned on me he didn't see me, that I was nothing to him, he was lost in thoughts of Myshkin and of the word "ruin" that accompanied him everywhere he went. He marveled that he could love such a treacherous word, that it drew rather than repelled him. Then I, too, felt flooded with love for that word though I couldn't explain it.

I wonder when you'll read to me again. I believe that you still want to.

Since you still haven't come, I've been remembering the early passages where Myshkin speaks of the Swiss village he was sent to with the hope he would recover. But there's something I still don't understand. Remember how soon after his arrival he notices a waterfall nearby—"It fell from a height on the mountain, almost perpendicular, white and splashing." At night its sound calms him, and often at mid-day he wanders up the mountainside to glimpse it. But he goes on to say, "If I walked straight on, far, far away, and reached the line where sky and earth meet...there I should find a new life a thousand times richer and more turbulent than ours."

But why would he want a more turbulent life? Why would he say that? Why would he even think such a thing? And he, especially, whose body already fills with turbulence as it seizes and then floods him with shame.

Do you understand what that turbulence a thousand times stronger would give him, what he would find in that new life, why he could think it a good thing?

It's been many days since I last saw you. I wonder where you are and why you aren't coming. I hope nothing has harmed you.

Last night I was finally well enough to go to her again. We read from Chapter 6, Part 1, where Myshkin remembers the destitute Swiss peasant girl, Marie, but then as soon as I finished she asked for it again, and then again. I keep wondering what it means to her, what she is thinking.

All day I've been going over the bare outline in my mind: how Marie, humiliated and sick, crawls back through mud to her small village, having been abandoned by the traveler she ran off with. But the villagers treat her like "a spider," mock her and refuse her food. Finally "she no longer opens her lips," but walks among the cattle that move in inhuman quietness through the fields. All she wants is to watch over them and tend them. Each day she does this until the herdsman sees her and drives her away.

But she slips back among them with her wooden stick. Even after she's grown too ill to walk, she rests on a nearby ledge and watches. This brings her great happiness. Her face thin as a skeleton's by then.

When we finished, I waited a few minutes to see if she might ask why I hadn't come the week before, but she said nothing.

Sometimes the nights are very long but at other times short I don't know how to account for this xxx And how can I be in this room when I am also on my rock ledge watching for my cattle Remember how Myshkin says of himself "I have no right sense of proportion" xx the waterfall still bright white inside him though no one in St Petersburg can see it xxx His gestures so often awkward misbegotten xxx "My words are incongruous" Myshkin says It is so hard for him to steady himself in a world that keeps shifting and confusing him though all he wants is to be kind xxx But after the herdsman chased me away I slipped back and for a long time he didn't see me and then one day he watched and saw I could be useful x xx he left me scraps of bread sometimes left-overs from his dinner xx But the cows where are they it's snowing xx If I could go to them if I could tend them—

I think you were here last night but I'm not sure why can't I be sure xxxx

And the cattle are lost in their white field their eyelids weighted down with ice xx I don't know how to help them xx I can't move from this rock ledge my legs too weak white air burning my lungs xx If I could go to them like I used to If I could herd them give them some dry hay and shelter but they shiver and move off and I fear they will soon freeze or starve xxx and the stray calves have separated from the others it's growing darker now where are they xxx they could be wandering lost by the ravine xx Why won't someone come for them now that it's too hard for me to walk xx The snow spreading its white harm all over their mysterious bodies their faces trapped in isolation xx xx

Is sleep also white it's been so long since I've felt it I can't remember its color or how it enters the body how it stays xxx Synaptic instability xxx Sleep spindles xxx Prions xxx xxx Once I was a good cow-herder but now—

I knew I was in Venice among canals and stone bridges, that my back was humped, my bones distorted, that I'd once traveled to San Servolo....

Still, as I closed the notebook for the night, I could almost smell that snow-white field with its cold cattle. And the one who waited to be read to, it seemed I almost touched her (though, as with Frieda, I would never actually touch her)—that I should try to soothe the sleepless pressure she was under. I didn't know how to think about the way she was in her room on the island and not, waiting to be read to and not, was Marie and still herself yet not, partly sheltered, protected, and yet not. Her sleeplessness carrying her somewhere malleable and porous even as filled with struggle.

But I'm remembering back to before Myshkin even arrives at the sanitarium xxx he is on his way there sick and half out of his mind with little hope of ever getting well xxx "I had no logical power of thought" he says xx often he could barely even speak xx had trouble understanding what was asked xx and these prions inside me xx On a stop in the marketplace at Bale he comes upon a donkey xx He has never seen one before but as soon as he's near its braying brings him peace xx xx But why would that braying bring peace what could be more odd x unlikely xxx "I understood what a useful creature it was—patient, industrious, strong, long-suffering, and when I heard it my sadness passed completely." Even after Myshkin says this I still can't fully stop my wondering x xxx I hold these pages looking for some answer but they blacken in my hands xxx Then I start thinking that though the donkey is long-suffering mistreated it inflicts no suffering or harm on others...it doesn't add by its own actions to the wrongness of the world xxx its voice grating inelegant honest without power xxx Myshkin hears it and instantly feels and understands this xx xx xx It is so easy to do harm and so hard not to xx though the donkey is misused and burdened its eyes aren't ugly its whole being is alive with feeling xx Is this why Myshkin grows less desperate—

Each time she sends a note I answer only with this quiet—I never send anything in return. When I am with her I read calmly, go over each page as many times as she wants. We go back to Marie moving with the cattle through the field until she is too weak to walk. We go back to the Swiss village, the waterfall, the donkey. But she never sees me when I fall, or the drained hours that come after when even words are lesions and those lesions are alive, they're creatures, and I know if I try to speak them I'll only cause them harm. My pronunciation's not right, sounds garble in my mouth, I am a beggar who doesn't know how to beg.

But tonight, I'm finally well again—my hands the snow of her cold field, her ground ice-white, new snow still falling, and I'm listening to how she is Marie and the rock ledge is there for her and the cattle, and this makes it possible for her to live. Tonight, I can't know myself apart from her, my thoughts inseparable from the words she sends me.

But each time a seizure comes, there's no bridge connecting me to anyone, not even her.

xxx But what if there is a patient hidden chaos within even the most tender-seeming word even the most kind most calming despite the donkey's eyes its usefulness its goodness A feeling of No earth No sun No moon xxx Instability xx Disorder—I wondered this last night after you left xxx I wish that I could see you as I write this xxx I know I'm not sitting on my rock ledge anymore but in this room where we've read so many pages xxx And yet I feel the rock ledge pressing xxx The hours laboring and folding xx the twelve trees x the courtyard

Today, continuing to sort the hospital's books and documents for storage (though I would rather not think of how soon we have to leave here) I came upon Spratling's <u>Epilepsy and Its Treatment</u>—the word <u>destroy</u> everywhere present:

"Destroys regulation"   *"Destroys equilibrium"*

"Destroys any peacefulness of being"

"Comes quietly and inevitably destroys"
"Insidious destruction, sudden loss"   *"Silent forms of destruction"*
"Destroys color"   *"Destroys constancy"*   *"Destroys unity"*

"Suspends or temporarily destroys"   *"Destroys attachment"*

"Destroys trust in the constancy of time"

"Destroys the basic feeling of what's real"

As I looked at that word, and, according to Spratling, all the things it obliterates: color, constancy, peacefulness, attachment, a feeling of the real, something quiet in me—I didn't know what to call it—felt like a face in a world-prison where I walked but could never be seen. And there were many others like me—but each was on a separate path and none could see the others.

His words slammed a hard, black door inside me. I knew he wasn't right. I could see the logic of what he said, but logic isn't justice. Though at first I grieved over what I'd lost I also knew (had no choice but to find out) that disordering can lead to a further, stranger order more prismatic and vulnerable, and in it there are questionings and reachings...so much still un-summarized, un-named,...new colors opening...

Each time I read to her I see this. Maybe breakage is the core of meaning.

*xx x And Myshkin tries to know the world but it keeps breaking inside him—
"everything was strange, I was crushed by the strangeness" xxx He understands
Nastasya will be hurt by Rogozhin who wants her only for himself though he knows
she doesn't love him xx and Myshkin can't find a way to stop this xxx Maybe you're
awake now maybe you are thinking of them also xx And Nastasya's father's house is
burning in her mind and her solitude her need for money her scorched orphanhood
her hatred of her fate her desire to not hurt Myshkin all of it red-hot and burning
xx Why are there so many fires in Petersburg so many forms of destruction xxx but
when winter comes the poor have no heat no one can save the freezing baby xx xx
Reticular formation xx myoclonic activity xx Is this why Myshkin shivers often*

This morning I had another seizure. It was as if for a moment—or was it a few hours, I don't know—all space suddenly stopped, and I saw the flightless bird catching fire in a red-black sea. I didn't fall, my limbs barely shuddered, but my mind and body stiffened, imprisoned in a vigilance much harder and larger than myself. Everything alert but also blind.

When it was over my mind was a stage-set, my hands a marionette's, yellowish, waxen, unreal.

What if chaos isn't quickness and movement after all, but stillness, empty space? An abyss freezing in its own confusions. A disarrangement, a shattering, but frozen solid.

If there is no way to say "I"...if one doesn't belong to oneself, not really...

It's said that within the human brain not one of its billions of neurons actually touches another. That they're linked by wire-like signals traveling through the spaces in between, and those signals are fragile, discontinuous, unprotected, rawly open to chaos and disruption.

If the brain is isolate at its core...if isolation and disruption are built into the very structures and mechanisms of thought...

x xx

I remember she wrote: A feeling of No earth No sun No moon.

But I am ver very tired now. Always afterwards it's like this. As if a great wave has lifted and then dropped me. I want only a tall glass of water.

I was walking along a shore I didn't recognize. From the edge of my sight, a distant figure moved closer. Its eyes were dark and much too large. Then I saw they weren't eyes but two black lenses. The head turned quietly, it was the epileptic. He held a book in one hand, and with the other reached to remove one black lens so he could read it. But his hand was stiff and small as if someone had whittled him carelessly, too deeply. His eye was bruised, the pupil greatly enlarged.

I didn't speak and though he looked at me it seemed he didn't see me.

xxx There is a place inside the brain known as the Nucleus Solitarius—did you know this xx—I pace inside my room and think about this lonely name forgive me xx How long has it been since I last saw you? The twelve trees in the courtyard lightly swaying The lagoon stock-still yet wandering xxx Your window dark but maybe you can see my lighted window xxx "Electric wires with silver contacts are applied to the sleepless patient's brain surface or scalp" xxx "Even in the later stages there can be intermittent periods of lucidity" "The first human EEG was recorded by Hans Berger in 1924—"

In these hours when you're not here sometimes Dostoevsky's life comes back to me I don't know why xx xxx he was born in the Moscow Mariinskaya Shelter for the Poor but maybe you already know this xxx his father was Resident Surgeon there xxx the whole family of ten crowded into two small rooms on the hospital grounds where he and his elder brother slept in a corner behind a makeshift screen xxx xxxx Years later his father was murdered by his servants but I'm getting ahead of myself xxx What I wanted to tell you is when he was 10 the family acquired a small country house in Daravoe and it was there an old peasant man, Marei, suddenly reached out his hand and stroked the boy's face for no apparent reason xxx Dostoevsky wrote of this years later "It seemed I'd completely forgotten, but in prison the memory came back to me and helped me to survive." xxx xx But why did Dostoevsky's father's servants pour liquor down his throat until he drowned xxx And where are my cattle they are so trapped inside their need their hunger xxx This rock ledge coated with fresh snow xx—Maybe in this darkness you can't find me—

xx But why did Marei stroke the child's face xxx Did he sense some need in him some sorrow xx The cattle move so quietly in their separate language xxx in these hours I will never understand xxx

As her mind moves further into places Spratling didn't understand and wrongly labeled, I sometimes worry that our reading troubles and frightens her, but mostly I believe it helps her—that as we read Myshkin is there with her, and Dostoevsky, the white field, the cattle. No earth No sun No moon Instability Disorder but Myshkin listens as she says this and she feels him listening. And his listening is what's real. She knows he's beside her. Like the feeling I call "fire" that crawls or floods in me before a seizure (but in fact there is no word for it, or even its true color) isn't the real composed of countless things I can't name or even see. And as I read Dostoevsky's book with her, and also read it on my own, it seems he finds the many wordless, invisible things and speaks to them and in their own way they speak back. Each night as we read, I've never felt closer to what's real. His book is beautiful the way human thought is beautiful—how it hurts and disorders itself and finds new hurts, new orders...and doesn't find...and loses, and brightens and gets lost...and finds and throws away...looks for and discards and darkens...too many routes to follow...it doesn't care about routes, doesn't care about following...forgets about following..."and fell from a great height...he did not say anything but listened intently...and was with children, always children...her eyes gentle...do not ruin the strangeness"—

Dostoevsky spent 4 years in a prison camp did you know this? I try to think of what it did to him what it took from his mind from his body what it gave Your window dark across the courtyard the branches of twelve trees between us xxx On the night of April 22, 1849 he was arrested for sedition xxx accused of having been involved in secret discussions to overthrow the enserfment of the peasantry Three officers in light blue uniforms searched his apartment confiscated his papers xx But he confessed nothing Refused to be "destroyed by an empty word" After that came solitary confinement in the Peter-and-Paul Fortress 7 months on an island on the Neva his cell window smeared with oily paste to prevent any daylight seeping through xx Then one morning he was ordered to dress quickly and was taken to Semyonov Square where he was informed he would be put to death but was sent instead on a long journey over snow to Siberia to the prison camp in Omsk He was allowed one letter: "Dear Brother, Today we were taken to Semyonov Square where we were read the death sentence, then allowed to kiss the cross, and given our white death-shirts to put on. I was the 6th in line for execution, standing in the 2nd row, and had no more than a few minutes left to live. Then suddenly a retreat was sounded. It was announced that His Imperial Majesty was granting us our lives. Apparently this had been planned all along."

The cows are cold on their hillside I need to find them a dry place, a salt lick, water—

You have been gone for many hours xxx our hour of reading went so quickly but there are things I would still ask you even though like me you have no answers xxx Why are isolation and separateness built into the human brain xx And chaos xx misunderstanding xx Dostoevsky's narrator says "We find it difficult to explain what occurred...it must seem very strange and obscure to the reader..." ~~and could not endure...and would vanish...~~ And on page 362 (I remember this from when I could still read) somebody says "there is something in every person which can never be communicated to another...and we die with it inside us." I wonder if you feel this also xxx And why does the narrator refer to himself in the plural as if he weren't trapped like all of us inside his separate mind xxx The white emptiness between the letters in each word—what lies there xx I have asked you so little of yourself who you are or what you've seen xx forgive me xxx x your window dark now xxx The lagoon a shadowed elsewhere pulsing—

But why am I suddenly so cold xxx My legs too heavy as if shackled And everywhere outside me there is snow now so much snow "Strange facts are before us in abundance" Dostoevsky's narrator says xxx I remember when you read this xxx I wonder where you are and when you're coming xx I don't know when I last slept it must have been so long ago—the protection of closed eyes that softness xxx Protein Activation Post-Synaptic Excitation xxx After the ride from the prison they gave us white death-shirts to put on—

Marei's hand touches my face but then it's vanished xx I have been in Omsk for nearly 6 weeks There are 150 of us crowded into a single barracks Not a minute goes by that I don't hear another's breath There's ice on the windows one inch thick xxx I'm told I will be here for 4 years xxx ~~synaptic instability sleep spindles prions~~ *On our journey we made one stop in Tobolsk where even the town bell is in exile from Uglich where it was publically mutilated and flogged xx found guilty of ringing for seditious purposes xxx Its sentence is eternal silence xxxxxx Often I am back in Semyonov Square as the guards untie the blindfold from Petrashavsky's eyes but then fumble clumsily and can't secure the shackles on his ankles He is so grateful and amazed to be alive that he eagerly leans down and with great dexterity shackles his ankles himself xxx xxx I don't know if you came to me tonight or what pages might have passed between us xxx Is Myshkin still remembering the marketplace at Bale xxx Or maybe his hands are trembling often he can't stop his hands from trembling* "The slower form of the illness can take several years to run its course. It is not unusual for the afflicted to act out their fantasies and dreams."

At daybreak we are led over miles of snow to the riverbank It is hard to walk in fetters over snow We are told to dismantle an old barge frozen into the river's ice while still salvaging the crossbeams intact We try again and again but each time we lift the beams they crumble xxx I begin to understand how the seemingly benign can be terrifying like the repetition of hands to no meaningful purpose xx I once read that a form of torture consists of forcing the subject to pour water back and forth from one jug into another for many hours of many days The pointlessness will cause him to go mad xxx There are so many ways for one person to bring harm to another xxxx Reality is infinitely various when compared to the deductions of human thought xx The cows are far away in their white field xxx I wonder where you are xxx Why no one hears them

This morning I was taken to the military hospital a mile and a half from the prison For weeks I have been having seizures xxx Dr. Troitsky speaks kindly Says I can stay here for three days I am given long stockings underlinen a night cap slippers From the next bed Ustyantsev tells me of a convict who scrapes plaster from the wall then rubs it into his eye so the doctors will believe he is still sick and won't send him back to prison Last week they cut a deep slit into his neck then threaded it with linen tape they pull back and forth through the wound to keep it open They believe this will cure him Ustyantsev says this treatment is also used on horses xxx But if Marei's hand could come to me now could reach clearly for me now...xxx And REM sleep is also known as Fast-wave sleep—long deprivation can induce hallucinations xx xx Yesterday after Mihailov died naked and stick-thin in the bed three feet away from me the smith was called to saw the fetters off before his body could be lifted xx Already it is spring now Outside the window many wildflowers are blooming xxx xxxxx Reality strives for diversification it cannot help it xx Sleep spindles xx Prions xxx Reticular Formation xx Dr. Troitsky's steady voice xx he slips into my bag a pencil a blank sheet of paper

Several times each week Commander Kirilov enters the barracks in the middle of the night to check if we're asleep on our right side or on our left then wakes us and insists we sleep only on the left Even at night we wear 5lb shackles on our ankles xxx We lie on bare boards covered only by our sheepskin prison coats too short to cover our feet Clumps of black beetles crawl across the rotting floor The temperature is 40 below xx I tell myself hard labor makes me strong the fresh air will strengthen my lungs but I continue having seizures The other prisoners shun me because I am "a member of the ruling class" "the iron beak that has tormented and torn us apart" Though this frightens me I know I mustn't show it Any sign of weakness and they'll rob or beat me xxx For work I turn the metal lathe pound alabaster shovel snow—

Last night after I left her, I dreamed I picked up Dostoevsky's book, but it was covered with black cloth and suffered a seizure in my hands. How could I not have noticed this before?—that in a sense the whole book is one long seizure. I've been reading it for weeks, holding it in my hands close to my eyes—and yet I missed this. Beneath the black cloth I could feel the spreading heat of its suffering, the light a dazzling hurt inside it.

Pilate sat with his dog in the cold moonlight, the air flooding with the scent of roses. He didn't know if he was on his terrace overlooking the flat plain, or in exile in some foreign land, or maybe in a prison by the sea. It had been decades since he'd spoken. "There is no safety of the mind," he thought, his temples pounding in the blood-red light. He couldn't tell if his head was bare or covered. Red wind made small incisions on his skin. Then he thought further: "In Sanskrit *safety* means *whole*, and in my language it means *intact, undamaged, surviving, extant, still holding.* Xenophon wrote: 'to be safe of mind, to be wise.' So to say a *safe mind* is to indicate a mind that is sane. But I think that is a vain, ridiculous wish"—he wanted to rub his right temple, but his hands hung heavily at his sides—"thinking is never safe, there is nothing more perilous in the world."

The red air turned suddenly pale, the roses faded—

Each day as I sit here opening her notes, thinking about where we have been and where we're going, I can't help feeling I'm wading into a widening sea from which I may never return or catch my bearings. Most nights I go to her and read, but who am I reading to? Her face the same as before, her still-careful arrangement of our chairs. None of that has changed. But somewhere inside she is watching the shackles cut from a convict's dead body, her brain is flooding with seizures and bright light, there's a white death-shirt in the wind behind her eyes. Always before, I thought of a face as singular, sharply boundaried, and even if resembling another, still inevitably distinct from any other, and the history of a life as the story of one single, irreducible life. But now I don't know. When the red fire moves through me it moves through more than who I am—for a long time I've sensed this. I'm not sure any more what a voice is, or the body that contains it—

HOSPITAL OF SAN SERVOLO, VENICE, ARCHIVE ENVELOPES NO. 912 AND 913, FOR STORAGE IN BOX 19

912:

PATIENT POPULATION:
Between 1725 and 1812, 1130 patients are admitted:
731 are eventually discharged
24 escape
105 are killed
4 commit suicide

913:

CHARACTERISTICS OF EPILEPTIC PATIENTS
December 1847–January 1848

Precipitating Cause of Attack:	State of Pulse:	Remarks:
Fright at a house catching fire	weak	extremities very cold
Scarlatina	very fast	drowsy and wild before fit
Sudden loss of livelihood	irregular	sight impaired in the right eye
Overwhelming grief	irregular	right facial paralysis, cold and weak
Fatigue after march in the army	very fast	fit preceded by pain in the tongue
Fright at the sight of an epileptic	quick	vertigo and crying
Excessive punishment	weak	blind for one year

Excessive physical labor	very fast	very talkative afterwards
Surrounded by rats	quick	systolic murmur at the base of the heart
Witnessing the injury of a child	weak	maniacal excitement
Witnessing the abuse of animals	weak	deafness on right side
Fright during exposure to a storm	very fast	contraction and atrophy of the left arm

Lately I have the sense that she's holding the whole book in her mind (she must have read it many times), and that when we're not reading she's traveling within it. She barely mentions the blurring pages anymore, or straining to see them. And tonight, right after I arrived, her eyes looking slightly downward as usual, her voice soft as usual, she asked if we could hear 221. She'd never asked for a page number before.

I opened the book and saw the passage:

> He fell to thinking, among other things, about his epilep-
> tic condition, that there was a stage in it just before the fit
> itself (if the fit occurred while he was awake), when suddenly,
> amidst the sadness, the darkness of the soul, the pressure, his
> brain would momentarily catch fire, as it were, and all life's
> forces would be strained at once in an extraordinary impulse.
> The sense of life, of self-awareness, increased nearly tenfold in
> these moments, which flashed by like lightning. His mind, his
> heart, were lit up with an extraordinary light; all his agita-
> tion, all his doubts, all his worries were as if placated at once,
> resolved in some sort of sublime tranquility, filled with reason
> and ultimate cause. But these moments, these glimpses were
> still only a presentiment of that ultimate second (never more
> than a second) from which the fit itself began. That second
> was, of course, unbearable.

We had never spoken about the times I didn't come. Or even about Myshkin's epilepsy or Dostoevsky's. All the nights I read to her and the world came to me more real than before, and I felt I was helping to bring her the real—I hadn't said a word.

Then I thought of Spratling's ugly words and read the passage.

Today after work duty Akim Akimitch tells me of a convict he met some years ago in Tobolsk The man lived chained to a wall xxx he had been chained there for eight years The chain was seven feet long and reached from the wall to the sleeping palette and back xxx The man showed him where it attached beneath his clothes and insisted he slept comfortably and even had good dreams But years later upon his release the sky terrified him he flinched at the smallest blade of grass xxx The snow is falling heavily it has been falling for three days xx Conformational influence xx Myoclonic Activity xx Everything is what it seems—

xxx And now Myshkin is saying If we understand things too quickly maybe we will never understand them as we need to xxx He mocks himself xx Says I am a Prince and of an ancient family! But "he stood, as it were apart, as though he had no share in it, and like someone invisible in a fairy tale"—remember—I can hear your voice reading—and now he thinks he may fall soon and is frightened xxx he is out on the streets alone and I'm looking for him but I can't find him xxx I don't know if I'm in the snow in Petersburg or in a room on an island off of Venice xx I don't know where he is walking xx I try to find him but the streets are unmarked   xxx ~~lesions of any nature effecting the vigilance~~ Everything shut tight too secret so how can I possibly find him how can I know what he needs what he is feeling xx And then the light is flooding his cells and the whole nature of the universe says yes…Everything's terribly clear and there's such joy…it's not even love…oh what is here is higher than love…x xxx…the soul could not endure…would vanish…xxx if I could come to you and know you—xxx But I'm still wandering through the streets and I fear that Myshkin's writhing on the ground or maybe his body is your body…Why are the streets so anonymous so empty Why is no one coming xx xxx How can I find my way without street signs xxx ~~neurochemical alteration of functions that remain to be uncovered~~ xxx Walking back from work-duty today Sokolov stumbled on a rock and injured himself badly xx Now he turns his face to the wall xxx tries to salve his wound with soiled paper xxx

But why is the Commander stepping into our barracks when curfew is still hours away xx xx   He never comes to us in daylight xx Are we in danger have we crossed some awful border is there about to be some new punishment beyond what we already know or have imagined xxx Then we see he is beside himself with grief this man who is so hard on us and cruel is sobbing over his dog Trezorska xxx We can hardly believe what we are hearing xxx He says the dog is like a son to him the only reason for his living but now Trezorska's fallen ill and the veterinary surgeon hasn't found a way to save him xx x He believes there's one among us renowned for treating animals in his village xx He commands him to step forward then leads him to the room where Trezorska lies on a white brocaded couch his sallow head on a silk pillow sunlight pouring in through the large window xxx The prisoner knows the proper treatment but pretends that there is nothing to be done xx xxxxx ~~And when you read to me I felt in you abiding kindness~~ Night comes very quickly in the depths of winter xxx No one in the barracks speaks of what has happened xxx

And what does Marei think as he touches me x He is poor and works from sunrise until nightfall in the fields Red lumps of scars on both his arms xxx x I will never know how he got them will never know his thoughts about anything xxx xx I belong to the class of people who call themselves "the best people" xx Marei is not allowed around them he is too dirty even to serve xx he touches me xxx I am given the white death shirt to put on this happens several times each month sometimes I wake screaming xxxx black beetles crawl across the barracks floor xx xxx In Tobolsk a man is chained to a wall for eight years I can feel his chain pulling xx I am in my bunk at the height of winter covered only by my prison coat xx Marei's hand has come back he is tired from his day in the fields he is touching my cheek he is kind xxx xx but why has this sudden light come into me why has my brain randomly caught fire xx the barracks are burning and the beetles the white shirt are burning x Marei's hand is safe it touches me the fire doesn't touch him xx what is the real what is it xxx how does it find a place inside the mind

It is spring again   xxx   Crusts of ice have melted from the windows Wildflowers bloom in the fields outside the barracks xxx We have adopted a pet goat and named him Vaska   xxx He runs up to us when called and jumps wildly on the benches though keeping animals is against the regulations His slender horns are long and curved a pale brown-gray with patches of pale blue xxx I don't know how he first came to live among us xxx We would raise many creatures if we could   xxx   Skuratov says if the sergeant finds out he will make us slaughter and then flay him that it is only a matter of time but the sergeant never looks and no one tells him xxx so far we've kept our secret xx Each workday he follows us to the brickworks at the riverbank and back xxx Packing up toward sundown we gather willow shoots and flowers Entwine them and place them on his head xxx He walks before us toward the prison in his wreath the only one of us not fettered—

The young convict Sushilov has taken to washing my clothes greasing my boots trying to find me extra bread I don't know why he does this Each day he walks the prison yard alone with lowered eyes Scars all over his bare back xxx Three years and scarcely any words have passed between us xxx Once I tried to thank him with some coins but tears welled in his eyes and he turned angrily and wouldn't take them It was the first time I had seen a prisoner crying xxx His mind dark to me I will never know his mind xxx And when you don't come I fear for you but don't know what I am fearing xxx x ~~temporal lobe~~ x ~~postictal~~ x My rock ledge bare The wind jarring and scraping xxx Why does Sushilov have so many scars on his back what happened to him before he came here why does he want to take care of me what could he be thinking xxx So much hiddenness inside each single being xxx xxx After I leave here I will never hear his name again or know what has become of him xxx never know why he chose me who he is—

And there is another one who also seeks me out his name is Petrov xxx He has been
here for as long as I but always acts in a great hurry as if he must rush back to
his real home in town because of course he couldn't actually live here xxx xx xxx
Every now and then he comes up to me and asks me questions Is Napoleon an
emperor or a president xxx Is it true as they say that there are monkeys as large as
a tall man with arms that hang down to their heels xx What are the Antipodes xx
Do people in Sumatra walk on their heads and not their legs Was Danton a real
person or invented What happened to Rome after it burned xx I try my best to
answer and when I'm done he curtly bows his head then rushes off in silence xxx
"And in spite of the most recent progress in sleep research it is still not understood
why the hippocampal circuitry begins to fail and can no longer control the flow of
information" xxxx

But this chaotic tenderness I feel xx and you in your room where I can't see you can't know if you need help or what you're doing xxx ~~strange facts are before us in abundance~~ Is there joy or has it broken xx This sudden light inside the mind this xxx This distance that engenders thought

If I could bring you a calm tenderness xxx a listening clear as a thin vessel of hurt glass xxx Myshkin's waterfall far off but it still falls inside his mind xxxxx the watchful place inside the donkey's eye xxx I still think of the kindness of your voice your hands the turning pages xxx Random words come back to me and hold me The hours so slow within your absence xxx Your window shut across the courtyard xx The twelve trees xxxxx

Sometimes after I've fallen, her words seem almost silvery, the faint traces of a vanished metal.

This morning I woke to that same silver. I had dreamed of the book again. It was still covered with black cloth. As soon as I picked it up, I could hear Myshkin breathing from inside the closed pages. I could hear his heartbeat. Then suddenly the beats lurched forward—tumbling erratically, too quickly. I worried he was having a seizure. I could hear Marie breathing also, the wind moving through her field, the muffled hoof-beats of cattle. When I tried to open the book the black cloth held it shut. Inside they were still breathing. I knew there was no way that I could reach them.

It is the depth of winter xxx xx Darkness comes too quickly xxx Daylight a brief slit in wind xxx For two months an eagle has lived among us It is one of the small kind of the steppes and stands in the prison yard's far corner dragging its crushed wing in circles xxxxx At first it refused any food but after three days it took our crumbs but only if we looked away and stood at a safe distance xxxx x Even now it eyes us with mistrust stays only by the farthest fence posts always watching the far steppes it can't get back to xxx And when you fell I wanted to help you but time grew strange to me x spilled pearls black beetles x and at first I couldn't move or find you xx x xxx In prison there is always the sound of others breathing xxx And when you fell I wanted to tell you that each time you read to me your words had brought me peace xxx

I am walking across the courtyard to you xx I am carrying a book xxx I want to read it to you the way you read to me I want to bring you Myshkin's joy I want to bring you Dostoevsky saying "This is realism, only deeper" xx Your window dark above the walkway the twelve trees no more than shadows xx But my legs move so slowly as in blackening water and as I walk I am thinking the scientists say there is no such thing as empty space but Dark Energy Dark Matter xxx Our galaxy our Sun and all we can observe with our finest instruments the barest hint of what exists xxx Dear brother today I was informed I am being sent to Semipalatinsk to serve out the remainder of my sentence as a soldier xx I must beg your forgiveness for the future disorder of this letter Already I am sure it is disordered

This morning the red fire started burning my right arm again, then flared and spread into my chest. When I came to, I didn't know where I was. Even my name was lost to me, I had no name.

I want to go to her tonight but how can I go to her?

It was night. I was carrying her across the courtyard to him. She held a worn book in her hands. We passed the twelve bare trees.

I was surprised my damaged bones could support her. My body alien in its strength and yet it was still mine.

Why did she trust me to carry her like that? I could feel the brittle softness of her arms, the hollow between collarbone and neck. My hand against her narrow spine. I began to realize that softness and hardness, suppleness and resistance, aren't separate or contradictory but move within and through each other.

I had never before held another person in my arms.

As we neared the lawn's far border, I glanced down at the top of her head, her dark brown hair against the still-dark air. I understood I was carrying Frieda.

For a moment I shut my eyes. When I opened them again my arms were empty.

If I could have partly become another, been released into the life and mind of another...

For a moment I thought I heard Frieda's voice.

But the room was empty, the night air still and quiet.

Titian was dragging a stick through the prison yard's dry dirt while the eagle sipped from a cracked bowl and pressed its bad wing against the farthest fence post. All the convicts were inside.

Why would Titian speak into such emptiness?—yet he did.

"Though I had no access to the brain's physiology beyond what I once observed at a dissection, how could I have done a single portrait without sensing the caudal divisions of the solitary complex, its strained synapses and subtle breakages, the periodic desynchronization of its waves.

Take my self-portrait of 1567, for instance, in which my hand looks blurred, unfinished. Many claim this is due to my carelessness, or maybe my impatience, but what if I was trying to convey the brain's vulnerability, how any grasp is partial and approximate at best."

For a moment he stayed silent, then:

"As for those who commissioned me to paint their portraits, no matter how much power they assumed they possessed, in truth they were essentially helpless. Though they convinced themselves my rendering would keep them safe and important forever, in fact mostly the opposite is true— what remains is the defiant vulnerability. Annihilation and pain claimed them all. I still feel each thin endangered edge moving through my hand into my brush. Why believe there is such a thing as protection?—though I still treasure the red cloth, the red moments it gave me."

No matter how much I pace back and forth I can't tell if it is morning or is it night or where I am But then I remember I am in Semipalatinsk xxx I am a Private 2nd class in the Siberian Army Corps 7th Battalion It is mid-March I have turned 30 my years in prison finally over xxx Loose sand drifts through the streets and sticks to the weatherbeaten houses xxx The town is called The Devil's Sandbox xx My army coat is red with a gray collar xx For the first time in four years I am allowed to walk without fetters xx xx Sometimes I wonder if freedom is more alien and inaccessible to the human mind than the many forms of bondage xxx Dear Mikhail I have received no word from you in four years I hope to hear from you soon How can I begin to speak of what has marked me xxx A flightless bird A ghost xxxx Everything I am will disappear xx These are the notes of an unknown—

xxx xx And while light has been traveling through space x space itself has been expanding This Dark Energy Dark Matter The days go on very busily here xx there is so much to learn about being a soldier Often I am very tired but at least I can be alone for a few minutes xxx I've been having frequent seizures xxx Afterwards my mind deforms the most ordinary facts even the white tents of the Khirghizes grow frightening xxxxx xx Or I try to read but my eyes are weak and scramble the words on the page—"the invisible either" "the volatile because" but then these words seem more interesting and true than the words in their right order xxxxx Lieutenant-Colonel Belikov has assigned me to discuss with him current books and newspapers he is so pleased with our meetings that he has given me his old greatcoat which is ill-fitting but warm xx But my cattle are so cold and I can't help them xx "And current research shows that the afflicted experience brief intervals of lucidity even in the latest stages xxx In their ongoing sleeplessness agitation and grief are not uncommon xxx Sometimes there are surges of great joy" xxx

Does she remember that I read to her again last night? That finally I was able?

Each time we read, I think of Spratling's "destroys"—each one a small, meaningless prison secured by electrified wire and the finest technology, strongest metals—but the locked cells can't keep the prisoners in. The cells are empty.

Dear Mikhail My discharge from the army has been approved on medical grounds as over the last week I suffered four attacks within five days xx After each one my arms and legs grow heavy my mind and heart submerged in thick black water xxx Maybe a specialist in Petersburg can tell me what this is xxx How the body crushes the mind and light is a terrible error pressing in xxx Last week I heard from Nekrasov who offered so little for my work no self-respecting author could accept his terms For some reason he finds this more convenient than overt refusal xxxx He believes my talent is gone that I am finished xxx As I don't hear from you I wonder if you get these letters—

The final sorting and packing of the library is almost done. All that's left are a few random boxes, and documents from the vault for Dr. Galzinga at the Archives of the Social and Cultural Emargination Studies Institute at Ca' Foscari University. They've already acquired the records and books from San Clemente, and last year what was left of the old San Servolo Apothecary. But part of me doesn't want to pack anything up anymore. The official announcement says a team will "conduct a systematic examination of a selection of clinical records to reconstruct the psychiatric apparatus of San Servolo from 1840-1904, from the point of view of both psychiatric practices and clinical nosography."

Now each time I pack a box of papers and folders to be shipped, it's as if Myshkin's skin is exposed. The tremor in his hands increases.

Pilate's mind was filling with red thoughts that pained him, but each time he tried to remember what they were so that maybe he could calm or heal them, he felt only the beginning of a migraine.

He knew he had committed an unforgiveable act, but couldn't remember what it was. He sat still on his bare summit, his dog sleeping at his feet. They sat this way for thousands of years.

His whole body was the Nucleus Solitarius, that mysterious and most solitary place.

But even though memory failed him, somewhere deep within he understood he longed more than anything for the one he had wronged to draw close and walk beside him.

I, too, think of the Nucleus Solitarius. I was hearing Frieda's shadow-voice now that her real voice had vanished. A hollow ache spread through my chest. *What could be more true, more sad, than those two words? Think of a voice that never touches another, that is unable to ever reach another. The wind is very cold tonight, the water's surface unbroken.*

The Minister of War has declared I can't live in Petersburg or Moscow so I am free but not free xxx But now I am in Petersburg after all I can't explain how this happened xxx Today the doctor confirmed my illness is epilepsy and that I will never get well xxx Some speak of being purified by suffering but I don't believe this ~~xx bursts of synchronous brain waves Insidious destruction xx~~ *my falling a brutal mockery of all the beauties and conclusions of reason xxx Walking back in the late afternoon I saw over the Neva new buildings rising out of the old but it was only the smoke from the chimneys xxx it still amazes me to walk without fetters xxx But why do we assume a mind is just one single mind xxx All these words I send to you xxx unsigned xx disordered xx and all the flowers of the steppes disordered xx and what if the universe is just a jumble heap of moments and all existence dependent on the existence of coincidences x xx And as it is the doctors can't keep my brain from catching fire x or help protect the scattered words inside me xx Dear Mikhail Dear Apollon Dear Sonechka I don't want to fall but I will fall x*

All of Petersburg is up in flames even the Apraksin Market and the Schukin Markets Men hurry through the streets destroying the wooden fences they designed and built with their own hands xxx they need to stop the fire from spreading further xx There are leaflets everywhere even on the Nevsky Prospect They are demanding justice for the peasantry and the overthrowing of the Tsar "The day will come when we will unfurl the red banner of the future We will move against the Winter Palace we will wipe out all who serve it We are prepared to hunt them in broad daylight through all the avenues and streets of the capital We will find them we will track them down..." But I can barely see the twelve trees anymore xx xx x And the flames are so close I don't think I've ever stood so close xxx Have you fallen do you need me xxx ~~interictal abnormal electrical activity~~ How can I cross the courtyard to you when this fire is so close and spreads so quickly xxx

I can feel the aura starting, the fire in my arm increasing. And now Myshkin's brain is catching fire...the flames seeping from his head and spreading...the whole book we read from is burning...there is no way to protect the pages he is embedded within them...How will I tell her there is no way we can continue reading we'll never reach the next chapter...and Myshkin's hands are shaking badly now...he has lost his whole world...his whole body is trembling...

This morning as I prepared one of the last remaining folders to be sent to Dr. Galzinga and his research team, I wondered if, like me, something in her would cringe and think of Myshkin.

•••

FOLDER A3. Dr. Henri Gastaut's working notes for his 1977 conference paper "Fyodor Dostoevsky's Involuntary Contribution to the Symptomatology and Prognosis of Epilepsy" delivered at the Annual San Servolo Epilepsy Seminar and subsequently published in Epilepsia Vol 19, 1978.

—

I will now illustrate my previous point with two quotes from Dostoevsky:

"My sickness is getting worse rather than better. Last month I had four fits, a thing that has never happened before, and I could hardly do any work. The fits are followed by a state of gloom and melancholy and I feel a completely broken man."

—1858

"O my friend Stepan Smitrievich, this epilepsy will end up carrying me off! My star is fading—I sense that. My memory has grown completely dim (completely!). I don't recognize people any more; I forget what I read the day before. I'm afraid I'm going mad or falling into idiocy. My imagination is overflowing, working in a disorderly way; at night I have nightmares."

—1867

Years before, when I first started working as a scanner, I glimpsed this passage: "Though by and large we think of the sun as silent, in truth its core is raucous, cacophonous, conflicting. The source of our planet's warmth derives not from silence or consistency, but from upheaval, volatility, disturbance."

Though your window has been dark for a long time I still want to ask you How does the brain know what tenderness is In what ways does it register its presence Are there chemicals assigned to it x Codings x Neural pathways xx Do you still come to me I can't remember if you come xxxxx Gray blur of sun gray-yellow nights xxx I haven't told you that last month a girl knocked on my door Her face dirty xx long black hair in messy curls xx She said her grandfather had died and she was looking for his dog Azorska xx That no one was left to take care of her so how could she take care of the lost dog xx I took her in and watch over her and feed her but for weeks she wouldn't even say her name xxx Something brutalized in her face Suspicion and mistrust in her black eyes xxx Today she finally said, "I am Yelena. I begged on the Meshchanskaya Street xx My mother told me before she died it isn't wrong to beg but it's wrong to suffer and stay hungry 'Stay poor, and after I am dead don't go to anyone for anything, there's nothing wrong with being poor, but it is wrong to be rich and hurt others.'" xxxx Are you hurt now are you sleeping have you fallen xxx "Everything human suddenly disappears" Myshkin says of his seizing xxx xx All of Petersburg is burning xx What has happened to the dog Azorska—

I meant to bring you Myshkin's joy xx not this garret or Yelena's begging xx xxx There are things one chooses not to say it is better not to say them I won't tell you what happened to Yelena xx xx The Neva is very beautiful in sunlight and all of Petersburg intricate with hundreds of canals and bridges xxx This other Venice of the mind I walk through xxx Nothing is stranger than the real

Titian's voice was soft, his tone sober, "I often think of the many beggars in Venice though I chose not to paint them. By the 1520's the whole city was sick with gaunt faces—so many had fled the provinces desperate for work. One night I walked among the swirling masks of carnival only to stumble upon three starved corpses sprawled beneath the portals of the Ducal Palace. There were no poor laws then, no edicts to support the needy. In his *Libri della famaglia* Leonardo Alberti put forth his cruel suggestion—all beggars should be expelled from the city if they remained without work for more than three days as a man would be better off dead than to live in misery and need. Within just a matter of weeks the price of wheat rose from 4 lire per bushel to 15.5—so how could the poor afford even a small loaf of bread? When the Senate finally ratified a law, it drew a distinction between the 'deserving' and 'undeserving' poor and proposed all foreign beggars be incarcerated or shipped from the city. 'All beggars who have arrived within the last year must depart the city in three days.' Sometimes I wonder what it did to my eyes to see their sunken eyes and bony hands, the emptiness they carried. I tossed my few coins and walked on."

Dear Chairman of the Society for Aid to Needy Writers and Scholars:

In preparing to go abroad again for three months for the treatment of my health and consultations with specialists in Paris and Berlin about my falling sickness, I am resorting to the help of the Society and request a loan until February 1, 1864, of 1500 silver rubles, without which, because of my circumstances, I would be unable to make my trip xxx ~~But this Dark Energy Dark Matter~~ xxx I give my word of honor to return this money with interest by February; I am firmly convinced that by then, having restored my health, I will have managed to finish and publish the work with which I am now occupied xxx ~~And when I think of you and when I try to reach you~~ xxxx In the event of my death, or if for any reason I have not repaid my debt, I offer to the Society as security the permanent right to possession and publication of all my works, I cede all my rights completely xx Sleep spindles xx Prions xxx This transfer of rights will be accomplished, as required by law, in a broker's office.

Fyodor Dostoevsky
23 July 1863

Wiesbaden Paris Baden-Baden Hamburg Turin Genoa Livorno The roulette wheel's blank eye spinning and spinning When I lose I am flooded with shame Each time the wheel spins my mind asks Does hope exist Is the universe kind or is it made of the most brutal power xxx Why do I still feel these shackles on my legs the prison cloth rough against my chest Today I lost 600 francs Yesterday 300 Nothing is calm or settled on this earth—

This morning before I woke I felt her standing at my door, upset that Azorska was still missing. Somehow I knew it was her, though she looked like Yelena. "I never told you that Azorska performed for many years in the circus. He carried a monkey on his back. This took enormous concentration and he did it with great dignity, but the audience only laughed and mocked him."

"When he grew too old to perform the circus-owner dropped him on a street corner and drove off. After that he sat with me every day on Meshchanskaya Street. But how can I share my scraps with him now that I can't find him?"

For a moment she looked away, as if seeing Azorska on the street-corner in the days before she'd lost him.

I waited for her to say more, but she turned her back and stared into the empty courtyard.

Dear Nikolay Nikolaevich Already it is March I am in Paris the so-called beautiful-far-away xxxx The Europeans speak of brotherhood but I sense in them a troubling isolation xxx I am alone most of the time then go to the roulette tables and lose all my money When the tables spin I feel a freedom like no other or like the shadow of the moment before I fall when there is no such thing as time and harm is more fragile than air xxx a pale invention of the human mind—

Last night, I read from the 9th section of Part 4 where the narrator says (but it's unclear who the narrator even is) "It is extremely difficult to continue our story...how can we describe that of which we have no idea or personal opinion...."

At those words, I felt my skin turn cold again. I saw Myshkin standing in a world that couldn't know him or even sense his existence. Then that world became the future, and intracerebral electrodes were being surgically implanted in his brain to track the epileptogenic zone's electrical activity—

A gray, automatic door slid open to admit him, then closed.

He lay face up on a gray table. Ten incisions were cut into his scalp, the electrodes secured at varied intervals to best register the angles of the zone's neuronal network. Brain-mapping had identified the key sites of high frequency oscillations. He was told to open his eyes, to keep them open no matter what. Bright white lights flashed in rapid succession, inducing the seizure.

Neon-green brainwaves lurched across the screen. Five horizontal lines of similar waves appeared, and on each line the waves started crowding together, quivering, still lurching, tightening into clumps of almost-solid green. Small, trapped specimens of roiling ocean beneath a sky wholly placid, stormless, unmoving. The waves were slowing, curving downward into mild undulations, as if they could almost undo themselves, would, wanted to, could reach into themselves and find some other nature.

All the while, a computer registered and interpreted the data.

Myshkin's eyes had closed. His hands were gray fists, his knuckles almost yellow. Soon another door slid open. An attendant wheeled him through.

The print-out lay on a metal shelf, tagged with his number and the date. The report was open, and I read it: "Aim of Testing: Our goal is to provide a robust approach allowing easy access to patients' brains in time and space. Our program involves the effective normalization of brains to a common anatomic atlas."

I thought of Spratling's "destroys," his prisons. I didn't want to look anymore. But like the time she asked for page 221 and I turned to it and saw what it was and didn't want to read it but did, I read more:

SEIZURE ONSET ZONE: amyg.   ant/post   Hc pHcG.   T4

FIGURE 1: Summary of the procedure to obtain a map of epilep-togenicity index at peri-onset time D and in a frequency band f, from stereo EEG signals and electrode positions.

ANALYSIS OF THE ONSET SEIZURE ZONE: Two seizures were recorded. Using a fixed-effect analysis, epileptogenicity maps clearly confirmed the bilateral involvement of opercular regions and of right precentral regions, (see Fig. 5). The seizure propaga-tion map contained only zeroes indicating very fast onset in all implanted regions.

RECOMMENDATION: Surgical removal of the epileptogenic zone.

I felt even colder. I heard his waterfall, the train hurtling toward Petersburg at full speed, its windows white with fog. He tried to see out but couldn't. The stranger across from him was about to ask his question, but in my mind I wouldn't let him. Maybe Myshkin hadn't gotten on the train. Maybe none of it had ever happened.

But where was he now?

Outside there were only nameless streets. The sky silver-yellow. It didn't look like Petersburg, I was sure it wasn't. I watched for a long time but saw no one. After an hour, maybe two, I saw him with an overnight bag strapped over one shoulder, walking down the long central street, still empty. His back grew smaller and smaller. If he walked long enough would he come to anyone he knew? Anyone who would recognize him and speak to him and listen as he spoke? Would he even want to?

Pilate sat in his stone chair in the moonlight. The migraine wandered in his brain, its red thorns strong as trees. Red petals calcified behind his right eye, pressing and crushing. Everything else was drained of color—the granite cliffs in the distance, the cracked soil. His chair was gray, and the robe with its silk lining.

The red separateness spread like a vast sea, words shattering, dissolving. Had he ever cared for another, shown kindness or concern for another? Had he married or ever had children? The red separateness couldn't remember.

For a second he vaguely recalled being a follower of Pyrrhon who posited that for any given proposition the opposite can be proposed with equal reason. "The man of wisdom, rather than declaring *this is so,* can only say, *This seems so.*" Then he sensed that once he'd had power over a man who, unlike him, felt certain and deeply believed, but the thorns stabbed again and there was nothing.

Thousands of years passed between one thought and another.

Procula—wasn't that his wife's name? Her hair wreathed with white flowers in six braids under a veil the color of flame.

The red thorns pressed in again. The crushing sea. Words shattering to useless pieces.

His hands stayed rigid on his chair as the gray land before him stretched farther than his eyes could see.

Again I was carrying the one who waited to be read to across the courtyard to the epileptic's room.

(Or was I carrying Frieda?)

When we reached the courtyard's border, I left her at his door, knowing he would let her in. The two of them sitting without speaking. Then he picks up the book and starts reading, and her sight isn't blurring. She's listening from a place in Myshkin's eyes.

I'm in the Basel Museum looking at Holbein's Dead Christ then I feel I'm falling but for once I keep looking and don't fall xxx The eyes are dull half-open the face a nauseous blue-green the skin on the verge of decomposing xx the mouth rigid unclosed There's not one hint of consolation xx Who would want to sit beside this corpse you can almost smell it rotting Nothing else on the canvas but these two horizontal forms Stone slab Brutalized hurt body xxxx xx The slab so much easier to look at than the other In what ways can compassion appear for the beautiful that is mocked and does not know its own value xxxxx And there is no such thing as empty space x the whole universe expanding xxxx every day in my notebook I ask myself this question

My dear friend Sonechka much has changed since we last saw each other xxx I am living in Geneva my brother Mikhail died suddenly last August xx It will surprise you to know that I am married xx I am at work on a new book xx I want it to be as uncompromising as Holbein's Dead Christ xxx xx Each day I destroy most of what I write xxx I am tired of beautiful words I never liked them xxxxx I don't know if I can do this—

xxx Dear Apollon I think it is impossible to know what goodness is until it is reduced to complete powerlessness xxx My hand fears what it must write xxx There is a Prince I need to hurt in order to reveal his goodness In order to begin to know him xxx

But where are you have you fallen xx Myshkin says that "kindness can rescue everything" but how can this possibly be true xxxx

Today I felt my skin grow cold again. I saw the gray table, the electrodes, the city with its empty streets. And he was on that table again and he was cold, his hands in fists, that same yellow-gray as before. (How many times must they make him go back? Why are they still taking the data from his brain? Will they ever finally stop?) I could hear only a few words: signal analysis, temporal, microvolt, asymmetry, resective.

But then as if from somewhere inside the prone body, and in a language I'd never heard and didn't know, someone, or something—was it him or someone else?—was speaking. And although I couldn't understand, somehow I felt its questions that weren't quite questions but a kind of questioning assertion— What colors come from the destruction of color, what new forms from the destruction of form, what new sounds from sound destroyed?

"The mind is a chaos of touches," Titian said. He was standing outside the locked gate of his former garden near Calle Largo dei Botteri. "This is why I've preferred my late works to stay unfinished, though it took me much too long to understand this. For many years I loved only the mastery of my hand, but over time I began to wonder about the shape of a donkey's cry, the black sound its eyes make, each impenetrable red thread before it's woven to another, nothing that my hand could render. Think of how in your language thread means wander, meander, pull back, and even betray. Nothing is ever just one thing. But for so long I didn't see this. Still, I will never forget the red cloth, the red pleasure it gave me."

xxxxx Already it is November I have filled many notebooks for my story about the Prince but he keeps slipping away from me xxx Today I read of another Prince— Antonovich—born in 1740 who at the age of one was imprisoned by his enemies and kept for twenty years in isolation xxx At twenty he could barely even speak his lonely mind filled up with dreams and visions xxx When the young officer Mirovich rescues him he tries to explain certain things about the world—how others might have to die for him etc. xxx But the Prince looks at him with saddened eyes and says with his few words If this is what the world is then I do not wish to live

As I put down the notebook, I remembered that Holbein had used for his model a dead body fished out of the Rhine.

It had been years since I'd remembered.

As a boy when I first glimpsed that painting in a book, its unsparing honesty shocked me. I had never seen a figure so coldly alone.

I learned that Holbein had a brother, Ambrosius, who had died. And maybe because he shared my name, my child-mind forged a link between the painting's brutal truth and the world I would go into and who I was. But that was a long ago, and for years I had forgotten.

It's said that Holbein died of plague 33 years before Titian.

His mind was an unswerving line and he painted its cruel edges.

For weeks after I saw that painting, as I lay in the infirmary bed I wondered what happened to the body after Holbein finished. Had he wondered about its age or name? Or if it was an "it" or had a family? And though I didn't really have the words, something in me tried to think about what beauty is when mixed with what's repugnant, and a goodness that's intact but also spoiled.

My small back was already sloped and crooked, sometimes it pushed in against my lungs, my shadow on the wall a sort of monster, lopsided, lumpy, over-spilling, a loose blackness where the neck should have been, head and shoulders fused together.

But I knew he'd paint my flesh, not shadow.

I learned Holbein worked under the patronage of Anne Boleyn and Thomas Cromwell, and by 1535 was named King's painter to King Henry VIII (his life so different from the body in the river). But when I flipped through the book for the day he died, I found this: *between October 7 and November 29, 1543.* How could that happen? He'd been famous, respected. It made no sense his death date was unknown.

He's buried in an unmarked grave. Even now, no one knows where.

But as soon as I think *unmarked grave*, I almost feel Frieda beside me, the black dirt of the forest floor all over her hands, then her hands smelling of antimatter, burning metal, her eyes watchful from behind her black lenses.

And Apollon I tell myself to choose only the bare facts without reasoning or explanation Facts on the side of action and mystery not description or interpretation Often I fear what I will find xxx I sit here late at night and certain words come close to me and find me—Mental darkness / Striving / Isolation xxx Dear Apollon I am still living in Geneva I have a newborn daughter xxx Already she follows me with her eyes and seems to know and love me but how can she depend on me when even on the morning of her birth I had a seizure xx From the first day I have already failed her xxx So why do I even think I have the right to envision a beautiful man xxx To try to write on my pages a beautiful man xxx And now the small creature who resembles me though she is beautiful and I am ugly lies sleeping in her crib beside me—

xx Dear Apollon Though I have written many pages I am still struggling to bring my Prince into focus xxx How can I show his innocence and compassion without violating the ways he is also unaware and enigmatic xxxxx Without pretending that I understand him x

And Apollon Last night as I filled my pages Rogozhin assaulted Nastasya Filipova and broke both of her hands xxx The brutality of the act horrified me yet it came from my own mind xxx xxx My child smiles when I sing to her and rock her xxx It is so cold in Geneva I think we must leave here very soon maybe for Florence Milan or even Venice xxx These nights are very long xxx A flightless bird A ghost xx There is a harshness I am trying to understand

But why should I expect anything but harshness xxx Facts are brutal and ordinary xxx I am falling many times each week xxx Alpha waves Beta waves xxxx Why is no one coming

Do all distances vanish when you fall until even the white sky's inside you xx Do you feel a sudden light like Myshkin's xxx

Maybe because we'll be forced very soon to leave the island, I've been having many dreams. Last night I was walking down Meshchanskaya Street, empty except for a man in a black coat approaching from the opposite direction. After a while I realized it was Myshkin. When he drew close, he started speaking, his voice soft but steady: "I used to believe in a firm footing, if not for myself then at least for many others. But I see now I was wrong. Whoever you are, whatever you do, don't try to follow me, don't even think of it, don't try to go where I am going."

Then he reminded me that Holbein painted his dead Christ without a hint of comfort or transcendence.

Yet as he spoke I saw something beautiful, maybe even transcendent, in his face. Something that had to do with his effort to care for and protect another.

A few hours after my dream of Meshchanskaya Street, the red aura started building, until finally I fell. Even now I'm not sure how long it lasted.

When I came to, I knew that I cared about someone named Myshkin, though I couldn't remember who he was or why I cared. Why would I be thinking of a Russian?

My temples ached, blood trickled from the corner of my mouth.

For some reason I was also thinking about a dog Azorska who had once been in a circus. And of a girl who explained why begging isn't wrong, and a donkey in a marketplace.

I felt a newborn's breath beside me.

I could make no sense of anything I thought.

Then I remembered the one across the courtyard. She must be wondering where I am, if something happened. I need to go to her as soon as I can—

Pilate sat in his stone chair on the desolate summit, his eyes focused on the icy moonlight. All around him, bare rock and arid soil.

If he was bleeding in the darkness of his brain, self-stabbed by his own cruelty to another, could there ever be a way he could begin to learn tenderness or kindness? But how could he begin to find them, trapped as he was within a cruelty that would last forever, the awful act he could never undo?

I am waiting for you by the ocean—no—I am in Geneva in the depths of winter— no—I am carrying your voice in my mind I am near Venice it is raining—but no— no—We are reading many pages the twelve trees are bare your window lit across the courtyard—no—but no—xx Dear Apollon my baby is dead xxx She contracted an inflammation of the lungs and even three hours before her death the doctor said she would still live xx xxx We buried her on May 24 xxx She was barely three months old xxx Words mean nothing Thoughts mean nothing—But where is the poor vulnerable being that I love—

I don't believe you will ever come to read to me again I don't know why I feel this
xxx ~~Black Holes Dark Matter~~ xx I am searching for the donkey in the marketplace
my cupped palm filled with sugar xxx And as I walk I remember the theory that the
universe is splitting it is doing it right now though we can't feel it xx And I remember
also that Columbus was said to be most happy three days before discovering the
New World xx before anything was safe or settled xx I can't remember where I read
this xx Have you fallen are you waking has your brain momentarily caught fire xx
and the "serene, harmonious joy" do you feel it xxx and this is not tenderheartedness
x and vanished xx and no longer xx and if the universe goes on for long enough every
conceivable accident is likely to happen xx No earth No sun No moon Instability
Disorder xx Holbein painted his dead Christ bruised and broken without any trace
of comfort or transcendence xxx When my baby lived I sang to her and she smiled
xxx Do you still think of me do you still look across the courtyard

All day I've been asking myself if now with that dead child inside her mind she would build a barrier between herself and Dostoevsky if she could, turn her eyes from him and never look again. And Marie would be gone and the rock ledge gone. And Marei's hand nonexistent, the boy's face he touched nonexistent. None of it ever existed. She sang to the child and knew it loved her, then suddenly all breathing ceased. Nothing protects anything. So it seems only sensible she feels no one in the world can find her.

———————————

Though we've never touched, sometimes I almost feel her in my arms—her shoulders and small hips, her narrow spine. How she grows softer and more brittle as she moves into a solitude I've tried to reach but can only partly understand.

I wish she could believe that I still go to her, that our hours of reading haven't ended.

Titian was standing before a wrought-iron gate set into a wall of pale pink stone in front of his last home on Calle Larga dei Botteri.

"By 1534 my fame had spread all over Europe. Charles V made me a Knight of the Golden Spur, my works were found in the great courts from Mantua to Urbino. I owned two saw mills at Ansogne, extensive lands and buildings in Cadore, 18 fields in Milare, and numerous other tracts as well. But how can I explain what I felt as I stood before my canvases? Color and form asked questions I could barely grasp.

Finally I came to understand that my brushwork must be left open and visible, my human failings part of what I paint. This was done out of honesty and love, though of course at times I questioned my motives.

But this late change brought mostly mockery and condescension. My effort to be faithful to the textures and angles of what I saw left me largely in a private darkness (though of course there was Orazio).

Mary, Regent of the Netherlands, claimed my late work could be viewed only from a distance and even then only in the brightest light. Vasari wrote that I painted 'in rapidly dashed off patches so that the pictures cannot be viewed from up close.' Nicolo Atoppio was simply convinced I could no longer see, that even if my mind was still alert my hand was feeble. And as if that weren't enough, in 1675 Joachim Sandrart wrote that I'd ruined numerous works of my youth by repainting them when old, and my assistants had taken to mixing wood oil into my paint to keep it from drying so that when I was absent they could wipe away my changes. I don't know if this is true.

I often think of how precarious color is, how mercurial. Though it is also joy."

Maybe you can't believe in Myshkin's joy anymore and that's why you no longer come xx I believe that you no longer come xx Ever since my baby died I xxx And these prions inside me xxx But what if Myshkin's joy doesn't leave him even in the darkest hour what if it still lives inside him xx "And sense the whole of nature and suddenly say yes" Is it wrong of me to think this xxx And the waterfall the donkey the twelve trees xx Soon I will enter the room of Nastasya's death I will part the green curtain xxx Behind it the deathbed where she lies xxx I will do all this without you xx I remember the pages I once read Myshkin's helplessness within them his hopes completely over xxx And the universe x splitting and splitting x Where are you have you fallen I would bring you a warm blanket these blurred pages—

It had been a long time since I'd last opened the copy of *The Idiot* I'd found on the Rio dei Assassinini. But that night after I closed the notebook, I spent the next few hours following Myshkin and Nastasya into their grim, concluding pages. I watched her become increasingly convinced that Myshkin's need to protect her could only bring him harm. When he realizes she's fled, he searches the streets with an unfolding sense of doom until behind a green curtain in Rogozhin's room he sees a body covered head to toe by a white sheet. The floor is strewn with flowers, torn ribbons, a white dress.

"Go nearer," Rogozhin coaxes. Then after a while, whispers, "It was I."

"What did you do it with? A knife...?"

"It was all so strange...the blade went in three or four inches...just under the left breast...yet no more than a half tablespoon of blood flowed out."

Myshkin's whole body is trembling, his chest is on fire and he can't move.

Dear Apollon How can I accept what is happening on my pages even as I know it would be wrong and dishonest to pull back xxx Isn't there a way to know Myshkin without subjecting him to useless pain perverse suffering x why did I even think I could begin to know him xx x But why do you never ~~e~~ come anymore why do you xxx the twelve trees dissolving xxx the courtyard gray and fading xxx and Rogozhin places four cushions on the floor by the green curtain xx the dead body behind it xx He insists Myshkin lie down on the ones on the left because they are "the best" then undresses and lies beside him on the right xx ~~T~~ Tears flow from Myshkin's eyes onto the murderer's cheeks as they talk about flowers the knife the drops of blood xxx xxx And "Rogozhin tenderly and eagerly" takes him by the arm—remember—xxx But how can the word "tenderly" survive after all that's come before it xxx how can "eagerly" survive And Myshkin's hand is tender as he strokes the pale crazed man beside him xxx How can his touch contain such kindness given all that's happened why does he reach out to soothe him xxxx Am I in Petersburg or on an island off of Venice Am I across from your lit window or is your window ~~d~~ dark now and you're elsewhere xxx Why is my hand stroking a murderer's face xxx xxx How can this possibly be happening xx Why do I feel a strange love for him xx Why don't I pull back in horror xxx

———————————

Even though she says I no longer come to her and read, and she believes she is going on without me, most nights we are still reading. Last night we read from the passage where Nastasya says "I have renounced the world...I have almost ceased to exist and I know it."

I didn't want those words to leave my mouth.

But already she is in Rogozhin's room, she has parted the green curtain....She sees the torn ribbons, the white dress. Lies down on the "best cushions." Holds the murderer close, her tears falling on his cheek.

So where is there left for me to take her, and why would she even want to go? In her mind the green curtain is parted again and again, she will never stop parting it.

And her hand will never withdraw from Rogozhin's face, his breath on her skin, tears falling from her eyes onto his cheek. She won't ever stop feeling this strange love she can't understand.

Soon it will be morning but it's never quite morning. Sun filters in through the window, touching the unsleeping bodies.

How could I have ever thought she would allow me to go with her. How could I not have known that this would happen.

But why is Myshkin so kind to Rogozhin xx He knows he has murdered Nastasya yet "he passes his trembling hand softly over Rogozhin's hair and cheeks" caresses him and holds him xxx   How can this happen what does this say of him And the flowers the white dress the ribbons the green curtain xxxxx And when you still came to me and this island wasn't drowned in quiet xxx No earth No sun No moon Instability Disorder xx So many boundaries blurring xx And how can I know what is beautiful what is ugly in what ways do they blend into each other xx Dark Energy Dark Matter xxx "Crushed by gravity...destroyed...but a star is simple" xx When the police enter Rogozhin's room they see a delirious man raving in another man's arms but the man who holds him won't answer anything they ask x only looks at them with empty eyes—

I am walking across the courtyard to you the night is very cold too quiet xxx In the far future the stars will all burn out there will be no life-bearing planets xx the inhabitants of earth will see only black sky they will think we lived in a delusion x their sophisticated technology their instruments their calculations will support this xx what is the real why is it so difficult xx and Dostoevsky said "they dismiss my approach as 'fantastic' but for me it is the height of realism...their realism cannot illuminate a hundredth part of the facts that are actually occurring." I am close to your room now xx I am not thinking of cold planets x I am not thinking of carbon or black space or computational processes xx I arrange the cushions on the floor the best ones on the left for you the other ones for me xx We lie down not speaking never touching though in my mind I stroke your hair my tears fall on your narrow cheeks xxx I want to know what you are thinking but you look past me with empty eyes

And if my eyes, like Myshkin's, are empty to her now, why would I even hope she could believe I still see her?

It seems a form of suffering—to be cared for and companioned by another, yet unable to feel this or remember.

Is this partly why she lies beside Rogozhin? She touches him, and doesn't doubt he's beside her. But if she were to turn her eyes from the green curtain, if she were to lift her hand from his face for just one second, there'd be nothing left for her but a world where she believes she's completely alone.

Each day I go to her, and each day she doesn't know it.

But when Myshkin first enters Rogozhin's room, a "strange dreaminess" comes over him even before the green curtain is parted and "words suddenly seem to mean something quite different" from the words that are being said. Why can't I find a way for her to hear those different meanings from my mouth? Those meanings I hear each time I fall—

xxxx *And when they came looking for me and found me and I didn't answer any of their questions they took me away xxx And then I didn't know how to go on in the world anymore xxx I don't know if I can live in my own body xxxx But why is the floor still covered with white flowers surely someone must have come and swept them xxx And the donkey's eyes in the marketplace—remember xxx What is joy where does it come from do you think it still exists or has it vanished xxx No earth No sun xx but those long hours the white dress the green curtain xx Am I in Petersburg or on an island off of Venice Am I looking at black sky or is it morning xx Gray sun dissolving xx Gray-black light xxx If I could bring you a warm blanket some cool water xxx xxxx Are you falling are you lost like Myshkin xx A flightless bird A ghost xx I can't see the waterfall anymore though I still hear it rushing through itself and through itself the way feeling struggles through the body to become thought—*

xxxx Dear Apollon I write the word "dark" and cross it out write "joy" and cross it out xxx cross out ~~peace eternal freedom consent~~ write "new terror"—cross it out xxx cross out ~~disordered intellect sick soul~~   xx Each word a torn shroud across the mouth xxx Sleep spindles xxx Proteins xxx Your window shut across the courtyard xxx The prion is a flightless bird a ghost xxx

They have sent me back to the sanitarium in Switzerland xxx have given me white pills they say will calm me xxx but mostly I hide them in my clothes the bitter taste not touching my tongue xx Every now and then someone moves my chair onto the hill so I can sit in the warm sunlight xxx But this ~~g~~ green hill is so cold and without shadow why can't they see that it is cold xxx ~~and the universe splitting and splitting~~ xxx I don't expect them to see it xx And the cattle are hungry as they move through their white field where there's no one left to tend them xxx It's been so long since I've seen them xxx Marie's rock is bare she stayed with them as long as she could xxxx why must time harm itself why does it need to live inside a body or maybe I am wrong and it has vanished xxx I think that I will never speak again xxx Do you still see the courtyard the twelve trees xxxxx Words are vulnerable and hurt I have buried them in secret places

Now that Myshkin was cold on his cold hill, unspeaking, I thought back to the book's opening pages where Myshkin's eyes "possess something gentle," his voice is "conciliatory and gentle." Little more than a year elapses between the first chapter and the last, yet everything has changed. By the end, his eyes are "empty," his voice completely silenced.

In those first chapters, the word "gentle" appears often. And in them a train is hurtling toward St. Petersburg "at full speed." In one of the third-class carriages two young men, two strangers, sit across from each other, tired, bored, but seemingly eager to speak. It is morning, November.

The dark-haired man speaks first.

"Cold?"

To which the fair-haired traveler across from him replies,

"Very."

These are the first words to ever pass between Rogozhin and Myshkin.

As he listens and then talks to the stranger, Myshkin's face is "thin, open, without suspicion."

I used to think of those first pages as the brief lull before Myshkin is pulled back into the world's confusion. But already Rogozhin has said "Cold?" and that coldness gleams like a bright knife between them. The same knife that will enter Nastasya's heart and kill her. But Myshkin doesn't know this, he doesn't feel it. He doesn't see the bright glint that follows him out of the station and then everywhere after. How from that moment, when he enters a house the two words "cold" and "very" enter with him, and when he walks down the street they are there also, and when he speaks to Nastasya. They are there in his seizures, in his eyes when he looks in a store window. They are faithful and they never leave him.

And when, after a time, Myshkin feels his tears flowing onto Rogozhin's cheek, "but perhaps he does not even notice they are his own tears…and a new sensation gnaws with infinite anguish at his heart," is this when he feels the cold knife, realizes it has followed? That it's been following since that first moment on the train.

Or maybe he doesn't realize and it doesn't matter. He is holding the murderer, his tears fall on the murderer's cheek, and he is trembling. Sunlight begins to filter through the window. Every now and then the murderer mutters, grows agitated, stiffens, and Myshkin softly touches his hair, his face, calming and soothing him. And he isn't cold. Rogozhin's question doesn't matter anymore. Maybe he was never cold.

Florensky had written of the body's "isolation." But it seemed there should be a word for an isolation that can never be healed yet still feels at its deepest core the unfathomable, beating presence of another—

———————

And your voice so tenderly xxx and your breath your moving hands—

xxx And folding wrongly in the delicate tissues of the brain xxx xxx xxx a rapid process of misfiring xxx The soul of another is a dark place and what chaos is found there xxx

Why must I remain here xxx This wooden chair so stiff on this green hill xx Why can't I stand up and leave here—

In the days when we were making our way through the passages where Myshkin cradles and comforts Rogozhin until light seeps in through the closed shutters and the police finally arrive, I felt I was bringing her a nearly unbearable world.

Yet in those pages, one man still tenderly touches another. Strokes him, comforts him. Myshkin does this without reticence or question, and no matter how much he trembles, he doesn't flinch or even once draw back his hand.

But by morning he's mute, his eyes blank and impassive.

And now, in these last pages, in Switzerland, he's completely alone.

As I watch her follow Myshkin further and further into his unceasing isolation, the prions folding wrongly in the tissues of her brain, I wonder if she feels that no matter what he did, or whichever way he turned, he would still end in isolation.

Even when a visitor stands beside him, Myshkin's eyes show nothing. No words emerge from his mouth.

There is no sign he will ever speak again.

I lie down beside you x The twelve trees are still saplings x The darkness kind and forgiving The book we read from has flown off like a white bird but we still feel it xxx But no I am on my green hill in Switzerland the hard chair-back pressing the quarter moon stiffly brightening xxxx I don't know what has happened to my hands x where are they x why are they no longer with me xxx and the universe splitting and splitting xx I don't know what to do with my eyes now that I can't see you now that I am sure you aren't coming

I didn't think this wind could grow even colder but it has xxxx my skin moonwhite and listening xxxx But ~~is~~ skin is unimportant eyes are unimportant xxx But how can my hands have so suddenly vanished x Where are they where could they have gone to how could this possibly ~~h~~ have happened xxx And what can they remember now that they have left my body xxx If you fall who will bring you water a warm blanket I wish that I could help you xxx But how can I help you without hands xxx "and tenderly and eagerly" xx and the material the galaxies are made of is embedded in a sea of Dark Matter xx Are your hands turning pages xx Do you feel the redness spreading xxx ~~is~~ Sleep spindles Prions xxx Once I was a good cow-herder but now

Now that she believes her hands have vanished and she sits on her green hill in Switzerland, cold and blankly staring, why does she still remember me and worry that I've fallen or think to bring me water? Even now she sometimes feels the turning pages, imagines lying down beside me. So how am I to understand the blankness of her eyes, or Myshkin's?

And sometimes, when I don't go to her, or have gone and then come back but she thinks I didn't go, I picture Myshkin cradling Rogozhin. How no part of him remained protected. And though the ones who think they know him lament "his afflicted and humiliated condition," the only fact they can truly know is that his visible responsiveness is over. Everything else is conjecture. They can't know what goes on behind his eyes.

xxx But how can I even be writing to you now that my hands have vanished into whiteness xxx I didn't expect to be so cold I forgot the earth could be so cold xxxxx I don't know where the waterfall has gone to ∔ I can't hear it anymore or the donkey in the marketplace xxx and tenderly and eagerly xx xx What is sound when everything is stripped and silent xxx This chair-back stiff and heavy xx Dear Mikhail Dear Sonechka Dear Apollon xx The heavy sound of you not reading xxx The sound of you not walking toward me xxx

---

And I would ask you again xxx what is a voice when no one hears it?

xxx but where is the small, vulnerable being that I loved and who followed me with her eyes and looked like me though I am ~~u~~ ugly xx and she was beautiful—

In a book about Titian I found in my first week in Venice, the author, whose name was Hope, wondered if one of the most important things about him is the way that we can never know him. "There is no lack of information about his day-to-day existence...but in a period when artists' comments and even their eccentricities were eagerly recorded, Titian is remembered for almost none....Michelangelo is famous for his *terribilita*, Raphael for his social assurance and aristocratic manner, Leonardo for his enigmatic personality...but Titian exists for us in his paintings and near-silence alone."

As I held the epileptic's notebook in my hands, a quiet dread came over me, as if I had forgotten my own name.

~~I~~ It is late and I want to go to her, ~~v~~ want her to ~~t~~ know that I still read the notes she sends though most likely she doesn't remember that she sends them. ~~H~~ her wooden chair so far from her gray courtyard xxx How ~~ca~~ can I let her know that I still think of her still feel her—or maybe she doesn't want to know xx but the red aura ~~vv~~ keeps burning through my arms and spreading even further through my chest and up my neck xxx the air surging in hot waves then crumbling ~~unstable~~ I've never felt it surge so strongly. ~~I~~ ~~xx~~ I keep waiting to fall but I don't fall. Everything wavering, splintering, uncertain. I'm still trying ~~t~~ to paste her notes into these pages but can't read anymore what they say. Even ~~thi~~ this paper xxx is red flame.

This air so hot now. I didn't know that air could be so hot—

The epileptic was burning on a wooden pyre. Only his face remained untouched. His eyes were wide open, filled with tears, his eyelids swollen. I was sure he wanted to speak but didn't know why I felt this or who he wanted to speak to or what he might say. When I tried to get close to him to help him, I realized both my legs were broken. Then even his face began to burn.

This air's unbearably hot now xxx I can hardly x see ~~m~~ ~~nn~~ my hand for all the redness xxx

I can't see her pages or ~~ss~~ anything she ~~n~~ means to tell me xxx

When for one second the fire turns less fierce (but ~~rr~~ then it starts up again even more violently than before) I suddenly remember how ~~N~~ Myshkin said "I don't ~~l~~ know how one can walk by a ~~xxx~~ tree and not be happy at the sight of it ~~xxx~~ ...And what beautiful things ~~H~~ there are at every step" ~~xxx~~

I was walking on the slope of a green hill where a solitary figure stared into the distance, a blanket draped across his narrow lap. I thought it must be Myshkin and that I must be in Switzerland, but when I got closer I saw it was the epileptic, his eyes red with tears. He was trying to paste new pages into his notebook but they scattered to the ground like ashes. It was clear that he could barely see. I wanted to gather them and read to him what he could no longer read for himself, but knew this was impossible, though I didn't know why. For a moment it seemed Frieda was near me, but when I looked up there was only empty land. I understood I had to keep walking, but had no idea where I was going or from where I had come.

But do you remember "kindness can rescue everything"—how we read this once on an island off of Venice xxx Or maybe I was never on an island Maybe you never came to me at all xxx Even my arms are white mist now and my legs xxx Have you fallen are you hurt now are you sleeping xxx I still wonder what you think of what we read xxx Do you believe that kindness is so powerful there's a way that it remains no matter what xxxx...and could not endure...would vanish...Do you still hear the word "cold" spoken by a stranger xxxx and tenderly and eagerly xx No earth No sun No moon I wish I still had hands to write to you to find you

Can it be true that there is no such thing as empty space but *Dark Energy Dark Matter* xxx xxx The cow-herder sent me away but I came back xxx I must part the green curtain xxx It still amazes me to walk without fetters x xx xx and the stars will go out and there will be no life-bearing planets xx and what's here is higher than love and there's such joy

As the pages thinned, the notes were often pasted sidewise, sometimes even upside down, bulging awkwardly and wrinkling. What effort did it cost him to still keep the notebook, though from the start he said he meant to burn it?

I wondered, had he fallen? Or was the redness spreading even further?

And she, who sat on her green hill with vanished hands, who was herself and not, was others than herself and not, was remembering and not, dissolving into mist and not—was there some way she understood that although he was gone he hadn't left her?

This hard chair is mist now   xxxxx your vanished voice enfolded in the air xxx

---

But could the joy be unbroken even so—

And sense the whole of nature and say yes

Even my face is white mist now and my hair xxx xxxxx The green hill has vanished the green fields xxx But how can the earth survive like this when it's so white so insubstantial xxx xxx xx xx Remember the fragile island we once lived on xxx I write the word "dark" and cross it out write "joy" and cross it out xxx Where are the twelve trees the night filling with our turning pages xxx The Nucleus Solitarius is such a lonely name forgive me xxxx White mist of vanished footsteps xxx vanished eyes xxx

There were no more pages left to turn.

I imagined the epileptic feeling the redness finally drain, or maybe it would stay forever. And the one he read to, what comfort was left to her once he could no longer come?

Had they lived to see their island emptied? Where could they have gone to after that? I knew that I would never know.

I pictured her writing in white mist. The word "vanished" taking form beneath her hand.

As Frieda had vanished, and the one across the ocean who'd faded into silence.

Vanish: "To pass completely from existence." "To assume the value zero."

From the Latin: *vanus, evanescere* – "empty." "To dissipate like vapor."

But I didn't know anymore what emptiness was, or what it really means "to dissipate like vapor."

PART III

MARGARITA FLYING

I knew I should leave Venice.

Just pack up my few things, walk out to the ferry, make my way back to the airport.

But when I tried to think of where to go my mind went blank. As if the earth were taken from me and yet it was still there.

My whole body the Servetta Muta, that white mask Frieda held before her face.

My white walls mask-like also, a vivid stillness that I couldn't name.

Florensky had written of the "beautiful continuity of light."

"In a space filled with light it is impossible to single out an area that does not communicate with any other region. It is only our granular optical environment which obscures the presence of this ongoing communication."

But now, as I sat in my room, nothing felt continuous.

I saw only my four walls, my computer, my coffee cup, my cane. The closed notebook beside me.

The material world exacting and opaque, insistent.

"What lies past the single horizon, the single scale?"

It had been months since any letter had come from the one across the ocean.

And Frieda—what had she been to me, who was she? And the one who was read to and the one who crossed the courtyard until he could no longer cross?

I heard the soft sounds of the canals, but it was as if something jagged, almost predatory, was moving underneath their waters.

Why didn't you turn to me? What would it have cost you to turn to me?

I raised my eyes but saw only a mute figure seated in a chair on a parched summit staring at the barren moonlight.

Her face was nearly featureless, her hands unmoving.

But as I thought of the one who read and the other who waited and worried he was hurt—so much care had passed between them—I finally turned to show that I could see her. The black smudges of her eyes stared straight ahead. I had waited much too long. There was no way I could know if she had seen me.

Pilate sat on his dry summit in the moonlight. His dog lay by his side, the wooden splint on its right, front leg wrapped in layers of white gauze; a silver muzzle covered its mouth. As the centuries passed, they watched comets fall through the sky, whole stars imploding. Atoms wavering, unlocked, unstable. Atoms caught in giant machines, split, recombined, broken open. They had no words for what they saw, what they were hearing. Sometimes when the moon thinned to its most razored crescent, Pilate tried to remember the philosophy he once learned, or just the names of fellow pupils, a few teachers. But even those mostly escaped him. What was it Xenephon had posited?—something about safety...And Democritus..."the wrong-doer is more unfortunate than..." But more unfortunate than...what...or whom...? He couldn't remember, though a chill with a bright silver edge went through him. Once he recalled an entire line from Anaxagorus, "The seed of everything is in everything else." But this he'd never understood from the moment he first learned it. And once, after a green incandescent comet sheered much too close to his summit, he remembered a fiery redness, and for a moment, though he didn't know why, the bones in his neck and shoulders frayed to a thread-like fragility; his right temple burned and pounded, as if a shard of the comet, too minute for even the strongest microscope to detect, had entered through his skull and lodged there. Long ago, after an important death, he'd seen an eclipse of the sun, the sky on fire, burning embers in free-fall, but whose death could it have been? Every now and then, the injured dog sighed quietly from behind its silver muzzle, but Pilate no longer heard it. Its legs twitched in a reflex of pursuit or fleeing. But mostly it lay still. It had never been trained to know distance, or what a wrong-doer is, or a seed, or *unfortunate*. All it knew was that white light poured all over its skin, but that light, though bright, resembled darkness, and was filled with an enormous silence.

I still needed to figure out where to go and what to do. I decided to head outside, maybe buy a few groceries, see if distraction might lead to an idea. I'd never thought of my life as a project to be managed, assessed, fine-tuned, and couldn't think that way now. I had been an orphan, an invalid, a book scanner, a seeker of a notebook—all these simply happened.

But shortly after I stepped outside, I glimpsed, by mistake, my hump in a store window's gilded mirror. At first I didn't recognize the strange, unlikely creature I was seeing.

Hadn't my whole life been a resistance to the question of this hump I carried? How it was made of an essential wrongness—a wrongness I couldn't undo.

I had never even said the word aloud.

The air was warming. I walked for several hours. Passing beside a canal, I saw my bulbous shadow, faceless, barely visible, as it moved across low walls and shadowed water.

Titian had been silent a long time.

I missed his red cloth, the dyers' shops, the blurred hands of his late portraits. How he'd spoken of the beggars huddled under the portals of the Ducal Palace even as he refused to paint them, and when the plague came he didn't flee with the city's privileged others, but stayed near the locked doors and their white X's. How he brought close the vulnerability of color, and light and form asked questions he could barely grasp.

Walking the narrow cobblestone streets near Calle Largo dei Botteri, I wondered if his feet had touched them also.

His silence a red wall...or...no...not red...but a hard gray.

And as I walked, I remembered he used his bare fingertips to smear red pigment into the hollows and crevices of bodies. He'd seen his own child die, and killed countless others in his paintings, his eyes steady as he hung Marsyas from a tree and flayed him. He even let a small dog lap from the pooled blood. He painted the pope in old age, ailing, tired, and tore his cap from his head, the barest touch of his brush crushing the stooped shoulders. He painted his own face aged, lined, bony, and left the hands unfinished.

But even he, with all his red watchfulness and power, hadn't pried the black lenses from Frieda's eyes.

Day after day of wondering, walking...Each time I went out I made sure to avoid the store mirrors. My legs sore, my right foot swollen, dragging (the result, I assumed, of a small fracture). And always as I walked I remembered the hundreds of thousands of wood poles submerged beneath the city's squares and buildings. Stone facades barely masking a too-quiet instability. The fragility beneath me.

And then one afternoon this came:

Dear A,

It is dark most of the time now, but sometimes for a few minutes or even hours, suddenly my sight comes back—I don't know how or why this happens. Everything briefly clear again—my room, this paper, the books I love that follow me even in this darkness. But mostly now I live in sounds—I didn't know they have so many colors—and nuances, insinuations—they bolt and change so quickly. Always I feel them on my skin—this constant, shifting pressure—so in a sense I am never alone.

Sometimes it is hard to know if what I'm seeing is in the world or in my mind. Or maybe both. Or does it even matter?

I never told you what I found in those last weeks before you left for Venice. Back then I could still see even though my sight was dimming.

I was standing at my work station scanning. The next book in line was a copy of Dostoevsky's The Idiot. Maybe you remember that we'd received a shipment from a library in Venice some months before. The copy was tattered but intact. But as I turned it over to press onto the scanner, a few loose pages fell out. I could see right away they were handwritten, not printed.

I looked over at you but could tell you hadn't noticed.

The first stages of my illness had already begun to take hold. For weeks I had been sleeping less and less. And now, as I read those few pages, it was clear they were unsent letters from someone who suffered from my same affliction. But what was even more uncanny was that she was writing of a man named Ambrose who Dostoevsky had visited after the sudden death of his child.

What was I to make of this convergence?—my sleeplessness and your name on the same page.

I felt the air grow hot, a narrow fire spreading through my spine.

But my eyesight's starting to dim again. I still want to tell you more. Often I feel your name beside me. I will write to you again when I am able.

It seemed nearly a lifetime ago that I stood beside her in that basement office, scanning. And nearly as long since I received any letters. I'd grown used to her silence, to wondering if maybe she had died, and to the fact that I'd never know her name.

Again I remembered Ovid's words—the ones I recalled when I first encountered Frieda: "All things which I denied could happen are now happening."

Had she sensed I'd found the notebook and that the voices inside it were now closed to me, that once again I was alone?

But why was she even thinking of me? Why did she want to explain what had happened?

For a moment I wished I could ask her. And that I could show her what I found, even if she'd already sensed I'd found it. (My hand lightly touched the notebook's worn cover.)

I thought of how startling the world must look to her in the moments when her eyesight briefly returned. So many intricate makings and re-makings. The plainest line a thing of wonder.

But I realized I was barely concentrating on the actual contents of her letter—how she'd found pages containing her illness and my name. Pages in a book from Venice.

My hump felt heavy. My shoulders stiff, unwieldy.

All night I lay awake and wondered—after the island of San Servolo had been emptied of its patients, how had its library come to end up in that far-off basement room?

That copy of *The Idiot* the epileptic read from to the sleepless one, and that she held in the long hours of her aloneness, had been a living skin to them, and yet it had remained with neither.

I pictured him holding it open as he read, and she holding it also on those long days he didn't come, her eyes fixed on pages she knew but couldn't un-blur.

Their fingerprints all over it and yet no one could see them.

When I'd finished the notebook, I believed it held all the notes the sleepless one had written to the epileptic—he had taken such pains to paste them in. But given the letter I'd just gotten, maybe there were others. Again I felt my hump press firmly down, my lungs constricting, faltering, too narrow.

Dear A,

At first I found the loose pages somewhat confusing. They began straightforwardly enough—the writer referring to chemical changes in her brain, but soon she was writing of Dostoevsky and his visit to Father Ambrose at the Monastery of Optina Pustyn. And then suddenly she seemed to be Dostoevsky but she was also sitting on a hill in Switzerland, the lost sound of a waterfall inside her. And she was longing for someone from across a courtyard who had come and then no longer came. She worried he was hurt. I must have kept the letters somewhere, I probably still have them. But my sight's fading again, the darkness returning.

Dear A,

This morning I found one of the letters—

If I could write to you If I could find you xxx What is a mind
what is breathing when inside them there is always a dead child
xxxxxx Always now I ask myself this question xx I have come to
the Monastery of Optina Pustyn to see its Staret Father Ambrose
xx xxx xx xxx xx He speaks into my blackened mind his cane
propped against the wall his body hunchbacked straining frail "Do
not try to be consoled, but weep and grieve. Your tears will turn in
the end to quiet joy" xxx xx But what if joy can't break through
this Dark Energy Dark Matter What if it can never reach me xx
And how can I be here when I am also on my hill in Switzerland
xx x The Nucleus Solitarius is such a lonely name forgive me xxx
Are you hurt do you need water have you fallen xxx Your window
dark across the courtyard xxx My hands completely vanished now
the branches of twelve trees dissolving

Dear A,

As I read that letter, how could I not think of you? For months I watched you at your work station. Your hunched back, the way you often seemed in pain, the cane you leaned against the wall each morning. I knew your name was Ambrose. I didn't see why you would do the work you did with the body you'd been given. And yet those books seemed living things to you—the way you held them. Of course anything I thought was just conjecture, but I sensed a wounded gentleness in you and also something dark like Dostoevsky. At first I didn't think much more about it, but as my illness grew and deepened, I felt you near me even when you weren't there. But how could I feel this when I didn't even know you?

Dear A,

One night in my sleeplessness I found myself wondering about your name, turning over its history and syllables, all the ways it seemed to fit you as it fit the Staret of Optina Pustyn. The "am" in it, the "rose" that followed. I learned that Ambrose of Optina fell ill as a young man and never fully recovered. "Weakness is a teacher of gratefulness and patience"—he wrote this years later. His happiest hours were spent in solitude translating Greek texts—one of them was called "The Ladder." In 1884 he founded a convent for the destitute, the blind, the sickly. At that time this was uncommon. When appointed Staret he replied, "I would prefer to live in solitude and silence but this is not allowed me."

Then I found another Ambrose—this one Bishop of Milan from 374 until his death in 397, who wrote in his De Officiis, "What a splendid thing is justice—to be born for others rather than oneself." I hadn't thought of justice in that way. His definition seemed to me a thing of beauty.

He believed our human deeds inflict a violence on the world that's left it fractured, gravely wounded. But "what has been weakened and warped can in some measure be restored." I noticed he said "some measure"—again I felt the exacting pressure of his words, his acknowledgment of harm and limitation. How there are elements beyond all healing.

The more I paced and thought of him, the more I felt the rose inside your name, the many roses in the air before me, red petals bruised and opening. And still I knew I didn't know you. But the less I slept the less that seemed to matter— everything more vivid and more real, less real, at once. Or maybe the idea of realness began to seem too limited, <u>imprecise</u> in some essential way. The air turned darker, tinted with deep reds. Small sounds I'd never heard entered me like pinpricks, swelled in growing waves around me.

Dear A,

In my sleeplessness I paced back and forth among rows of blackened windows, thinking to myself, "am rose," "am rose."

And then one night inside my sleep (in those days I could still sleep for a few minutes) I felt a weight along my back and understood it was my hump and that my hump was filled with roses. Thousands of bruised petals trapped inside that weight I carried. There was no way I could release them. In the hiddenness they couldn't open.

No matter how I stood or walked the hump was hard to carry.

When I woke, I felt a sense of mourning and revulsion, though I tried to tell myself the hump was just a part of me and wasn't ugly.

I thought of St. Ambrose's hurt world. Its fractured wholeness. Of healing's lacks and limitations.

But why had I dreamed myself as you? Why had I become your body?

Dear A,

Even now, I worry you'll believe I thought you ugly. That the revulsion I felt after my dream was what I felt toward you.

But nothing could be further from the truth. After a few weeks in our shared work space I understood you wouldn't lift your eyes to see me, that we would never speak. (Of course I lived in my own silence also.) I wondered if your hunchback shamed you, if it had built a rigid fence inside you. But that hump was beautiful to me—I don't know how else to say it. The very thing that was a site of shame to you seemed to me inseparable from your goodness, your hurt gentleness that wondered and observed and questioned, even if you couldn't see it. Even if you hated what you were.

Of course, as I already said, this was conjecture. There was no way I could know what you were thinking.

In those days I was reading Bulgakov's The Master and Margarita on my lunch breaks. Maybe you even saw it on my work station. So when I got to the part where Margarita requests of the devil that he prevent the handkerchief from being brought to Frieda, for a moment I imagined I was her but my request was different—I asked him to free you from your hump. But as soon as I spoke he glared at me with weary, disappointed eyes—I realized he was seeing my blunt ignorance, misunderstanding. The task was not to take away the hump but to understand it wasn't ugly.

So when I woke from my dream of revulsion and bruised roses, I felt ashamed. Wasn't it my own mind, not your body, I was dreaming—the limits of my thinking? The cramped darkness I moved within as sleep grew less and less. My fear of what was next.

And still at night I paced and thought "am rose," "am rose," the boundaries between us loosening even as I didn't know you. Even as we didn't speak.

Dear A,

But why did I need to dream myself into your body, to feel your hump as mine, the dragging weight of it, that coarse, unbalanced heaviness you carried?

Dear A,

Those last weeks in the office I kept the loose pages in my pocket. Felt their hard, slow burn inside me, the white-hot pressure of the writer's vanished hands. Often in her notes she returned to the idea of her lost hands—that because of this she couldn't write. And yet her words were there before me. There was someone across a courtyard who she missed and had no way of reaching.

By then I had almost finished scanning The Idiot's final chapters. It was the last book I ever scanned.

One afternoon I paused at the passage where Myshkin holds and comforts the murderer Rogozhin until the whole world and what passes between them becomes more than he can bear to live with or ever absorb. After that he sits in the sanitarium in Switzerland, his body like those vanished hands.

I wanted to tell you of those letters in which the world had vanished to white mist, and Myshkin was alone in his cold chair, and your name was shared by a man who had comforted Dostoevsky. It had been weeks since I'd slept more than a few hours.

But why did I want to tell you? Why did I feel you'd understand?

We who'd never even spoken.

Dear A,

In mathematics there is an entity known as the empty set. Maybe you have seen the symbol Ø which stands for this emptiness, this set with no elements. There are many ways to speak of loneliness and isolation. For instance, think of how the empty set is said to be both closed and open—all its boundary points (of which there are none) are confined within it and so it's closed, and yet for every one of its points (of which there are none) there is a surrounding openness, and therefore it is open.

Maybe you have felt this in yourself—an openness within the confines of an equal isolation.

I believe this is what I sensed in you.

I have seen it called the "proper name of being."

Dear A,

Back then when I tried to understand the concept of the empty set, my mind knotted and strained beneath the weight, and it still does. But I found a theorist whose angle partly helped me—what if the empty set isn't empty after all, it's just that we can't fathom what's inside it? Then he went on to wonder if although we think of a set consisting of "like things," maybe this is wrong and instead it consists of things that are different but in ways beyond our comprehension and so we see them as alike. What if things that we assume are unalike are linked and bonded in ways we're too limited to see?

What I am trying too awkwardly to say is that the less I slept, the more I felt we were alike and different and the line between the two began to vanish. I couldn't live inside my old distinctions. Inside each face, each body, so many paradoxes, anomalies. I should have known this all along, and yet it took my sleeplessness to lead me. The vanished hands in the letters were different from my hands and yet they were my hands, Myshkin's silence in his chair was yours but different, his cradling of Rogozhin an act that couldn't fit within a single, rigid category, containing as it did kindness and compassion but also violent damage and destruction.

Each night I felt the complex weight of who you were even as I didn't know you.

Dear A,

I knew I'd never get to Venice. Never find the author of those letters. But it tugged at me—her vanished hands, her sleeplessness like mine. In one letter she wrote of someone named Marei touching a boy's cheek with unexpected kindness and that night as I paced that hand was on me also. Once she wrote, "Why should I expect anything but darkness?"—I read this as my world was darkening.

Then it occurred to me that you could go instead. Not in my place exactly but for other, vaguer reasons I couldn't quite get hold of, the way I couldn't understand the empty set or whether it was really empty, or if a set consists of likeness or unlikeness.

And after all, I reasoned, like the Staret in those letters your back was hunched, your name was Ambrose.

But how could I ask this of you? How could I even begin to suggest it? My mouth was mute like Myshkin's, the nights lengthening beyond my seeing.

As I read her letters, I realized that even as I claimed all along I didn't really know her, and of course we hadn't spoken, there was a part of me that had constructed some idea of her and carried it with me. But as she spoke of the hump on my back and the roses in my name, my cells remembered every cold and sterile waiting room, each test and brace and body cast—those things I never spoke of, though for a while I'd wondered, if not for them, would I have been less silent? The words I lived with seemed, so many of them, ugly: *mutant type 1, negative type 1, management implications, rodding, deformity, intramolecular disulfide.* Shortly after my diagnosis, I came across a reference to an Italian doctor, Dr. Ambrosi, who published a paper in 1905 on "Diseases of the Bone," mine included, but all I remembered of it was *calcareous bodies*, and that his name was close to mine, and that closeness hurt me. I never knew what word might hurt me next.

So now, as she longed for the part of me I found most ugly, and feared I would misunderstand her longing, I tried to imagine giving her what she wanted: I loosened my hump from my back and, standing by the bed where she lay face down, gently placed it on hers. I pressed for several minutes until I was sure the two had fused. Then I tucked a warm blanket over her, and from the chair beside the bed watched the rise and fall of her tender, almost-secret affliction. And as I did, it occurred to me that the prions inside her left no outward, clearly visible sign, that maybe this troubled her and so she imagined herself into my body, so visibly disfigured. I watched over her for many hours, though it's possible she wasn't really sleeping, but in some other state where the roses, now hers, not mine, could open.

Dear A,

In those first weeks of sleeplessness strange things often came to me, small facts or random details I'd once known but had forgotten. Plants which don't form clusters are called solitaries. The painter Titian's death date was August 27, 1576—why would I remember such a thing? The hours of darkness were increasing, but I could see in them the red that Titian painted, and the lotion Margarita rubbed into her skin until she glowed like roses and found she was invisible and could fly. I saw white boats, a barren summit, terraced gardens.

Dear A,

As I paced, I remembered other things as well. One night a phrase I had once learned came back to me. At first I barely heard it, blurred syllables not linking to make words but lost inside a hushed confusion. But after I paced more I could hear clearly: "the flight of the alone to the Alone." I think the phrase is from Plotinus. I kept pacing and the phrase extended, "The flight of the alone to the Alone is and must be wordless." As with many things that happened in those weeks since I'd stopped sleeping, I didn't really understand and yet I deeply felt them. As if each required a kind of crumbling and rebuilding, a departure from assumptions I'd carried without even knowing they were with me. Each thought mercurial, sharp-edged, almost lawless, or even awkward, lumpy, as it pulled from what had bound it. I thought of how "alone" and "Ambrose" both begin with "a." It seemed the smallest thing and yet it calmed me, as if the word "alone" which I had felt as cold and filled with distance, could also be a site of sharing. Though I still sensed a separateness in you wordless and enclosed beyond my knowing.

Dear A,

Even though I knew I couldn't really know you, one night I started writing you a letter. At first I was sure I wouldn't send it—that it would be like those unsent letters that had fallen from The Idiot. By then I was shifting in and out of darkness, often for many hours I couldn't see. The color-sounds were sometimes comforting but also lonely, even threatening, cut off from some essential steadiness or sheltering I still remembered but knew I was losing. Sometimes I didn't want to know them, but then, without them, the darkness grew too flat and gripped too tightly. I knew I couldn't return to the office. But even as my thoughts began to take shape on the page, I still considered thinking basically private and withheld, not visible or shared like action.

My hands like the hands of the one from San Servolo—vanished hands.

Dear A,

I realized something in me considered action—as opposed to thought— aggressive and intrusive, the way we speak of "military action" or "the exertion of force by one thing on another." So to write to you was one thing, but to send the letter was another. And how could I ask you to go out into a world I sensed you felt hurt by and avoided? How could I suggest you cross an ocean? Yet I watched as my hand sought out an envelope, my mind considering how my words could reach you. And still I thought of how an action is something taken in court <u>against</u> another, or even subtly invasive or intrusive as in Einstein's "action at a distance" where if one entangled atom is prodded its entangled twin must feel this also even if there's half the universe between them.

But I also thought of Bulgakov's book and Titian's paintings. How actions made them possible. And though my actions weren't important like theirs, maybe there was a place for some degree of gesture, though I feared that by sending you the letter I'd unwittingly hurt you and myself.

Dear A,

But there is so much darkness now. I hear words inside my head, but mostly I can't see to write. The air grows rough with unsent words. This grinding red of interruption. My heartbeat silver-gray. Wired hiss of sunset. Black rocks beneath the waves.

Dear A,

Of course you know what happened next. I left the letter and you found it. So many roses in the air between us. The bruised petals crushed inside my back. I worried I had wronged you. Somewhere I had read, "When thought is free then what can bind us?" But my thoughts felt chained even as I tried to set them free. Even as the color-sounds sometimes sought them out. I started wondering if maybe the true nature of thought is that it can't be free at all, not really. Often I still think this. So by sending you that letter, was I enchaining you as I'd enchained myself?

And yet something in me trusted you, and wondered, though I feared I'd bring you harm, was there some way my words could also be in some small way like Margarita's ointment.

Dear A,

It wasn't until I was sliding the folded note into the envelope that I decided to leave it on your desk instead of send it through the mail. This seemed more intimate than the postal system's computerized conveyer belts and zones and bar codes. But maybe it was also more entrapping—maybe you'd find it harder to ignore or put aside if you found it in the space we shared, that shared space with a silence woven by us both with threads that, though sound-proof, were embedded with microscopic eyes, though neither of us admitted they were there.

I addressed the envelope quickly—I only had to write one letter, A.

With the darkness slipping toward me, I'd been trying to learn what I could about the eye's physiology and functioning. In the end I got a lot wrong, but back then I thought I could at least pin down the basics. So I learned there's a small, curved depression, the fovea, located at the center of the retina's macula luten, the only place where the retina's layered folds spread aside and light falls directly on the cone cells, which are the cells that register images most sharply, and are also the most responsive to the color red. I thought then (though I soon learned I was wrong) that red would help me see better, more acutely. (Later I found out the rods in the eyes, not the cones, function best in darkness. The cones with their sensitivity to red, work best in light.)

I wrote your initial in red ink. The red looked somehow brave. This pleased me.

Dear A,

But did I really think you'd cross the ocean just because I asked you? At first I told myself that even though of course you wouldn't go to Venice, I had shared with you the world I had begun to live in, and that sharing pointed to some bond between us, an unspoken sense of kinship. I'd sensed your kindness even as I didn't know you. Then once again it struck me how the word "alone" derives from "all" and "one" as if it holds within its core a silent, unacknowledged sharing. But as the hours went on, I came to understand I believed all along you'd do exactly what I wanted—fiercely sensed this even as I claimed to doubt it. And so my act felt largely cruel and coldly selfish. How could I send you into hardship, the unknown, maybe even into unexpected harm? Why would I do that to you? Always I thought of your hunched back, your cane, how hard it is for you to walk. Why wasn't I protecting you? And still I imagined you traveling across the ocean, the sound of the Venetian canals entering your body.

Then suddenly for a full week the letters stopped. I worried she had grown too ill to continue, or maybe even died (though her letters weren't feverish like the ones from the one who'd waited to be read to). And of course I couldn't reach her. But even as I missed her and worried for her safety, part of me withdrew into a different, separate silence that was troubled by her certitude I'd go to Venice. I hadn't guessed she would have felt this. The more I thought about it, the more I felt a spreading coldness. If she'd been sure I would go, did that mean there was a part of her as ruthless and enclosed as Pilate? (She'd almost hinted this herself.) Yet what she sensed I could find in Venice, and what I found, was filled with everything Pilate tried so hard to disavow (care, tenderness), even if in the end he couldn't. The cold stayed for many hours, as if the only covering I had, had been lifted from my body. Though I missed the hurt colors in the words she sent me.

A white sheet was covering her from foot-soles to waist as she lay face down on a gurney. I leaned over, my hands in latex gloves; my right hand held a scalpel. The room was white and windowless, the only noise the buzz from the florescent lighting. A quieter, more focused light attached by a metal cord to the ceiling, hung directly over her as I inserted the scalpel and cut from the hump's base to her shoulders. Then, parting the wet flesh, I cut deeper into bone and sinew. When her hump was fully opened, its skin pulled back on either side like curtains, I slipped in my hand to loosen and set free the roses—not hundreds as I supposed, but many thousands—wave upon wave of crushed and brown-edged petals. But though I tried for many hours, the petals wouldn't budge, as if dampened with a lotion the opposite of Margarita's. I wondered if the roses had lived outside her hump, and then something forced them into her, or if they were born there, and if they were, did they always have brown edges? There was nothing else to do but to sew her up again as best I could. I labored to make each stitch as neat as possible, though with each one I remembered the crossed-out words in the notebook, the silence that followed.

Dear A,

Maybe it's been days or even weeks since I last wrote you, I lose track each time the dark comes back. But I remember clearly what I wrote you last, how I was certain you would go to Venice. And that certainty felt cruel. But once you left I thought about you constantly even though you didn't know it, the way Margarita worries about the Master after he vanishes, having left behind him only a handful of scorched pages and pressed roses. He'd lived a solitary life until she came as if from nowhere and stayed with him among his many books, red furniture, heat from a small stove. Lilacs grew outside his door in summer. But on the day he vanished the bushes were weighted with snow, his worn coat had no buttons. Often, as I thought of you in Venice, I thought also of the silence they both lived in after that—she unable to find him, he too ashamed and hopeless to be found. So when I stopped writing to you, it was as if I was both of them at once, each wrapped inside their separate silence. There was no way you could know that I still thought of you, still cared what might befall you, so wasn't my silence inflicting an even harsher, further cruelty? One night I dreamed your cane splintered into hundreds of charred pieces.

Dear A,

Of course by then my eyes were failing badly. I lived mostly in dimness and in dark, so I tried not to blame myself excessively for the cruelty of my silence. (The sound-colors were still coming and going, and though I lived with them, I didn't know how to trust them, or understand what they were.) Even when I wrote to you in my mind I couldn't get the words on paper. And still I felt I was to blame. Every now and then I grew convinced you had forgotten me, that my not writing no longer mattered. You were walking along canals named Rio dei Santissimo and Rio di Santa Margherita; down streets with enchanting names—Calle Valmarana, Calle Arco, Calle del Sansoni—or maybe passing the Old Pharmacy, or the bronze face of Pietro Arentino above a doorway, or the Orsini Glass Kiln with its Library of 3,000 shades of enamels. So why should you remember me? With that new world before you, wouldn't the idea of the lost notebook be drowned within a million new sensations?—

Dear A,

And yet in truth I didn't doubt you still remembered me. That no matter how many winding streets or hidden courtyards you discovered, you were essentially like Myshkin in the book I scanned—unable to forget the reality of another. Or like the epileptic in the few letters I found, who crossed the courtyard to read to the one who needed him and waited.

Dear A,

Some years before my illness, I'd read about a "foundling wheel" in Venice that was built in the 1300's. It was a kind of rotating cradle inserted in a convent door where parents could safely leave their newborns. The parents placed the child inside, then rang a bell so the nuns would know to turn the cradle and retrieve the abandoned child. The opening was bordered by a grille so narrow only newborns could fit through. One day as I was pacing, the darkness pressing down inside me, for some reason I envisioned the infant you once were inside that cradle. Your clenched fists and lumpy back, your twisted spine. I didn't know if your eyes were closed or open, the cradle's wooden arms around you—

Dear A,

Weeks later, when I managed to sleep for a few minutes (every now and then I briefly slept), I woke from a dream in which I came across a wooden cradle. But when I reached inside to lift the sleeping infant, my hands found only hundreds of bruised roses.

Dear A,

How could I miss someone I didn't even really know? And yet I missed you. One day when you'd left work before me, I noticed a notecard on your table—a grocery list you made but had forgotten. Bread, milk, coffee, eggs. But on the other side you'd copied this: "the soul's strange solitude, H. More Ψυχωδια Platonica sig. P4." So even though I didn't know you, there was a way you came to me like light on water, or as when one glimpses through a window a stranger's face that suddenly feels intimate, or a new room that feels familiar.

Dear A,

But as time went on I sensed more and more you didn't miss me. That although you'd crossed an ocean as I'd asked, I'd ceased being vivid in your mind. It's not that I believed you had forgotten, I still felt you were like Myshkin. That you would never turn your back on another. I didn't even doubt you were trying to track down the notebook. (Maybe you had even found it). One night as I was pacing as I always did, I pictured us in outer space—me locked inside the spaceship's narrow capsule, you tethered and spacewalking outside. I tried to pull you back but you resisted, entranced by all you moved among and saw—flashes of white light, sounds like grinding metal mixed with static, blue pearl of earth, the many-colored stars, etc. After a while, I could only glimpse the silvered rim of your left boot, one strip of shoulder. Once I feared my silence was a cruelty I'd inflicted, but now I, not you, was locked inside it. I felt the weight of your hunched back in mine, even as I knew I shouldn't.

In my mind's eye, an astronaut was spacewalking outside the capsule. It was the summer I was eight or nine. Both legs were in casts, new rods had been inserted. The astronaut was testing the newest prototype of protective gear from NASA, a suit equipped with a PLSS device that enabled him to walk untethered. Even mission-control couldn't reach him.

What if he refused to come back? How would they force him?

Space smelled charred but fresh— that same space-smell he smelled every time, and every time found impossible to describe.

Streaks of blue-white light flashed by. The earth turned minutely below, its surface strewn with dirt pits of shattered bones, trenches and grave-yards, and billions of other bones still laboring in moving bodies.

I was him and I was floating. What was I hearing? Something like a wind tunnel, but metallic—cold and at the same time fiery.

Then I was on earth again. The days felt long, I spent them reading free government pamphlets I'd ordered. A new one had arrived, *Spacesuits: A Short History*. But why did the word *protection* appear on almost every page, and often more than once? I wanted to read about the latest "Z-series" of space suits, which included a prototype for planetary vehicular activity and "increased tether-free mobility." But instead I saw: *protection against micrometeoroids….protection consisting of five layers of aluminized insulation….without this protection human flesh expands to twice its usual size….* I tried to skip past it, but only came to: *the blood will boil without protection, the lungs will fill with boiling water….It is crucial to have protection from radiation…. protection for the DNA…Pressurized DNA molecules will shatter apart from the inside….*

It seemed the more minute the entity, the more volatile, explosive.

On the next page was the Apollo 1 fire, and a photo of The Block I AIC nylon pressure suit that went up in flames and melted.

I didn't know how to picture my astronaut after that, what to make of his supposed freedom.

Special lights are embedded in the fingertips of space-gloves. "The future promises an even stronger, self-heating design, manufactured with laser-scan technology, stereo lithography, 3d computer modeling, and CNC machining."

But *protection* had built a wall inside me. I couldn't feel the freedom it was supposed to enable.

So that day when I came to her dream of me outside the spacecraft not wanting to return, although I knew it was really about her, not me, I felt again that part of myself that never stopped wanting the astronaut, the space walk. That part that never believed in the fire. The fire was a lie. The fabric never melted.

Dear A,

The more I sensed you had forgotten me—or at least that in some fundamental way your attention had turned elsewhere—the more I began thinking about Margarita and the Master. Her life after he vanished. How she retreated to the darkest room of her Moscow apartment and unlocked a bureau drawer where from beneath some fabric scraps she took the only possessions she still valued—a photograph of the Master, some rose petals wrapped in tissue, the singed remnant of the manuscript he'd burned. Only a few sentences were left and she read them again and again, always arriving too soon at the end of the last, which was unfinished, "vanished as if it had never existed..."

I didn't have a photograph of you, or rose petals in tissue, or any words except that notecard with the grocery list and quote. Of course I'd deliberately ensured you couldn't find me. I tried to remember why I'd been so set on that decision, so sure it was important. What was I trying to accomplish? But though I tried many times I couldn't remember. I didn't even let you know my name. The sound-colors came and went.

The ocean stretched, a vast blank night, between us.

Dear A,

As I already mentioned, in the letters that fell from The Idiot, the writer sometimes seemed herself, but sometimes she was Dostoevsky, sometimes even Myshkin. Early on this troubled me, but as I paced and the darkness deepened and sounds took on more shapes and colors, at times I began to feel that I was Margarita. I sat on a bench beneath the Kremlin wall dwelling on the Master, "If you've been exiled, why haven't you let me know? People do manage to let others know. Have you fallen out of love with me?" Or I'd walk along the Moskva River thinking, "Why am I cut off from life?" I didn't know how long it had been since you'd left for Venice. Time and space collapsed like folded paper, or sometimes opened into sprays of roses—I never knew which would come next or how or why. I lived within a kind of quiet anarchy, a much-too-quiet-disarrangement whose laws —precise, exacting — governed me, though I couldn't know what they were or how to follow. I walked by the Kremlin wall, held burning paper, thought about Bellini ferrying his servant. Nothing linear or clear left in the world.

Dear A,

Many years before, I'd read a book about the properties of time and space— how though we live within them they defy our understanding. What if time isn't bound by a predictable rearrangement of atoms? What if it is another dimension of space, and our sense of its passing is our way of trying to feel and briefly capture it inside us? What if the future isn't a logical outcome of the present? Or even a partial consequence of the present? What if the laws of physics aren't static but malleable, ever-changing? Theories rise and crumble. As I walked along the Moskva River, or read the notecard I still carried, or wondered about the lost notebook and the writer of the fallen letters, my skin grew less than air but also full of light and color.

Dear A,

Even though I felt you had forgotten me, every now and then I thought back to Margarita's stoic answer to the question Woland asked at their first meeting, "Is there perhaps some sadness or anguish that is poisoning your soul?"—and Margarita answered plainly "No, there's nothing like that" though inside she was suffering. Maybe it was then that Woland realized he could trust her and decided to show her his globe. He could see she possessed a sense of tact, proportion. And though Woland didn't say this (after all, he was the devil) it struck me that such qualities are part of what makes possible kindness and caring toward another. That awareness of being a small part of a darkness much vaster and deeper than one's own. (As the sound-colors belong to something much older, more experienced than myself.) So even though my eyes no longer saw, and I feared you had forgotten me, I tried like Margarita not to give way to my own leanings. I imagined you walking the Venetian streets, your back briefly healed in a canal's unwitting kindness, its undulant, distorting water.

Dear A,

But suddenly I'm not sure what's happening—my skin's invisible and light as air, the muscles in my arms and legs are strong again and taut and I am weightless—It must be Woland's ointment that has done this. I'm flying over St. Mark's, over the fish market's stone columns carved with water fleas and wind roses, over the crooked balconies of Palazzo Pemma, the remains of the old Anatomy Theater. The air shines a clear, bright blue then slowly darkens. I'm flying over the bas-relief of a shoe on the corner of Calle Crosera, and over the botanical gardens of Ca' Morosini, the Ospidale Civile with its graffiti of a hand enclosing a wounded human heart. I'm flying over the Church of Santi Rocci e Margherita.

I am looking for you in the corners of the poorest districts, in the rope factory's narrow alleyway, the crumbling streets beside the women's prison. But when I try to descend below the rooftops I can't land. Why won't Woland's ointment let me? I want to draw close to you, to find you. If not to talk to you at least to briefly glimpse you. But from the air all faces blur, bodies stay unfocused. The lost roses of your name pull closed inside me.

Dear A,

It's still dark and I can't find you. But for some reason (have I paused in air?) I see cloud-letters slowly spelling out a word that I can't read but I see now that it's "care." At first the meaning's clear. "To take care of, to look after."..."The charging of the mind with anything."..."An inclination to or for."...But like anyone's lost or fading sight—like mine—it complicates itself, layers build and coarsen—"From the Germanic; "bed of trouble, sickness, grief." "Mental suffering and sorrow." "Dress of mourning." "Burdened state of mind." Why do words unhinge themselves? Wanting turning into mourning, charging changing into sorrow. Once I read, though I can't remember where, "to cast water on a care-scorched face"—so care is also fire and scarring. So when I tell myself I care for you even without really knowing you, when I imagine soothing your hunched back, or repeating Woland's claim that "everything will be made right, that is what the world is built on," when I imagine my care for you making possible your flight beside me, and how I'll say when you are tired, "Sleep will strengthen you and I will guard your sleep," how can I not feel my words infected by that other meaning even as I focus on the first? In this darkness I can't reach you.

Dear A,

I'm flying over the Grand Canal, over the tourist shops and bakeries, the lazzaretto islands where the plague victims were taken. I'm flying over the white boats no longer there, the blistered hands and ghostly purple faces, the pits where they were thrown and buried. I am still circling, circling, I can't seem to leave the white boats behind, I don't know why. I want to look for you on the calles near St. Marks, or among the small stone bridges that span even the narrowest canals, but the white boats keep reappearing. Why can't I break free of this white circling? Even the closed rose inside your name is white now, and the bruised petals I touched inside the cradle. How can this whiteness be so strong when I can barely even see? Your white notecard in my pocket, its white ink—

Dear A,

But even if I could stop this white circling and try again to find you, what if this ointment makes me stay invisible forever, what if there's no way to rub it off? What if this white flying means that you will never see me?

Florensky had pointed out the random gaps in our knowledge, the astonishments that lie past understanding, the impact of a searing light whose intensity is "pure potential—a light that is not, however, there." In a way that's how she felt to me, vivid as Florensky's light that's there except it isn't. In her flying she was tireless, rejected nothing. But in her real room across the ocean, was she living in a dimness that grew emptier, grayer, the prions weakening and hobbling her further, even as her thoughts caught fire? The mind is a chaos of touches, Titian said, and although I carried my body's weightedness and fractures, I tried to feel her flying more real than her hurt body, or the walls of the narrow room she lived in.

I was walking toward Calle Largo dei Botteri looking for the remains of Titian's house, its vast gardens and views of the lagoon. But when I turned the corner, the street was cluttered with hundreds of white boats. How could so many fit into that narrow street ending only in a garden, and why were they on land instead of water? Behind one and slightly to the right, Titian was on his knees, his hair yellow-white, his clothes tattered. His bony fingers were sifting the dry dirt, as he stiffly turned his head one way then another. He did this many times. It seemed he was looking for Orazio who he forgot had died of plague. I walked closer and stood beside him but he didn't see me. I wanted to touch his shoulder, let him believe I was Orazio. But as I reached out my arm (I thought of Marei, Dostoevsky), something behind me pulled me back. It was Dr. Ambrosi, author of the famous paper, "Diseases of the Bone," the one who shared my name and used the words *calcareous bodies*. I felt his breath against my hump, as it pressed through my shirt, my skin, and finally down into my blood where it circled and then settled in my eyes that were still watching Titian, though I couldn't speak to him or reach him—

Dear A,

I've landed on the Lazzaretto island—but how could this have happened? Suddenly the air released me. I see long rows of wooden barracks, incineration pits, the quarantine warehouses stacked high with piles of silk and leather. And everywhere the smell of burning juniper and rosemary. Several times each day feathers and clothes are plunged into boiling vinegar or dragged into the sun for airing. Armed boats patrol the shore. Seneca wrote that we must seek out that which is untouched by Time and Chance. He says this is the soul. But I think this must be wrong. I walk back and forth on this island where nothing is untouched, yet everywhere dark souls are beating. I don't know if I'm invisible, or if you'd see me if I finally found you. But when I turn around, except for the armed boats, the water's empty. The stables hold 100 healthy horses.

Dear A,

Since my sight is mostly gone I try to count the coldest hours then add them up with the idea that because they're cold they must be nights, then try to figure out how long it's been since I last wrote you. But the numbers drift and crumble. I am still on the Lazzaretto island, I don't know if it's been days or weeks or maybe even months. Where is Woland with his globe, his belief that manuscripts don't burn, and "everything will be made right" because that is what the world is built on? Where are the Venetian rooftops I flew above before I landed? There's so much suffering and strife here—the sailors far from home, black sores appearing. It's said that the dead who stay unburned before they're buried hold and chew their white shrouds like milk in their mouths.

Dear A,

Maybe you remember Woland's notion that "a fact is the most stubborn thing in the world." But as I walk back and forth in my invisible skin and waves crawl on this shore where plague doctors in oiled black coats and masks walk toward the barracks carrying white sticks, I'm not sure anymore what a fact is, only that I see your roses opening somewhere far away in safety, white petals tucked in their white cradle. So maybe, unlike here, Woland's cold and bitter midnight hasn't reached you. Woland says a fact is anything that comes true, but what's true isn't always possible to see. And often it isn't just one thing. The truth that's Venice from the air is different from this truth since I've landed. Can't even facts grow wobbly, unsure, confuse and obscure themselves, sometimes lie or partly disguise themselves to others, even to themselves? Ever since this sleeplessness began, the solid world, which must be one of Woland's "facts," is different from what I thought or ever expected— its truths decentered, restless, prismatic. Its angles more vulnerable and porous than I imagined or that my eyes or mind can see even when they're there. "If" is a fact, and "doubt," and "contradiction." Mystery is fact. The limits of my knowing, fact. Once I thought facts were my shoes on the pavement, my hand on the scanner, my paycheck, my morning cup of coffee. But now none of that feels real. Remember that book on time and space I mentioned? How it said though we live in time and space they defy our understanding. Our human minds can't grasp them. So how are we to say what's fact? All I know is that this sleeplessness is sometimes water sometimes wind and that it carries me. And maybe if everything keeps shifting, there's solace for you even though it seems there's not. Sometimes I sense that it exists for you, I don't know why I feel this but I do. Why should I care if you remember me as long as the roses in your name can briefly open? But then I feel your hump again. The fractured bones. The bruised rose that also closes.

Dear A,

I wish that I could fly to you, that you could tell me if my skin is still invisible, but I can't fly anymore, I don't know why, and I can't find you. And as I walk this shore I have no means of leaving, colors appear like sentences that have no endings or beginnings. Remember the Master's scorched page, its sentence with "vanished as if it never existed," but no ending? Often I think of that burned page and wonder, why did humankind decide to build these structures we call sentences, why choose to move within their narrow rooms, their walls, look out from their clipped windows?—If the laws of physics aren't static but malleable, if the future isn't a logical outcome of the present or even a partial consequence of the present, then why should a sentence move only forward, and most always toward an ending? (Yet I'm writing to you in sentences... though sometimes I doubt I'm even writing—I'm walking on the sand and I was flying.) If order, at least as we know it, doesn't exist...if it's different from what we think it is...is there some other kind of sentence not a sentence...some other way to make you hear me...You are far from me and silent

Dear A,

And now, as I walk back and forth, this salt-air heavy on my skin, I see a man in white, tattered clothes sitting on a rock in the full sun. He's holding his bowed head between his hands. I can't see the plague barracks anymore, and the air no longer smells of juniper and rosemary—it's heavy with the scent of roses. I edge closer, but don't want to get too close. His face is oozing with black sores, his arms and legs purpling and blackening. His lap is covered with a white and crimson cloth. And now I also have a cloth, white with a frayed border, and I'm carrying a pail of water, though I don't remember where or how I got them or why they're with me. I don't want to let the man's oozing face any closer, but for some reason I'm still walking toward him. Maybe my white cloth and water are supposed to soothe his spoiling sores, though I don't want to know or touch him, and anyway it wouldn't really help him. I don't know if he wants me to come near. I don't know if he even sees or hears me. But I'm still stepping closer, I don't know why my legs want to do this, then finally I stop and stand as still as possible...wait to see if maybe he senses me—if maybe he'll lift his eyes and see me—

Dear A,

He lifts his eyes and sees me. At least he <u>seems</u> to see me. I'm not sure. Then he parts his cracked, black lips, he's speaking: "I'm from Rome but lived away in Yershalaim for many years where I carried out my official duties as was required. When I finally finished out my service and was permitted to return home, the journey back was arduous and took many weeks in a caravan over difficult terrain. But every day I saw any number of amazing things—hundreds of bird's nests woven of fish bones and seaweeds, animals with four ears or one blue eye, the other black or gold. Jeweled, minute birds flying backward. Ladders arranged in a circle surrounded by miles of empty sand. Silver nets and handprints in red air. But when I finally reached Rome, the city seemed more alien, more strange, than all the things I just mentioned. At first I thought I confused my route, made some navigational error, ended up in a foreign land at carnival, its streets brimming with bright banners, burning torches, flutes like the flights of wild birds. I stood apart near an alley at the edge of an open square. After a while someone must have noticed the mute, baffled man leaning by himself against a wall—a stranger approached me: "'The Emperor Tiberius is dead, smothered in his bed clothes.'"

He stops, lowers his eyes. Turns his oozing face toward the water.

Dear A,

When he looks up again he's looking at my pail of water. (I still don't know if he sees me, though when he speaks he says "your" so it seems he believes someone is there): "Your word pure derives from our Latin, purus, which means unstained...but isn't living itself an impurity? So no one really escapes. I can see that such staining can at times and from certain angles be beautiful, though much of it is coarse and ugly. Of course some of us are much more badly stained than others, or even worse, are ourselves a source and implement of staining. I understand I am among the worst...By the time I returned to Rome I'd carried out Tiberius's many brutal wishes and in turn thought up many of my own. I condemned an innocent man to death by crucifixion. Yet when that man stood before me bruised and beaten (I ordered him beaten many times) he treated me kindly. He even knew I suffered painful migraines— though I'd never said a word about them. So when I learned Tiberius was murdered in his bed clothes, I stood alone, face to face with my own ugliness. Tiberius's brutal heart was destroyed but nothing could undo the horrid act I committed."

Dear A,

The air begins to cool, the sky grows dimmer, I'm still holding my white cloth, my pail of water. I want to wash his oozing sores, the black crusts along his lips, his legs and arms blistering and swelling. Then the sky dims even more, turns flatter, duller, almost dark—a dark that's also oddly white—and slowly I realize there's something in me that doesn't want to know his story. As I start to think this, I hear his words turning to coarse sand inside him. Wave after wave of it sifting back down his throat and back inside him.

Why have I silenced him like his? Why don't I want to know his story?

Then I close my eyes and hear my mind saying to itself, I'm him.

Was I wrong to send you to Venice, did I harm you, was I blind and cruel like the one who sits beside me? Was I impetuous and selfish like him? Cowardly, destructive, arrogant, unwise, like him? Am I filled with burning sand like him?

How can I know if I hurt you, if you suffer even more in your bones because I sent you—

I need to try to fly to you, to find you....

Dear A,

But the man hasn't finished, there are still things he needs to say...It's morning again or afternoon, it's too hot to be staying on that rock, the sky's completely cloudless, too bright. Then I feel my mind taking back the sand that's falling down his throat into his body, the isolation that can only make him suffer. He is so thin, his collar bones like the tips of arrows through his skin, his cheek bones sharp beneath the oozing sores. I still don't know if he sees me, if maybe the ointment has worn off. But maybe his hurt mind would be incapable of seeing anyone.

"Do you know what the man I condemned to death said at our last meeting? 'Every kind of power is a form of violence.' That night after he was gone and over the next days I followed my usual routine, ate my favorite meals and enjoyed them. I even briefly convinced myself my migraines had dissipated— the dead man the irritant that had kept them going. I assumed I would forget him. But a slow blackening was spreading through my body. One day it simply sharpened into anguish, and that anguish clawed at me and at all my selfish parts. I knew there was something crucial we hadn't finished saying. My nights grew hot with dreams of the two of us walking side by side, endlessly conversing, so rapt we hardly noticed alterations in the land, or light or darkness. But always by the time I woke I had forgotten every word. That forgetfulness carved traps inside me. Ever since, grinding sand pushes at the insides of my head and burns with piercing redness."

Dear A,

As I keep listening to the stranger and telling you each word, I feel your hump fused to my back again, pressing down along my spine and spreading. How can I begin to know the ways I harmed and wronged you?

I was wrong to send you to Venice. I am sure now I was wrong. I was wrong to make sure you couldn't find me.

―――――――――

...But why do I believe you even think of me or want to find me? Why should I imagine that once you got to Venice I was anything more than some vague, dragging thought connected to a notebook (though I still think that I was wrong to send you) your eyes filling with new names, streets of water—

Dear A,

I'm still standing near the stranger, I still see him. His voice hoarse as if a rock were rubbing raw his throat. "After Tiberius's death, there is no record of what became of me, I simply vanished. Some believe I died by my own hand, others that I went into exile somewhere in Italy. Others say I retreated into a grim house on a dark hill where every living thing around me suffered—even the evergreen oak became tormented because it hadn't resisted being made into a cross. Still others believe I branded my forehead until it oozed and blackened like a plague sore, so I was forced to wander endlessly over the earth in an attempt to drive away the pain. Still others believe my enemies consigned me to a well so deep that my sobs, though continuous, could never be heard. And even others believe I was sent to live beside the sulfurous lake, Ameria, whose waters are known for healing fractures. But given my hateful act, why would I be sent to any place of healing?"

But everything's starting to blacken...I don't know if the stranger's beside me. I hear only my heartbeat, the small, clipped waves, your absence.

Dear A,

Why do I still talk to you...Why do I keep insisting I need to find you, knowing that I wronged and harmed you? ╫ Why can't I let this darkness pull me back to where I have no thoughts of flying or even remember that it happened? Why do I still feel my back as yours ╫╫╫ the awkward hump with its thousands of bruised roses?

Dear A,

The stranger is very quiet, maybe he's been this way for many hours, or even days, I don't know. I can never tell how long I stay inside the blackness. ⫩
My eyes are still blurry but I can see the silver pail, silver water inside it. I dip my white cloth, the water covers my fingers so I know it's still cool— ⫯
I take the cloth and press it to the stranger's forehead. But the second he feels it touching him he flinches, and with great effort grabs my wrist to stop my washing. With great effort he pushes me away.

⫪

+ +

With each new letter, her handwriting was growing larger, more erratic.

I reminded myself that even as she held her cloth and pail of water, she was in her real room across the ocean, her real sleeplessness building.

(I couldn't know the ways that illness—intricate, ingrained, destructive— both held her and didn't. Dostoevsky would say this is the real.)

And as I thought this, I glanced over at the notebook from San Servolo still open on the table beside me—though I was sure I'd left it closed— my eyes blurring *Myshkin* to *My skin*.

For a split second I couldn't see, as if a thin sliver of the light that entered Myshkin's brain before he fell was slipping into me—that same light that moved through the epileptic's hands as he read, and into the hands of the one who waited until she didn't wait anymore but sat with vanished hands on her green hill, the same hill as Myshkin's.

My skin was very hot.

Did the sliver of light touch her also, the one across the ocean, whose back was my back and filled with roses?

For several weeks there were no letters.

―――――

‖‖

Dear A,

‖ ‖

The stranger is gone from me, and the white rock, the gray-black sand. (Or maybe I should say, I'm gone. In all likelihood he probably still sits there.)

I'm in a room that's mostly bare except for a round wood table covered with red cloth, and on the room's far side, across from me, a long, rectangular table (maybe it's a work desk) beneath a large window. On top is a carafe of water. There are lilac bushes outside, and here, on the round table, a vase of roses. There's not much else—just a wood stove in one corner, some books and papers.

I don't know who the room belongs to or why I am here.

Loose piles of papers are scattered on the floor, some written-on, some blank, others marked with just one word.

I look down and my eyes land on the single word: <u>ruin.</u>

‖ ⊢

Dear A,

But I never told you what finally happened on the island before I found myself suddenly in this room.

After the man on the white rock spoke that last word "healing"—"Given my hateful act, why would I be sent to any place of healing?" I waited for many hours...and then days...weeks maybe, maybe longer (time is still a perplexing thing to me). But he never spoke again.

Even so, I kept listening for his voice. Concentrating. Focusing. Even as I didn't want to know his story or even be near him.

The blackness had come back, I was listening from inside it.

十 十

I worried that his words might spill out in a faint whisper and I'd miss them. Or that the pale reds of the sound-colors might cover up a death rattle, or that maybe he'd change his mind and ask for the damp cloth, though I saw no reason he'd let himself have it. In a waking dream I heard the word Procula, and for one second mistook it as coming from his mouth.

But why did I care if he spoke, or if I missed it? Why was I listening like that, knife-sharp in the blackness? (The prions inside me still spreading, destroying...) If I wasn't feeling sorry for myself, why was I wasting any shred of caring on him? I didn't know a word for what I felt—it wasn't pity, or tenderness, or compassion, but something more impersonal, maybe not even human.

Why did I feel I had to wait in case he spoke? He had done terrible things. For a while I had even turned his words to sand inside him, but then I'd relented. And I was probably still invisible, he never gave a sign that he could see me. 卌

And still I stayed nearby him, listened.

Dear A,

And then one day I was just here. My arms on the chair's wooden arms. Lilac bushes outside the window.

+

I started thinking, maybe now that the man on the white rock was far away—or I was far away from him—I could feel the hump growing on my back again, and the trapped roses, and feel I was near you.

But the more I thought of it the more I knew that as long as I had harmed and wronged you—remember I finally decided I was wrong to send you to Venice—the roses would no longer come back, and the coarse sand would build in me, even though I wasn't on the island.

I couldn't fly, and I had no right to find you.

+

+

Dear A,

I sat inside this room, just waiting, though I didn't know for what. The blackness came and seemed to stay for a long time. The sound-colors wove bright threads in me, though sometimes they suddenly turned white like the man on the island, and I'd wonder if my sand was rushing down his throat again, was he choking?...Or maybe someone else had stumbled upon his rock by now and he was telling the same story...maybe that just happened over and over.

And then one day the blackness lifted, and with my eyes still blurring (the glass vase hurt air, not solid, the lilac bushes bruised, unstable), I noticed a stapled article on the floor and picked it up and, after my eyes cleared more, started reading.

It was from <u>The American Journal of Medical Genetics</u> (after that came: 122A, but I had no idea what that referred to. Then: 201–214, I assumed those were the page numbers. And then the year: 2003.)

Its title was: <u>Personality and Stereotype in Osteogenesis Imperfecta: Behavioral Phenotype or Response to Life's Hard Challenges?</u>

Of course I thought of you. As I said, my eyes were very weak and it was hard to see, but this had been the case for a long time. There was a magnifying glass on the sill beneath the window. As I walked over to pick it up, my back was lithe above my hips—much too light, too slender, unburdened. The floor against my shoes too flat, predictable. No roses inside me.

At first I felt relieved to hold the letters and know she was alive. It had been many weeks with no word from her. The handwriting was no larger or more awkward than before. But when I thought of the article she mentioned, not only myself but everything I looked at or touched seemed fragile. It was hard for me to explain even to myself that my illness, though flagrantly visible, felt to me essentially private, fenced within a mute, concealing darkness. Just as I'd never once spoken the word *hump*, there was a larger kind of silence, maybe *a silence of thought and feeling* I'd built for it as best I could.

But now I remembered clearly:

> Rodding: 'Internal splinting' of the long bones by means of the insertion of a metal rod. Under general anesthesia a long bone (e.g. leg or arm bone) may be cut in one or several places, straightened and 'threaded' onto a metal rod. The surgery generally involves an incision long enough to expose the bone where it is deformed. The procedure is most often used to treat children with moderate to severe Osteogenesis Imperfecta. It is recommended to control the repeated fracturing of a long bone; however, it does not necessarily *prevent* fractures—the bone may still fracture—but the rod will provide an internal splint that may help maintain proper alignment.

I was sure that by now she had read similar words.

I grew hot again like before when I first felt the light-splinter enter.

———————

+

+

+   +   卌

~~Dea xx~~

Dear A,

As soon as I found it I knew you wouldn't want me to read it. I had already harmed and wronged you. Trespassed. Trampled. Made assumptions. Asserted my own wishes. Interfered where I had no right and sent you to Venice. I knew you were deeply private, strongly sensed this from the beginning, that morning you first came to work. And of course, all that time in the office you never once looked me in the eyes (though I know the same is true of me with you). But I'm sure all this is clear already, and anyway of course you know it. That privacy, your lowered eyes, was part of the hurt gentleness in you—the thing I noticed most—that made me trust you and feel I knew you without knowing you and could send you to Venice.

Though I know now I was wrong to send you.

So when I picked up the magnifying glass, right away I wondered if maybe I should just smash it right there, throw it against the wall (though I quickly realized that wouldn't be effective) or find an axe or hammer—some way to destroy it as the Master destroyed his manuscript, though Margarita tried to lift it from the fire and Woland said "manuscripts don't burn."

I didn't want to hurt you but I still wanted to read it. I scanned KEY WORDS in a box in the upper right-hand corner: osteogenesis imperfecta; behavioral phenotype; stereotype; genetic conditions—psychosocial aspects.

The words were ugly but I wanted to read on. Even though I knew I shouldn't. Even as I thought of the bruised roses—

卌

Dear A,

The article was a scholarly research paper, peer-reviewed and thoroughly vetted. In an asterisked note at the bottom of the first column of the first page, was this: *Received 1 July, 2002; Accepted 17 March 2003*.

Then: *Grant sponsor: National Science Foundation. Grant number: SBR-9407268*.

It was divided into 7 sections with numerous sub-sections. The main sections were: Introduction, Materials and Methods, Results, Response of Subjects to the Stereotyped Features of OI, Response of Subjects to the Assertion of Euphoria, Discussion, Conclusions. (I noticed that last was plural.)

As you can imagine, "Euphoria" caught my eye—What was that doing in this paper?

But I didn't know when the blackness would come back, and decided I would go through the paper methodically, in an orderly fashion, so that if I were left for a long while in blackness before I finished, it wouldn't turn into a jumble inside me. Even in the darkness I could consider the parts I read without confusing them with parts that might come after. So though I wanted to, I didn't skip to "Euphoria."

Of course I wonder, will that word catch your eye also when you see this? (Though maybe you don't read the things I send. Why should I believe you read them?)

And as before, I still wonder, is it wrong to read this article, and send this? To almost pretend that we've spoken. (You've never once sent me a letter; though of course I made sure you couldn't. But even if you could it doesn't mean you would have.) Is it wrong to learn these details that belong to you, not me, am I trespassing again?—the procedures, the roddings, the body casts, the long hours of isolation, surgeries, x-rays, "resilience" and "perseverance"?

~~I am so tired I~~

and how once, but it seems so long ago, I wrote
to you of Una note bianco, a night in white

I sent you to Venice I   I was wrong to send you

Why am I cut off from life   the soul's strange solitude

and that sign above our work stations...digitized...
delivered in a variety of media that have not yet been invented

Sometimes I still almost sign my name. I remember my flying—

⊬⊬

Though it pained me that she was taking into her eyes what I most wanted to keep silent and hidden, and to imagine her wondering how each detail might apply to me, which procedures, how many and at what intervals, to what extent etc., and though at times I resented her eyes that never had to hide from a store mirror—(though I never forgot her sleeplessness, the prions)—I also realized I had lost myself in the epileptic's notebook, his red auras, his seizures; and in the lazzaretto islands; in Marie too weak to tend the cattle; in Myshkin's and Dostoevsky's joy and then their falling....

But what my mind and reason told me was different from what I felt.

My skin was still hot. I was starting to feel dizzy. For several days Frieda's eyes came back to me, smudged black as that last time I saw her when I turned to her but couldn't tell if she saw me. As I held this newest letter in my hand, I felt those smudges slowly spreading until they were black water—it seemed almost endless—and my body inside and beneath as I tried to swim toward her word *tend,* her kindness and all the ways I had hurt her, her hands covered with dirt, the newborn child still alive and in her arms, or the child drowned or buried, or lying in its broken bones, or lifted by Frieda and carried out of the woods into daylight where Marie sat on her rock or walked among the cattle with her stick and Myshkin's waterfall still fell inside him—

Dear A,

As soon as I started the Introduction—<u>The positing of behavioral phenotypes has come into fashion with</u>—the black print beneath the magnifying glass reminded me of the Venetian streets I saw from highest up while flying, though not beautiful like them and much more rigid—those streets I couldn't begin to make out without swooping closer down. Signs and intersections, closed dwellings like small traps below me. The article's printed words (small traps) were cold, more body cast than fragile, broken bone.

How could I possibly find you in those words? What could they begin to tell me? I was sure I wouldn't find you.

I told myself you were like the Master's vanished pages. The ones that burned before Margarita could reach into the fireplace to retrieve them. That all along I should have known this.

My temples ached, it was hard to read through the glass eye. I didn't want to continue.

But then I thought of Bellini ferrying his servant across the water, singing, I thought of you in the office, scanning, standing for many hours though it's hard for you to stand. And of Bulgakov rewriting his book from the beginning. Of other arduous things: Dostoevsky's years in the prison camp, his definition of the real and the ways he faced it in his books even as others labeled him extreme, the plague islands you can still glimpse from Venice (they are that close), the many lives in the many books I scanned. I even thought of the one almost certainly still on his rock on the island, his head festering and spoiling, the carved traps inside him.

How long did I sit by that window? I enlarged several words at a time, then moved on to the next cluster, held it under the glass. Underlined. Highlighted. Circled back when I had to.

And all that time the blackness didn't come. I could hardly remember it being so long away. Though I told myself this meant nothing—

—|—

But after I read for a while, though the magnifying glass grew heavy in my hand, I didn't want to stop. And as I read, I remembered how something broke in me that time of my first blackness when suddenly I couldn't see. But what did it do to your mind to live in a body that broke from the beginning, before words had even entered, or a feeling of wholeness.

I see you standing in the office.

Your back is yours, not mine. The plain fact of it. No roses inside it.

—|—

~~Dear A~~

~~I couldn't fly to you and I had no right to find~~

        is it wrong to learn the ⊢ details that belong ~~t~~ ~~to you~~

x-rays   ~~protect~~   certain meals   ⊢

⊢

⊣

Dear A,

I copied down some of what I read. It's on the other piece of paper. I hope I'm not wrong to send it

~~I am so~~

            ~~I am so tired~~

But there was no paper.

I pictured her too tired to pace, too tired, even to imagine the window, its lilacs, the Master's torn coat and burned pages, or Woland's assistant offering his lotion to Margarita.

In reading of my illness, was there a way she had also become more like Dostoevsky who never would have seen my hump as filled with roses? Once she saw my back as mine, not hers, and the roses left her, did her darkness clamp down even stronger, more frightening?

She sat in her room in her real skin and had no way to fly or turn invisible or turn partly into me., her back just her back, the prions hurting her brain further, her room just a room, wherever it was, and with no way of leaving.

Was anyone even there to take care of her? (For a second I thought of the tape that held her glasses together.)

My skin was flushing even more. A grinding dryness had settled in my throat.

I told myself I wanted to download the article. That it wouldn't be hard. Except for the author's name, I had all the basic information. I would see for myself what she'd been reading so painstakingly with her magnifying glass beside the window.

But I kept hesitating. I brought it up on the screen, closed it, brought it up, closed it again. I wasn't sure I wanted those words coming into my eyes, though I also knew that like steel rod bone, they were already firmly in.

My night was restless. Taut bands of heat slackened and then stretched from my right eye to my shoulder and then into my right hand. Taut bands clenched in my chest. Sweat moistened my forehead and my temples ached. I tried to think of her and tried not to think of her. *(I was wrong to send you...picked up the magnifying glass...my back is not your back...If you go there I will write to you, I promise...)* I had downloaded the paper but hadn't yet read it. As soon as it was light I took her letter from the envelope to read again and this time found on its blank side faint chains of words in pencil lines so thin they were almost invisible:

you learn certain metals

you observe

genetic   *a birth defect*   *often reading*

<u>*a different sphere of perception*</u>

Why were the words in pencil, and so faint? And so few of them, so scattered? What could *you learn certain metals* possibly have to do with my illness?

She had underlined *a different sphere of perception.* Was the article claiming that's what happens to people like me, but what exactly was a *sphere* of perception?

If perception is "the process or state of being aware"; "insight or knowledge gained by thinking," then why divide it into different spheres? And why place me inside one?

(I remembered reading "the universe of disabled persons in our society.")

Spheres, universes—those terms like the discomfited glances I saw as a child, when strangers glanced at me with alarmed half-curious eyes, partly wanting to stare, party wanting to quickly look away.

The next day, another envelope came, and inside it other scattered words:

protect

self-preservation

constantly re-injured

pieces of metal shoved into a body

increased rate of cellular oxidation

painful and gruesome procedures   *long periods of immobilization*

cyclic AMP

by age four

could read an x-ray

euphoria / protective function

I worried even more that she'd grown weaker, sicker. Was this all she could manage?—near-ghostly words faintly penciled, atomized, too fragile.

The bones in my left wrist were broken, and two ribs, and my right ankle. And one of the three bones inside my right middle-ear—I forgot what they were called—maybe *malleus, incus*...I couldn't remember the third. I had broken one once before as a child.

I still worried about her, thought of her faint as her pencil marks, her books beside her blurring or completely dark, the magnifying glass by her side that, if she could see it at all, might seem like the plucked eye of an enormous bird. But then I also began to wonder if I could be wrong that the scattered words were signs of weakness and increasing sickness. Was it possible they were some form of unlocking, her sentences releasing...And then, as she'd wanted, she'd no longer be trapped by the idea of an ending, the forwardness of time, completion...

The waves of heat kept spreading through my skin...

...my turning to you without speaking, this slow darkening inside me...

And still I kept wondering what *learn certain metals* could possibly have to do with my illness.

Though part of me wanted to delete it, I brought the downloaded article up on the screen and started reading. At first I read quickly, impatient with the all-too-familiar words I was finding: *physical restrictions, isolation, environmental factors.* A boy's voice unexpectedly caught me:

> You're lying there in a bed in a full-body cast and you're alone. You're a child, and you want to play. But what have you got to play with? Then you realize you have your mind. You talk to yourself. You observe....My mother and father were in the kitchen. I could tell you what they were doing, whatever room they were in, how many steps they were taking, which shoes they were wearing. I could feel when sounds got born. At the least little sound, I knew what was making that sound....They're in the kitchen, and you learn certain metals. If they picked up a fork, if they picked up a spoon, or laid a spoon down—different sounds between a fork and a spoon. Different sounds between a ladle and a knife. A cup. Which cup? Some are made of plastic and some ceramic. You occupy your mind.

His pronouns shifted as mine often did as a child. Was I Ambrose or Anselm?...Was the steel rod inserted into my leg, or his, or yours?...Was he lying in the infirmary or was I, and he the one standing outside peering in at the body cast...And the *precise site of the deformity* in the bone—who did it belong to as they probed for the operation? Did you or I or he feel the rodding?...I felt his observing mind grow so focused it turned into pure sound. He listened as his mother and father walked in their separate lives in the kitchen wearing their clearly identifiable shoes, and the clock ticked unnecessarily loudly, and the cup understood it was a cup—it possessed a distinct sound all its own—and the fork understood it was a fork, and the spoon it was a spoon...but he, who had turned into pure listening and then into pure sound as he lay in his bed in the full body cast, kept slipping back and forth from near to far, from there to here, from "you" to "I" to "you"...He could find no single place or word to hold him.

The waves of heat were coming back again, I'd almost gotten used to their slow building that never crested but grew loosely undulant like the lagoon's shallow water.

The infirmary walls were swaying and melting but still standing. I understood that they would stay forever, no matter how long they burned, no matter how high the flames or what the flames were fed with, or how much wood or gasoline...or how empty the beds...or if all the caregivers vanished and there was no cup to know it was a cup and no fork to know it was a fork, and no footsteps or loud clock. The walls would still be there and the boy would still be listening and then turning into sound as he taught himself each lock, each pair of scissors, each set of keys, the different metals.

As the waves surged and then released, I wondered if I'd ever hear from her again:

...I am looking for you in the corners of the poorest districts, in the rope factory's narrow alleyway, the crumbling streets beside the women's prison...I want to look for you on the calles near St. Mark's and among the small stone bridges... even the closed rose inside your name is white now...how can this whiteness be so strong...what if this flying means that you will never see me...

Dostoevsky was sitting in a small, cramped room in Switzerland, or was it Italy? The wood had burned out in the stove, it was almost morning. His skin was sallow, his right eye bruised from a fall some days before. The seizure had left him too tired to speak but he refused to stop writing. He knew he was about to break Nastasya's hands, there was no way to avoid it. Rogozhin would do this and he wouldn't stop him. As he wrote, he remembered his arms lowering the white death-shirt over his head and naked body, but at the last minute the guns were withdrawn, there would be five years of hard labor...On the way to the prison camp they stopped at Tobolsk where a bell from another town was in exile, convicted of sedition, its sentence was eternal silence. He remembered a man chained to a wall for eight years who after his release grew afraid at the sound of grass, unfolding flowers. And another who worked in the fields and touched a boy's face in kindness. Though the stove had gone cold the room was growing hot, then hotter, and when he put down his pen he realized he was in Venice but there was no way he could have gotten to Venice, and he knew no one there. He was looking for a notebook, he was on the Island of San Servolo, he was having a seizure, he was falling. The air was red, he was on the floor, he was thirsty...And my walls were growing hot like Dostoevsky's study, then red as Titian's cloth, then redder. Someone was flying above me, her skin was invisible but I knew she was there. Twelve trees were swaying in a courtyard. And in a room overlooking them a woman who could barely see was being read to, until she wasn't being read to anymore and she knew she had to go on alone, and she parted the green curtain alone.

My sheet was drenched with sweat. My right ear was pounding. The walls shivering, leaning.

A week passed. I had taken medicine, had rested, gotten stronger. My ear no longer ached, the red waves abated.

I was ready to get back to the article. I still wondered what she thought as she read it. What happened when she arrived at the section on euphoria she'd been eager to see. But when I looked at the computer screen, my sight was blurry, a black spot floated at the edge of my vision. I could take in very little:

.................................*genetic*...............................*defect*..............................

body cast...................................*leg braces*...*mind*......

......*historical perspective*................................*Constantly being reinjured*........

KEY WORDS......................*INTRODUCTION*........................*CONCLUSIONS*..............

....*kindly, benevolent face*..............*behavioral genetics*.............*determined to*....

.................*equanimity and meaning*..

The walls were leaning in again. I didn't feel hot. I didn't know what was happening.

Dear A,

─┼┼─

Remember when I wrote you about finding those letters in The Idiot? I said the writer sounded clinical, almost business-like at first, but soon she was on a hill tending cattle, and then she seemed to be turning into Dostoevsky...In a way this article was like that also. It begins by dryly laying out the basic data: number of subjects interviewed (fifty-five adults) etc. And it makes broad assertions: certain behaviors are "genetically determined." It uses terms like "secondary phenomena," "behavioral phenotypes," "genetic environmental interactions."

Such ugly words, but I brought them under my magnifying glass, read them cluster by slow cluster.

Then I came to one brief paragraph that laid out the broad parameters of your illness, and gave sources:

Glauser, Wacaster, Antoniazzi et al, Cherval and Meunier.

Maybe these names mean something to you. Maybe one of them even examined or treated you when you were a child, or performed an operation, but I don't think so. (It is hard for me to imagine you letting anyone near, it is so against your nature, but now I realize you must have been prodded and poked at often...It seems in such children's lives there is so much solitude and isolation but almost no privacy...I think of your averted eyes, your silence...)

I read that afflicted children can routinely suffer over 100 fractures before the age of 20. This is not uncommon. And the breaks are often deforming. I should have known this, but it's hard to absorb the fact of a body routinely breaking—to truly understand that this is real.

In one sub-section, maybe it is "Profile of Subjects" (many aspects and concerns overlap from section to section), the author points out that a small, quiet sound, even music, can shatter the delicate bones inside the middle ear—this has been documented. These are the smallest bones in the body. But of course you would know this.

I can see now there are so many things you'd have no choice but to know.

Some of what I read was very strange. Under "Behavioral Phenotypes in the Literature" the article states that people with this genetic mutation tend to "have a kindly benevolent face." It even cites a source (Dilts et al, 1990). I learned such thinking is part of the field of "behavioral genetics"—one major proponent is a man named Money.

My favorite section is "Response of Subjects to the Stereotyped Features of Osteogenesis Imperfecta"—in which the subjects, all now adults, recall themselves as children (and of course this means all the remembered children survived).

There's a boy who lies alone in his room in a full body cast and teaches himself the distant sounds of different metals. He's the one I think of most. Another writes to Jacqueline Kennedy, asking for a wheelchair. She says she's ten years old and "tired of being carried everywhere like a baby." Another learns to read x-rays by age four: "My doctor wanted me to trust my own eyes the most in case I ended up in the hospital." Another quotes her pediatrician cautioning her parents, "You let her go, she'll break up a storm, and she may not live. But if you tie her down and try to stop her, she will never have even a chance at living." (As I read that, I reminded myself that child is still alive.)

I wonder what you would have told them if you had been part of their study, though of course you'd never agree to such a thing.

This letter is much too long, and I'm too tired...I'll try to write again tomorrow—   #

Dear A,

As much as I wanted to tell you what I learned about the children, in a sense I avoided saying the one thing I think about most and that still leaves me confused. It begins with this passage:

> The increased rate of cellular oxidation that is a component
> of the generalized metabolic disturbance characterizing
> Osteogenesis Imperfecta may influence central nervous system
> and cognitive maturational patterns. Of special interest is the
> possible relationship to alterations in cyclic AMP [adenosine
> 3.5-monophosphate] metabolism...Thus, considerable evidence
> links OI with altered cyclic AMP activity...a mechanism asso-
> ciated with numerous forms of euphoria.

As you can imagine, at first I could barely make my way through it. But when I finally did, at least enough to get the basic point (I looked up adenosine monophosphate etc.), I finally got to the word that startled me from the beginning when I read the Key Words.

Though the article treads cautiously, it definitely implies that "subjects" who suffer from this particular genetic illness often experience euphoria, much more so than the "general population," and a great deal more than those beset by other afflictions.

At first this seemed absurd. (Of course, one could think of the saints...but this is different—they're claiming this happens to a significant percentage.)

But soon it becomes clear that quite a number of "highly respected" researchers insist this euphoria is in no sense an effort to compensate for the hardship and pain of affliction. It's nothing psychological. The brittle bones and euphoria aren't even really connected, except insofar as both are the result of the illness's specific biological processes. Euphoria and the breaking of bones coexist as separate, unexplained, but very real manifestations of this particular genetic mutation.

This doesn't mean that experts should be trusted. But the explanation surprised me. I wish I could know what you think.

I've tried to lay this out for you as close to how I read it. To not stray or make unnecessary asides. It's very hard for me to be this methodical. And always I think of the blackness. It should have been back by now I don't understand what's happening I ~~xx~~

~~*I will try to write one more time*~~   *xx*

Dear A,

I don't know where the magnifying glass is anymore ┼┼ Why can't I find it? And the lilacs outside the window—how could they have vanished? Or maybe they're there but I can't see them (though the blackness still hasn't come back, or the sound-colors that come with it...I have no way to understand this). As when I read about time and space—how we can't feel or know their true nature yet they're there xxxx ┼┼ we live in incompletion always ┼

Woland takes me to his room, gives me slippers of spun rose petals to put on, tells me it's all right to feel anything I wish "but not indifference." I don't tell him I don't want his slippers or anything to do with roses. I'll take them off as soon as I leave here. I understand now your roses aren't mine. And I was wrong to imagine myself into your body. I try so hard to see you...I still think of your privacy, your quiet. How we worked side by side but didn't speak.

Remember the boy who taught himself the sounds of different metals? Why do I so readily think of the boy and his metals but not the thousands of times he sat in a paper hospital gown in an examining room, the air too cold, waiting with his one broken bone or another, or his several broken bones, maybe looking at the garish seascapes on the wall, or looking only away, or at the photographs of trees taken by a doctor who decided he needed "a new hobby"? What does a fracture feel like, can you tell me? Or a fracture that recurs many times in the same place?

I still remember our months in the office. The books we scanned, the silence between us. The fake daylight we worked in. The signs above our work stations. The real daylight we often didn't see. We knew the new technology would replace us, it was just a matter of time. I wonder if by now it's ready. And the low hum of the machines, remember? Fluorescent buzzing from the ceiling. Computers. Scanners. Everything close and far away at the same time. Even our own skin.

The man on the rock, where is he? I never should have turned his words to sand and wished them down his throat. I tried to help him with my cloth, cool water, but he didn't want it, and I knew it wouldn't really help.

Why didn't you push my hand away like he did? (Though I know that you would never touch me.) Why did you open my first letter, why did you do as I asked? The article says you have a "benevolent face"—it says that you "possess a remarkable capacity for empathy."—that maybe this is built into the structure of your genes, the same mutation that's the cause of your illness. How can we ever begin to understand how we are made, how we function, the forms and processes that drive us? So much elsewhere outside and inside us...The article says there is something in you resistant to holding on to hurt— it calls it "benevolence." It calls it a "particular form of mild euphoria," "the power of bearing well." "Indomitable and tenacious spirit."   ✝ ✝

But I sent you away, I—But maybe the notebook gave you something after all, though you don't know my name or where I am and you can't tell me. Venice. The lagoon. San Servolo...Maybe they gave something and you're not sorry that I asked you, that you went.

And this light is too bright now when all along I expected the blackness. I don't understand what could account for this. But now it's getting dark again, so I don't know... "Sometimes mercy slips through the narrowest cracks," Woland says, but I want to leave his room, go back to the room with the round table, the large window, the papers on the floor, the word "ruin." Dostoevsky felt such joy before he fell, remember?

"increased rate of cellular oxidation...a component of the generalized metabolic disturbance"

"Behavioral phenotype" is such an ugly term—

Her penciled words had been so faint I'd barely seen them. And those words so few, so scattered, as if they were the only ones left and, as in her description of Pilate, the rest were sand sifting back and down her throat to where no one could hear or feel them.

So when these letters came, and I tried to accept they could be possible, it was like trying to accept a notion of time and space that exists in accordance with laws all their own and apart from us where we never truly know them.

My fever was coming back again. I'd felt its slow rise for several days, though at first I denied it. So as I sat in my red room, and held her last three letters, I was also thinking maybe they had never come, maybe I was holding nothing. Thinking I had never read them. That they didn't even exist. Or maybe I had written them—she was dead and I missed her. And as I thought this, I thought also of Frieda, how her voice entered the air after so many years of not speaking, and how strange it was for her to suddenly hear its willingness to place itself in danger, though the white handkerchief remained inside her.

The infirmary walls were much too quiet. The caregivers had given me my name, then left me. No one lived there anymore. The air smelled of Pilate's roses. Then the roses left and it smelled of rosemary and camphor, and after that the acrid burning of computers.

I was in Venice, I was on the plague island with Frieda, I was watching the doctor write his name in the plague ledger, sign it. I was in the courtyard, the twelve trees still saplings. I was in the office, scanning. My bones were broken. I was wearing a leg brace, a body cast, a wood splint, I had my cane by my side, I was in a wheelchair, I was holding crutches. My bones had never broken.

The penciled pages were blank. I had been right the first time. There were no words on them. There were never any words.

There had been no *cyclic AMP*. No *you're alone you observe...I learned the sounds of metals I was alone and I knew what was making that sound...you're alone and you learn certain metals...*

Or maybe the letters were there, even the ones in faint pencil.

How did the Master's manuscript come back after it burned, and what else could come back or could nothing ever come back? Why were my walls so hot...why were they still melting...A fork...a spoon...a cup...I am alone and I learn the sounds...you're alone and you learn the different metals...

But why does Sushilov have so many scars on his back....the nights are very cold in prison, there's ice on the windows one inch thick....and the cattle are cold in their white field, I want to tend them like I used to but I can't move from this rock....the red cloth is very beautiful, isn't it...."behavioral phenotype"...."grant sponsor"...."purpose of this study"....who will bring food into the city....only the poor remain in the city....I understand that I am nothing, that my suffering is nothing....but this white handkerchief inside me....why do I still believe that you might hear me?....I have put on my black lenses....I have wrapped myself in resin and blackness....he showed me the kindness of red cloth....a fluttering thing of pale gray blue and white....A flightless bird A ghost....

I took the medicine. Why would the hot waves slip back and rise and slowly spread again....and this black spot in the corner of my eye....

....the article is "Personality and Stereotype in"....as soon as I found it I knew you wouldn't want me to read it....I held the words under the magnifying glass, read one cluster then another....I write the word dark and cross it out write joy and cross it out...."behavioral genetics"...."systematic research"....from the air all faces blur, all bodies stay unfocused....Woland gave me the slippers but I didn't want them....I worry that I wronged and harmed you....why did I see your hump as mine...."the materials and methods of this study"...."the history of euphoric attribution"....I am looking for you in the poorest districts, in the crumbling streets beside the women's prison, I am flying over St Marks and the gardens of Ca' Morosini....we must learn to find beautiful laws, we must understand more fully the nature of order....

....Why won't you show that you can hear me I believe now that you never heard me....

....And the scientists say there is no such thing as empty space but Dark Energy....Dark Matter....

....And all the stars will go out and there will be no life-bearing planets....

....Myshkin believes that kindness can rescue everything but how can this possibly be so....

....All beggars are ordered to depart the city in three days....I still wish that you would show if you could hear me....25,000 have already fled the city....the magistrates have fled, the councils have emptied....but it is suddenly as if the whole universe says yes, everything's terribly clear and there's such joy....But there is so much darkness now....What lies past the single horizon, the single scale?....and Myshkin strokes Rogozhin's face with such tenderness but why does he do this why doesn't he get up and leave him....Why do I keep coming to you, why have I found you?....you are alone and you learn to observe, you are alone and you learn the different metals....how can I explain why I need you to read to me....the light across the courtyard the twelve trees....the Nucleus Solitarius is such a lonely name, forgive me....Protein activation....Post-synaptic Excitation.... and when you read to me your reading brought me peace

Dear A,

But everything is dark now. I still feel you though my eyes can't see you.

I am sitting in a chair on a green hill in the cold sunlight.

I see the different grasses under my feet, some rough and dark, others slender, thread-like, almost silver. I see the splinter of black wood jutting out from the chair leg. Mostly I remember Rogozhin's room, my tears falling onto his cheek as we lie close, side by side on the cushions he arranged on the floor, the two on the left for me because they are "the best." Many hours pass. I hold and stroke him. We talk about flowers the knife the drops of blood. And Marie is too weak to leave her rock, but the sight of the cattle calms her as they move in their inhuman quietness through the fields. She worries they are cold and hungry. And the waterfall, I still hear it, and the donkey in the marketplace. I am still holding Rogozhin and now it is impossible to tell which is his skin and which is mine. My tears are falling on his face I am trying not to tremble, I can see the green curtain, the tip of a bare foot beneath it, scattered petals, a white dress, white ribbons. I am holding a white handkerchief, the shore is empty then it's littered with white boats. The green hill grows darker, colder. I am in Daravoe, a man is touching a boy's face in kindness. The hours pass slowly, I have put on black lenses. I see the plague doctor's beaked mask filled with rosemary and camphor, I see the white mask of the Servetta Muta. I am on my cold hill, I am putting on my white death-shirt I am lowering it over my head my naked body I am sixth in line for execution. I am traveling over snow I pass a bell sentenced to eternal silence. I am in a prison camp and a man is remembering Daravoe, a hand touching a boy's face with kindness, I will stay here for four years. I am on the plague island with Frieda and won't show if I can hear or see her. I am in a room with a narrow bed, a coffee cup, green lamp, small table, the room is red I am hot and cold at once my fever is building. The long bones in both my legs are broken. A soft music has fractured one of the bones of my middle ear, the smallest bones of the body, I am alone and I am listening for the sounds of different metals. I am alone and I learn the sounds you learn to know them, a fork, a spoon, a cup, each one is different. Marei has worked all day in the fields, he is old, red scars on both his arms. Why is he so kind to me? A man is crossing a courtyard to read to a woman whose sight is failing. Then the courtyard is empty, the man lies on the floor he is having a seizure. The woman looks out on twelve trees, she can feel the man's hands on the closed book, she hears turning pages. The hill is very dark, the air sharpening, colder. My tears fall on a murderer's cheek, I lie on the "best" cushions I hold and stroke him. My breath mixes with his breath, I hear our breathing. I think of pulling back but don't pull back.

ACKNOWLEDGMENTS

This book is dedicated to Jack Shoemaker, to his dedication as a publisher, his love of books, his indomitable spirit and example, and to all that he stands for and has done over the past decades.

My thanks to everyone at Counterpoint, especially the intrepid Matthew Hoover, whose exceptional discernment, keen, clarifying, eye, and steady, problem-solving temperament were invaluable in taking this work from manuscript to book.

My thanks, too, to Kelly Winton who created the inspired jacket design, and to Domini Dragoone, the book's designer, whose acuity, and clear, persistent vision has enriched these pages.

Also to Megan Fishmann, for her invaluable judgment, guidance and spirited support.

Thanks, too, to Peter Mendelsund and Maggie Hinders, whose work on my first hybrid helped me to move forward with aspects of this one, as I tried to see through their eyes, and further think about surfaces—their complexities and contradictions, but most importantly, their ingenious plainness.

My husband made this book possible in the deepest of ways.

Thanks too, to my parents. To the gift of my mother's joy at seeing each book. To Susan Howe for her kind act, as well as her example. To my caring friends, and my cousin Karen. And to the Rinaldis, dear, wonderful neighbors, who made possible the environment in which much of this book was written. Sharon Cameron's radiant essay on Dostoevsky was an inspiration.

SOURCES

PART 1

The character Frieda is lifted and adapted from a few brief paragraphs in Mikhail Bulga-kov's novel The Master and Margarita. *In that book, the often-charming, world-weary, and even kind devil, Woland, says, "A fact is the most stubborn thing in the world." How-ever, in Ambrose's tellings, sometimes " facts" shift around a bit, and quotations may at times be approximate or altered.*

Venezia Isola del Lazzaretto Nuovo, Ministero per i Beni al Attivia Culturali, Venice, Italy, 1986.

The Abandoned Islands of the Venetian Lagoon, Giorgio and Maurizio Crovato, San Marco Press, Middlesex, England, 2008.

The Canals of Venice, Marcia Amidon Lusted, Lucent Books, Farmington Hills, MI, 2004.

Venice Incognito, James H. Johnson, University of California Press, Berkeley, 2011.

The Souls of Venice, Janet Sethre, McFarland and Co., Jefferson, NC, 2003.

Venice Is a Fish, Tiziano Scarpa, Gotham Books, New York, 2009.

Venice: The City of the Sea, Edmund Flagg, Charles Scribner, New York, 1853.

Life on the Lagoons, Horatio Brown, Rivingtons, London, 1900.

The World of Venice, James Morris, Harcourt Brace Jovonovich, New York, 1974.

A Literary Companion to Venice, Ian Littlewood, John Murray, London, 1991.

The Venetian Printing Press, Horatio Forbes Brown, G.P. Putnam, New York, 1891.

In Venice and in the Veneto with Ezra Pound, Rosela Zorci, Ca'Foscari University, Venice, Italy, 2007.

A Wanderer in Venice, Edward Verrall Lucas, New York, 1914, reprinted by Biblio-bazaar, 2007.

Venice: Its Individual Growth from the Earliest Beginnings to the Fall of the Republic, Pompeo Molmenti, A.C. McClurg and Co., Chicago, 1907.

The Makers of Venice, Mrs. (Margaret) Oliphant, Thomas Y. Crowell and Co., New York, 1887.

Daily Life in Venice, Maurice Andrieux, Praeger, New York, 1972.

Chioggia and the Villages of the Venetian Lagoon, Richard J. Goy, Cambridge University Press, England, 1985.

Venice Observed, Mary McCarthy, Harcourt, Inc., New York, 1963.

The Companion Guide to Venice, Hugh Honor, Boydell and Brewer, Suffolk, England, 1997.

Venice, Fragile City 1797–1997, Margaret Plant, Yale University Press, New Haven, CT, 2002.

The Stones of Venice, John Ruskin, National Library Association, New York, 1851.

Venetian Life, William Dean Howells, Houghton Mifflin, New York, 1891.

The Charm of Venice, compiled by Alfred H. Hyatt, Chatto & Windus, London, 1908.

Tropic of Venice, Margaret Doody, University of Pennsylvania Press, Philadelphia, 2007.

The Lazaretto of Venice, Verona, and Padua (1520–1580), Jane Stevens, Cambridge University PhD Thesis, England, 2007.

Rich and Poor in Renaissance Venice, Brian Pullin, Oxford University Press, England, 1971.

The Master and Margarita, Mikhail Bulgakov, translated by Diana Burgin and Katherine Tiernan O'Connor, Vintage International, New York, 1996.

"Bulgakov, Dante, and Relativity," Bruce A. Beatie and Phyllis W. Powell, *Canadian-American Slavic Studies,* 15, Nos. 2–3, Summer–Fall 1981.

Mikhail Bulgakov: Life and Interpretations, Anthony Colin Wright, University of Toronto Press, Toronto, Canada,1978.

A Pictorial Biography of Bulgakov, Ellendea Proffer, Editor, Ardis Publishers, Ann Arbor, MI, 1984.

Pontius Pilate, Ann Wroe, Random House, New York, 2001.

Beyond Vision, Pavel Florensky, Nicoletta Misler, Editor, translated by Wendy Salmond, Reaktion Books, London, 2002.

The Life and Times of Titian, Vols. 1 and 2, Joseph Archer Crowe, John Murray, London, 1881.

Titian, Filippo Pedrocco, Scala, Florence, Italy, 1993.

Titian's Portraits Through Arentino's Lens, Luba Freedman, Pennsylvania State University Press, University Park, 1995.

Titian: The Last Days, Mark Hudson, Walker & Co., New York, 2009.

Through the Eye of a Needle, Peter Brown, Princeton University Press, NJ, 2012.

"Sleep in Venice," Millard Meiss, *Proceedings of the American Philosophical Society,* Vol. 110, No. 5, 1966, www.jstor.org/stable/986024.

Venice: Past and Present, Thomas Osmond Summer, Southern Methodist Publishing House, Nashville, TN, 1860.

"A Venetian Plague Miracle," William M. Schupbach, *Medical History,* Vol. 20, No. 3, July 1976.

Secret Venice, Thomas Jonglez and Paola Zoffoli, Editions Jonglez, Versailles, France, 2010.

Blue Guide: Venice, Alta Macadam, A&C Black, London, 1986.

Venice on Foot, Hugh A. Douglas, Charles Scribners, New York, 1907.

Cultures of Plague, Samuel K. Cohen Jr., Oxford University Press, England, 2009.

The Body: Public Health and Social Control in Sixteenth-Century Venice, Michelle Anne Laughran, Dissertation, University of Connecticut, Storrs, 1998.

City and the Senses: Urban Culture Since 1500, Alexander Cowan, Editor, Ashgate Publishing, Abingdon, England, 2007.

Plague and the Poor in Renaissance Florence, Ann G. Carmichael, Cambridge University Press, England, 1986.

The Great Pox, Jon Arizzabalaga, John Henderson, and Roger French, Yale University Press, New Haven, CT, 1997.

Plagues and Peoples, William H. McNeill, Doubleday, New York, 1977.

A World by Itself, Shirley Guiton, Hamish Hamilton, London, 1977.

Hope and Healing, Gauvin Bailey, Editor, University of Chicago Press, 2005.

PART 2

In the sleepless woman's sections, some phrases and sentences have been adapted from Dostoevsky's letters and other writings. She and Ambrose quote briefly from the Constance Garnett translation of The Idiot *and* The Possessed. *Many details of the sleepless woman's illness as she mentions them come from D.T. Max's* The Family That Couldn't Sleep.

The Idiot, Fyodor Dostoevsky, translated by Constance Garnett, revised by Elina Yuffa, Barnes and Noble Classics, New York, 2004.

The House of the Dead and *Poor Folk,* Fyodor Dostoevsky, translated by Constance Garnett, Barnes and Noble Classics, New York, 2004.

The Possessed, Fyodor Dostoevsky, translated by Constance Garnett, Barnes and Noble Classics, New York, 2005.

Dostoevsky Letters, Vols. I–V, David Lowe, Editor and translator, Ardis Publishers, Ann Arbor, MI, 1989–1991.

Selected Letters of Fyodor Dostoevsky, Joseph Frank and David I. Goldstein, Editors, Rutgers University Press, New Brunswick, NJ, 1987.

Dostoevsky, Vols. I–V, Joseph Frank, Princeton University Press, NJ, 1995.

The Notebooks for The Idiot, Fyodor Dostoevsky, Edward Wasiock (ed.), University of Chicago Press, 1967.

The Unpublished Dostoevsky, Diaries and Notebooks, Vols. II and III, Carl Proffer, Editor, Ardis Publishers, Ann Arbor, MI, 1975, 1976.

Dostoevsky Reminiscences, Anna Dostoevsky, translated by Beatrice Stillman, Liveright, New York, 1977.

Problems of Dostoevsky's Poetics, Mikhail Bakhtin, Caryl Emerson, Editor and translator, University of Minnesota Press, 1984.

Dostoevsky, Andre Gide, New Directions, New York, 1961.

Dostoevsky Archive: First Hand Accounts of the Novelist, Peter Sekirin, Editor, McFarland and Co., Jefferson, NC, 1997.

Dostoevsky's The Idiot: *A Critical Companion,* Liza Knapp, Editor, Northwestern University Press, Evanston, IL, 1998.

Dostoevsky and The Idiot: *Author, Narrator, and Reader,* Robin Fever Miller, Harvard University Press, Cambridge, MA, 1981.

The Bond of the Furthest Apart: Essays on Tolstoy, Dostoevsky, Bresson and Kafka, Sharon Cameron, University of Chicago Press, forthcoming, 2017.

The Art of Dostoevsky's Falling Sickness, Brian R. Johnson, PhD Thesis, University of Wisconsin, Madison, 2008.

The Falling Sickness, Owsei Temkin, Johns Hopkins Press, Baltimore, 1945, 1971.

Epilepsy and Its Treatment, William P. Spratling, W.B. Saunders and Co., Philadelphia, 1904.

Epilepsy and Other Chronic Convulsive Diseases, W.R. Gowers, J. & A. Churchill, London, 1881.

Epilepsy: A Study of Idiopathic Disease, William Aldren Turner, Macmillan, New York, 1907.

The Family That Couldn't Sleep, D.T. Max, Random House, New York, 2006.

"Fatal Familial Insomnia: A Seventh Family," P. Silburn and L. Cervenakova, *Neurology,* Vol. 47, No. 5, November 1996.

"Fatal Familial Insomnia: Clinical, Neuropathological, and Genetic Description of a Spanish Family," *Journal of Neurology, Neurosurgery and Psychiatry,* Vol. 68, No. 6, February 2000.

Museo del manicomio di San Servolo la follia reclusa, Mario Galzigna, Curator, Foundation of San Servolo, Venice, Italy, 2007.

Il Recupero Di San Servolo, Claudio Carlon, Libreria Edirice, Province of Venice, Italy, 2004.

Epilepsy: The Facts, Anthony Hopkins and Richard Appleton, Oxford University Press, England, 1996.

Epilepsy in Our Own Words, Steven C. Schachter, MD, Oxford University Press, England, 2008.

St. Petersburg, Michelin Travel Publications, Greenville, SC, 1999.

In Search of the Multiverse, John Gribbin, John Wiley & Sons, Inc., Hoboken, NJ, 2009.

A Disease Once Sacred: A History of the Medical Understanding of Epilepsy, M.J. Eadie, John Libbey and Co., Eastleigh, England, 2001.

The Asylum Journal of Mental Science, Volume 4, John Charles Bucknill, Editor, Longman, Brown, London, 1858.

On Epilepsy, M.G. Echeverria, William Wood and Co., New York, 1870.

Una visita al nuovo manicomio criminale, Raffaele Nulli, Nabu Press reprint (1887), 2010.

Ecstatic Epileptic Seizures: A Glimpse into the Multiple Roles of the Insula, Markus Gschwind and Fabienne Picard, *Frontiers in Behavioral Neuroscience,* online Feb. 17, 2016.

Dostoevskii's Creative Misreading of Holbein, S. Kupper, Paper presented at the 2nd meeting of the Study Group for Religion in Russia, Gregnog, Wales, 2003.

Epilepsy and Literary Creativeness: Fyodor M. Dostoevsky, Franc Fari, *Friulian Journal of Science,* Vol. 3, 2003.

Lettres medicales sur l'Italie, Joseph Guislan, Gand, Rue des Piegnes, France, 1840.

L'Antica Farmacia Dell'Ospedale Di San Servolo a Venezia, Ernesto Riva, www. fondazionesanservolo.it.

"The Mental Asylum of San Servolo, Venice (1860–1978)," Mario Galzigna, *History of Psychiatry,* Vol. 20, No. 4, 2009..

The San Servolo Foundation, www.fondazionesanservolo.it.

The Province of San Servolo, www.sanservolo.provincia.venezia.it.

"Neuroscience Resources," www.neuroanatomy.wisc.edu.

"Neurophysiology and Neurochemistry of Sleep," Sergey Skudaev, *Cellular and Molecular Life Sciences,* Vol. 64, No. 10, 2007.

PART 3

"Personality and Stereotype in Osteogenesis Imperfecta: Behavioral Phenotype or Response to Life's Hard Challenges?", Joan Ablon, *American Journal of Medical Genetics Part A,* Vol. 122A, No. 3, 2003.

Fragile Bones, Unbreakable Spirit? Abstracts from 1st international meeting of OIFE and APOI, Lisbon, Portugal, 2012.

Neurobiology and Segmental Neurology of Sleep, Antonio Culebras, Marcel Dekker, New York, 1999.

"Sympathy for Pontius Pilate," V. Zayas, F. Maggioni, and G. Zanchin, *Cephalalgia,* Vol. 27, No. 1, 2007.

"Physiology and Neurochemistry of Sleep," Martha S. Rosenthal, *American Journal of Pharmaceutical Education,* Vol. 62, Summer 1998.